'I couldn't sleep.' Jenna's voice
~~v..................~~
**her throat and the rushed beating
of her heart.**

'I imagine not, after what almost happened
today,' Niall murmured sympathetically.

Not only that. But how could she admit that
she hadn't been able to sleep because of the
way he'd intruded on her thoughts. The way
she'd kept remembering the taste of him, the
scent of the wild outdoors that clung to him.
She couldn't, so she merely nodded.

He closed his eyes briefly. 'I felt sure the man
in the market was going to carry you away. It
makes me go cold every time I think of it.'

'Your arrival was timely,' she whispered,
gazing up into his eyes, mesmerised by the
heat she saw in their depths.

Slowly his hand lifted to her shoulder—a light
touch, but searing—and she welcomed the
contact, the feeling of not being quite so alone
as she had been since her father died.

His other hand cradled her cheek. Warm.
Callused. Yet infinitely gentle. She held her
breath, fearful and wanting. Revelling in his
touch when she .... him
away. And know

AUTHOR NOTE

It is not often that I can point to a particular inspiration for one of my stories, but I can for this one. My theme for HER HIGHLAND PROTECTOR came after a visit to Lulworth Castle in Dorset. It was built as a hunting lodge, and after several renovations was used during the Regency era as a country house by several illustrious tenants. It is now a burned-out shell. It was the picture displayed on one of the walls of that building that stayed with me long after I had returned home—a painting of the burning castle in the background, and neighbours and holidaymakers watching the 'show'. Over time, this lingering image became a major scene in this book.

I do hope you enjoy Niall and Jenna's story and will visit me at my website http://www.annlethbridge.com If you are interested in my rambles around Britain as I seek ideas for my stories you can find lots of pictures at http://www.regencyramble.blogspot.com

HER HIGHLAND PROTECTOR

Ann Lethbridge

Harlequin (UK) policy is to use papers that are natural, renewable and recyclable products and made from wood grown in sustainable forests. The logging and manufacturing processes conform to the legal environmental regulations of the country of origin.

Printed and bound in Spain
by Blackprint CPI, Barcelona

First published in Great Britain 2013
by Mills & Boon, an imprint of Harlequin (UK) Limited.
Harlequin (UK) Limited, Eton House, 18-24 Paradise Road,
Richmond, Surrey TW9 1SR

© Michèle Ann Young 2013

ISBN: 978 0 263 89837 8

Ann Lethbridge has been reading Regency novels for as long as she can remember. She always imagined herself as Lizzie Bennet, or one of Georgette Heyer's heroines, and would often recreate the stories in her head with different outcomes or scenes. When she sat down to write her own novel it was no wonder that she returned to her first love: the Regency.

Ann grew up roaming Britain with her military father. Her family lived in many towns and villages across the country, from the Outer Hebrides to Hampshire. She spent memorable family holidays in the West Country and in Dover, where her father was born. She now lives in Canada, with her husband, two beautiful daughters, and a Maltese terrier named Teaser, who spends his days on a chair beside the computer, making sure she doesn't slack off.

Ann visits Britain every year, to undertake research and also to visit family members who are very understanding about her need to poke around old buildings and visit every antiquity within a hundred miles. If you would like to know more about Ann and her research, or to contact her, visit her website at www.annlethbridge.com. She loves to hear from readers.

Previous novels by this author:

THE RAKE'S INHERITED COURTESAN**
WICKED RAKE, DEFIANT MISTRESS
CAPTURED FOR THE CAPTAIN'S PLEASURE
THE GOVERNESS AND THE EARL
   (part of *Mills & Boon New Voices*… anthology)
THE GAMEKEEPER'S LADY*
MORE THAN A MISTRESS*
LADY ROSABELLA'S RUSE**
THE LAIRD'S FORBIDDEN LADY
HAUNTED BY THE EARL'S TOUCH

And in Mills & Boon® Historical *Undone!* eBooks:

THE RAKE'S INTIMATE ENCOUNTER
THE LAIRD AND THE WANTON WIDOW
ONE NIGHT AS A COURTESAN
UNMASKING LADY INNOCENT
DELICIOUSLY DEBAUCHED BY THE RAKE
A RAKE FOR CHRISTMAS

And in Mills & Boon® Historical eBooks:

PRINCESS CHARLOTTE'S CHOICE
   (part of *Royal Weddings Through the Ages* anthology)

And in M&B:

LADY OF SHAME
(part of *Castonbury Park* Regency mini-series)

*linked by character
**linked by character

I would like to dedicate this book to all the people
who work on my beautiful covers, as well as the
wonderful staff at Harlequin Mills & Boon
who make it possible for you to read my stories.
I would particularly like to thank Bill and Lin,
who suggested I visit Lulworth and who cheerfully
put up with hours of my poking around
in odd corners, taking pictures. Thank you.

Chapter One

Heart pounding in her ears, Lady Jenna Aleyne gazed at the three shabby ruffians blocking the road and cursed her ill luck. The horse picking up a stone in its hoof the moment she was out of sight of the castle had been bad enough, but three men intent on mischief looked like a disaster in the making.

On a normal day, she would have been accompanied by a groom, but this morning she'd heard through one of the local lads that a tinker in the market carried news of Braemuir, if she was interested.

When Lord Carrick, her trustee, had insisted she leave the running of her family estate to him, it had made sense to the terrified fourteen-year-old orphan she had become so suddenly. But she had missed her home, all these years. Had longed for the day she would return to her people and take up her duties as she had promised her father.

The thought of recent news of Braemuir and its people had pulled irresistibly. Yet she was loath to mention it to her cousin, as she did not trust him to let her go.

So she had slipped out alone.

She offered the men a smile. 'What clan are you?' she asked in her rather rusty Gaelic, wishing she'd made the effort to practise more in her years of absence in England. 'There'll be a welcome for you at the castle, if it is food and drink you are needing.'

'Bloody heathen language,' the smaller of the three said. 'Can't anyone in this godforsaken place speak English?' He looked towards their leader. 'You are sure this is the one?' He moved closer with an oddly rolling gait and a hard glint in his eyes.

Not Highlanders, then. English sailors. Her mouth dried. Her heart thudded a signal to run. She wouldn't get twenty yards. Better to face them than turn her back. 'I'm headed for Carrick Castle and I am late,' she said in English. 'I shouldn't wonder if they havenae sent out a search party, so no need for me to keep you from your journey.'

Unimpressed by her implied threat, they moved in on her, spreading out, clearly intending to flank her like cowards.

A pistol would impress them, but hers was in its holster on the opposite side of the horse. These were desperate times in the Highlands, and while honour and hospitality ran deep among Highlanders, these Englishmen would have found little welcome. She winced. That probably accounted for their half-starved appearance and hard expressions.

The pistol was her best chance. Hands shaking, she passed the reins behind her back, jerking to make the animal shift side-on as if it was restless. 'Stupid beast,' she said. 'Picked up a stone.'

The animal half turned, tossing its head, favouring its forefoot. Just a little closer... Just an inch or two and she would be able to reach. The horse balked. She took a deep steadying breath. She needed a distraction, a way of taking their minds from what she was doing. But what?

A tuneless but cheerful whistling came from the direction of town behind her. She glanced over her shoulder and her stomach dipped. Another man, his walking stick swinging, his loose-limbed long-legged stride eating the distance between them. Heaven help her, was this another of these rogues? Her heart pounded harder.

The villainous fellow directly in front of her pulled a cudgel from his belt. The other two men followed suit. They were closer now and their expressions were grim, purposeful. She backed up against her horse, swallowing to alleviate the dryness in her mouth, while this new man kept walking towards her, his whistle never faltering. He looked nothing like the footpads circling around her from the front. Plainly dressed, yes, and a square jaw roughened by two days' growth of dark beard gave him a menacing appearance, but he also had an honest, open look in his expression that gave her hope. As he drew abreast of her she noticed a gleam of anger in his narrowed eyes. 'Three against one, is it, lads?' he said grimly, speaking English with a Highland burr.

Friend, she decided, trusting her instincts. But they were still two against three. She needed her pistol.

'Charlie!' she cried, throwing one arm about his neck and pressing her lips to his mouth, reaching out with her other hand to fumble for her weapon.

For a second the young man stood frozen, his parted lips shockingly intimate. Tingles raced from her lips to her breasts at the feel of his hot breath on her mouth, accompanied by the scent of wood smoke, heather and man.

So shocking and...and delightful all at once. Her eyelids drifted closed, the better to savour the sensations. The second lengthened to two as his lips melded to hers and a large warm hand cupped her bottom and drew her close. His tongue stroked the seam of her lips. The shock of feeling him, hard-muscled and demanding as he pressed against her, and the velvety warmth against her lips made her gasp. His tongue slipped into her mouth and explored gently and teasingly. Little thrills darted through her body like hot licks of flame. Delicious. Terrifying.

It was only the weight of the pistol as it began to slip from her grasp that brought her back to her senses. A hard tug freed it from the saddle holster. She stepped away, cocking her weapon and pointing it first at him and then the other three, who were staring at them, mouths agape.

The newcomer flashed her a breathtakingly wicked grin and, ignoring her pistol, he squared off to the three men. 'The odds are about even, I would say.'

'Bloody hell,' the smallest of the ruffians said.

She'd been right. The newcomer was not with them. She lined up beside him and levelled her gun.

'Gentlemen,' the man she'd kissed said with quiet confidence, 'you'll be letting this lady be on her way, now.' He swept his walking stick in a wide arc. 'The first one of you to step any closer than this gets his knees broken.'

She waggled her pistol, just in case they hadn't noticed. 'And the second one gets a bullet in the heart.'

The young man sent her a sideways glance, but kept his attention focused on their attackers. 'All right, my fine lads. Who wants to be first?'

The leader of the footpads gave his companions a desperate glare. 'There's only two of them.' His fellows stood frozen, staring at her pistol. She aimed it at their leader's head. 'You first, I think.'

He raised his hands from his sides. 'We need some coin is all,' he whined. 'For a bed for the night.'

'Ye'll make a bed in the heather like the rest of us,' the young Scot at her side growled. 'Oh, come on, man. Let me have at you. I haven't broken a head in days.'

The smaller of the men looked at his friends. 'Bugger that. She's got a pistol.' He tucked his cudgel back in his belt. The man to his left followed suit. Their leader glared at them. 'Curse you, you lily-livered sons of bitches.' He charged.

The Scot lunged for him. Unable to shoot, for fear of hitting her rescuer, Jenna kept her pistol moving back and forth between the leader's companions. In seconds it was over. The assailant caught a heavy blow on the shoulder. He screamed in pain, his arm dropping limp at his side. Moments later, all three of them were hotfooting it between the rough clumps of gorse and making for a distant line of trees. They were out of sight before Jenna finished counting to three.

She sagged against the side of her mare, who whinnied softly.

'Such cowards,' the young man said in disgust. He took her pistol from her slack grip. He stared at it for a moment, released the cock and shoved it back in the holster. 'You are taking a chance riding out with nothing but that for protection,' he said in dry disapproving tones. 'You might have brought one down, if you were lucky. It is no match for three.'

Her back stiffened at his obvious dismissal of her ability to look after herself. 'I have travelled this road scores of times without the slightest problem.'

'Alone?' he questioned, and she felt her face heat.

'Occasionally.' She knew she sounded a little too defiant, but who was he to question what she did? In truth, she'd been so anxious for news she'd given no thought to the danger. Not that she'd ever heard of footpads on this road before. Not so near to the castle. 'I would have been fine if my horse had not picked up a stone in her hoof.'

The look in his green-flecked brown eyes said he didn't believe it.

Infuriating man. The fact that he was right only made her feel more angry. At herself. She was lucky he had come to her rescue. But it galled her to say so. 'I thank you, sir, for your help. I do not believe I have seen you in these parts before.'

His frown deepened. 'Niall Gilvry, at your service.' He gestured to the horse. 'Which hoof?'

'Right front.'

He bent and lifted the horse's leg. 'Ah. Do you have a pick?'

She handed him the one still clenched in her fist. 'It's stuck fast, poor beastie.'

Gilvry gave a quick twist and the stone flicked out on to the road. He gently probed, looking for more debris. 'You'll have to walk, I'm thinking. It will be a while before she heals.'

He really must think her hen-witted if he thought she would ride the poor creature after it had suffered so, but what was the point of trying to disabuse him of the notion. She would likely never see him again. And when she recalled the thrills his kiss had sent racing through her body, it was probably just as well. 'If you think it best to walk, I shall certainly do so.'

He gathered her mount's reins. 'I will walk with you,' he said, without waiting for her agreement, 'in case yon fellows change their minds.'

She shuddered at the thought. Although, truth be told, his scowl—black brows drawn down across the bridge of a hawkish nose—was almost as frightening as the ruffians. Some woman might consider such rugged unshaven features handsome, but his height accompanied by his grim expression felt more than a little overpowering. Only his sculpted lips offered any hint of softness. A shiver trickled down her spine as her lips tingled with the memory of the feel of his mouth against her own.

It wasn't her first kiss. She'd encountered the odd amorous young gentleman who had caught her in a youthful game of blind man's buff. Awkward mashings of lips against teeth. Nothing so hot and so dark as his mouth had felt. None of them had set her ablaze, or made her forget what she was doing. Not for an instant.

Kissing him had been madness—now she had time to think. The very idea made her turn hot and cold by turns. But it was the only distraction that had come to her mind. *Rushing in where angels feared to tread*, her father had been wont to call such reckless actions. Embarrassing to boot.

'Lead on, then,' she said briskly. She had no wish to tarry because she had been telling the truth when she said a search party might be on its way. The folk at the castle might have missed the horse by now, though it was used so often by all and sundry they might not have, so long as Mrs Preston hadn't noticed her absence.

And now she would have to think of another excuse to go to the market. As they walked along side by side, she glanced at her rescuer from the corner of her eye. Tall and lean, he towered over her. This one had risked his life to protect her like a perfect Highland gentleman. A poor one, judging by his clothes. Not the sort of man she should be kissing no matter how good it felt.

Heat rose into her face at such wanton thoughts. She prayed he wouldn't notice.

'Where is your home?' he asked.

His voice made her jump guiltily. 'Carrick Castle. Lord Carrick is my guardian.'

A thunderstruck expression passed over his face. Or perhaps it was horror. She could not be sure, for his face quickly became a blank mask.

'Is there some problem with where I live?' she asked stiffly.

'I wonder at his lordship, then, letting you ride out without a groom.'

So would Lord Carrick.

'Or kissing strangers,' he added, and for an instant she thought there was a wicked gleam in the depths of his gaze. A challenge, like the one he had issued to the footpads. It faded too fast to be sure and his expression returned to its forbidding lines.

Had he really been so averse to her kiss? She was sure she had felt his breathing quicken against her skin in those few seconds of contact. 'I only did it as a distraction to get to my pistol,' she said, feeling the need to make it clear she was not completely wanton.

'I wouldn't advise such a method in future,' he said drily.

Because she was a poor kisser, no doubt. She really did not have much experience. Warmth suffused her body and crawled up her cheeks and she wished he would just go away so she could suffer her embarrassment alone. 'I will keep your advice in mind.'

He gave her a look of disapproval.

Drat the man. Who did he think he was to judge her? She gave him a haughty stare. 'I don't see how it is any of your business.'

It ought to be someone's business, Niall thought grimly. He still could not believe that the woman at his side—a lady from her dress, and an extraordinarily lovely one at that—was roaming the roads alone. All right, so his brother's wife, Lady Selina, hadn't been any less foolhardy. But she, too, could have been killed.

And that kiss. He still felt hot under the collar and elsewhere since she'd pressed her lips to his. Oh, he'd had better kisses from more experienced ladies, but none sweeter. And none that had left him so instantly mindless that he'd responded with such enthusiasm.

They were lucky he'd been able to turn and face those damned *Sassenach* criminals after she'd pressed her innocent body against him, because he hadn't wanted to let her go. And now he learned she was the ward of the man whose employ he was about to enter. A woman so far above him she should be ashamed to be seen in his company if she had even a wee bit of sense.

The sooner he stopped thinking about that kiss the better or he'd be out on his ear before he could turn around. He'd been lucky to get this position. Lucky to find any kind of paid employment here in the Highlands.

As Carrick's distant relative and a member of a sept that owed him its loyalty, his application had been accepted without question. Which didn't mean he would get to keep it, if Carrick wasn't pleased.

It was bad enough that Ian had asked him to secretly seek out information about Carrick's erstwhile steward Tearny, who had almost killed Ian's wife and had died by Ian's hand, without him getting tangled up with his employer's ward. If he wasn't careful he'd find himself scuttling back to Dunross with his tail between his legs and no chance for advancement. Or income. Back relying on his brother for his food and lodging.

His shoulders tightened at the thought.

Oh, he'd always made himself useful to Ian and the clan, taken on any task required of him, because it was his duty as brother to the laird. And he'd enjoyed teaching the clan's children at the tiny school in Dunross village. But if he faced the truth, it was hardly a challenge. And as Molly's father had been quick to point out when Niall had invited her to walk out with him, a man with no income or property was hardly a good prospect for a husband.

A blow to his pride, to be sure.

Even if his formal schooling had been cut short

owing to lack of money after his father died, he had plenty of book learning. It was time to put his brain to work, for his own sake and for the good of his clan. Here at Carrick Castle, he hoped to earn enough to permit him to go to Edinburgh and find a lawyer willing to take him on as a junior.

Meeting this young lady was hardly a propitious start to his new career. Not if she told Carrick about that kiss. He half-wished he had never set eyes on the lass. Not true. He did not like to think of what might have happened to her had he not come along at that moment.

He glanced sideways at her, looking down at the crown of a black hat fashioned like a man's curly-brimmed beaver with a bit of net tacked on. He couldn't quite believe how tiny she was. Her spirit facing those footpads had made him think her much taller, but in reality her head barely came up to his shoulder. How she had managed to kiss him he wasn't quite sure.

Oh, but he must have lent his aid to accomplish that bit of stupidity. Indeed, if he thought about it, his arm had gone around her to bring her closer. Instinct. Natural reflex.

The girl was, after all, devilishly attractive in a pixyish sort of way.

Her eyes were as green as mossy banks, changing to the mysterious green of winter forests with her mood. A bewitching face with creamy skin framed by unruly tendrils of auburn curls.

No one would call her pretty, but he found her fascinating. She reminded him of drawings of wee fairies in children's books. A haughty wee fairy. One that would turn you into a toad on a whim.

And she'd faced those ruffians without flinching. Extraordinary and worrisome. It spoke of a recklessness he had learned to abhor.

As they walked side by side, he tried not to notice the way her habit clung to the sweet soft curves of her slender figure. Curves that had plastered themselves against his body minutes before. A body that had responded with a will to her soft swells and gentle valleys.

His blood warmed again. He had the urge to float his hands over those curves, to savour again the taste of her full bottom lip…

No. This was his employer's ward. A lady to be treated with respect despite her surprising behaviour.

'And where are you going, Mr Gilvry?' she asked in her clear soft voice.

He had the feeling she wasn't going to like his answer. 'Carrick Castle. I am to start my employment there.'

'Not Mr McDougall's new under-secretary?' she said in a sort of wail.

He'd been right. She didn't like it one bit. 'Indeed.'

'I expected someone older. More—'

More what? Better dressed? He'd worn comfortable clothes for travelling first by boat and then on foot. He could imagine the sort of dandified gentlemen she was used to. 'I am sorry if I disappoint.'

She gave him a look askance that he could not interpret. Annoyance, probably, because he did not have a silver tongue like his brothers. He always said what came into his head.

He kicked at a pebble. By all accounts, where females were concerned, honesty was not the best policy.

The silence had been going on for some time now, he realised. She was looking at him expectantly. No doubt waiting for him to say something witty or charming.

It wasn't his style. He'd always felt completely left-footed with teasing and quick repartee. *Too much theory and not enough practice*, Logan, his youngest brother, always jibed.

The only time he'd ever tried anything of the sort had been at school in Inverness when he'd fallen hard for the headmaster's daughter. She'd been horrified at the temerity of a lowly third son even daring an approach. He'd never again wanted to go through such a mortifying experience.

Hence his rather cold-blooded courting of Molly. He'd been surprised at the relief he'd felt when her father suggested he look elsewhere.

The woman at his side was still looking at him, waiting for him to say something.

'It is a fine day for a ride,' he said finally.

'Except for the brigands,' she said, tilting her head and affording him a full view of her face and the teasing curve to her lips.

A smile he answered with one of his own. 'And the fact that your horse went lame.'

'And the chill in the wind from the north,' she added, her smile broadening.

'And the dust.'

'In fact, not a good day for riding at all,' she finished.

He bowed slightly. 'I stand corrected.'

She chuckled, a sweet soft sound that made his heart lurch as if it had stopped to listen. Inwardly, he shook his head at his odd imaginings. They were most unlike him.

They rounded a bend in the road, the castle, its towers and turrets, reflected in the loch at the foot of its walls. Damn. He'd forgotten just how tall those towers were. He hoped to God his duties didn't take him to the top.

'Carrick Castle,' she announced.

'I see it.' Of course he saw it. It was huge. 'I have been here before.'

Another of those quick glances up at his face

and he noticed that her dark lashes were tipped with gold.

'Not since I arrived last winter,' she said. 'I would have remembered.'

Now what did she mean by that? 'I was last here more than a year ago.'

She stopped and faced him.

As he stared into those clear green eyes fringed with sooty lashes, his chest tightened with painful longing. The kind he'd experienced as a lad when he realised he would never be like his brothers—dashing like Drew, or devil-may-care like Logan. Always analytical, he was the kind to look before he leaped into danger. To weigh the odds, while Logan scoffed at his words of caution. Ian simply made use of his knowledge as it suited him.

And now he wanted what? To cut a daring figure to this lovely young woman? Wouldn't that be hypocritical?

'I'd be obliged if you would not say anything to Lord Carrick about what happened today,' she said.

About the kiss. And a delicious kiss it had been, too. One he would not mind repeating, if she hadn't been under his employer's care. 'I'd be a fool to talk about it, now, wouldn't I?'

She gave him a blank look, then coloured. She caught her full bottom lip with perfect, tiny white teeth and he almost groaned out loud as his body tightened. A completely unacceptable reaction. He shuttered his expression.

'I meant the footpads,' she explained.

Oh, now he saw the trap. She planned to involve him in some web of deceit. 'I see,' he said, feeling unaccountably disappointed.

It must have shown in his face because she rushed on. 'You were right. I should not have gone without a groom. Naturally, I will not do so again.'

That did not explain why she had done it this time. What in the devil's name was she up to? Was she carrying on some sort of clandestine relationship? He would not put it past a female who would hold three men at bay with a pistol. This was not water he wanted to swim in. He started to shake his head.

She put a light hand on his arm. Her touch seemed to sear right through the wool of his coat to his skin. 'Please.'

Once more he stared into those green eyes and had the feeling he might drown in their depths. His gaze dropped to her mouth. His body tightened with the anticipation of kissing her again.

'Promise me, Mr Gilvry,' she said, tightening her grip on his sleeve. 'Please. It was a mistake I won't repeat.'

The touch burned, but it was the pleading in her eyes that made him feel weak. And then there was that kiss. Something he should not have allowed. Something she could have easily held over his head, yet had not. 'Verra well,' he said gruffly. 'I'll say nothing, provided you keep your promise.' Damn it all, he sounded like a stuffy older brother. Or a schoolteacher. Which he was, but not hers, for which he should be very thankful.

'And there is no need to mention I was on my way to town when we met.'

He huffed out a breath and nodded. In for a penny, in for a pound, as it were. 'All right.'

Her face lit with a smile that left him breathless. 'Thank you. For everything.' She danced away.

The girl was a witch. There was no other word for a woman who could twist him around her finger with such ease. He would not let it happen again. His future here was at stake.

He followed her under a stone arch ruptured by the teeth of an ancient portcullis overhead and into the courtyard. He looked about him. The castle wasn't large by Edinburgh or Inverness standards, but it had served its owners well over the centuries. Its granite tower looked out over the harbour and the town it guarded. A curtain wall encompassed several outbuildings added over the years.

A stable lad took the horse's reins from his hand.

'Careful,' she said looking over her shoulder. 'He's quite lame.'

The lad touched his forelock. 'Yes, my lady.' He looked enquiringly at Niall.

'Niall Gilvry,' he said.

'You are expected,' the boy said. 'You'll find Mr McDougall in there.' He jerked a thumb at one of the buildings on the far side the courtyard and walked off, leaving him to find his own way.

Niall turned to bid the Lady Jenna farewell, but she was already mounting the steps to the main entrance on the first floor. She didn't spare him a backwards glance. She'd extracted a promise and now he didn't exist. Good thing, too. So why this sense of loss when she was the most irritatingly reckless and undoubtedly manipulative female he'd ever met?

Cursing himself for a fool, he went in search of McDougall.

His assigned room was at the base of the tower, for which he was heartily grateful, and while it had no window, it was near the side door into the courtyard where his office was located. There was little he could do to settle in, since his baggage would come up from the town by cart, so he was glad when he was summoned to meet with Lord Carrick. He headed up one flight of stairs to his new employer's study and knocked on the ancient arched door bound in iron.

'Enter.'

A man of around fifty-five, Carrick was still

in his prime apart from a little extra fat under his chin and on his belly. The man had a pleasant hail-fellow-well-met look about him, until you looked into his pewter-coloured eyes. They had the power to strip a weaker man's inner thoughts bare.

Niall met his gaze steadily. 'You sent for me, Lord Carrick.'

His lordship lowered his brow. 'Ah, Gilvry. Niall, isn't it?'

'Yes, sir.' Niall kept his expression neutrally respectful.

'Sit down.' The older man leaned forwards in his chair. 'I understand you met my ward on the road today?'

So much for keeping it a secret. He'd known it wouldn't work. 'Yes, sir, I did.'

'And dealt handily with a pack of ruffians, too. You have my thanks.'

How did he know all this? 'The roads can be dangerous, sir, but Lady Jenna swore she would not go out again without an escort.' Now why was he trying to defend her?

Carrick sat up, his eyes sharpening with interest. 'Did she now? And how did you extract that promise?'

By making one of his own, which was clearly futile. He winced. 'I pointed out the error of her ways.'

Damnation, that sounded pompous, even if true.

'And here I've been thinking a good switching would do her some good.'

Niall's shoulders tightened at the thought of anyone laying a hand on the girl. He concentrated on not clenching his fists.

'Is that how you keep order with your students?' Carrick continued. 'Appealing to their reason?'

'In part, my lord. Occasionally I resort to the removal of privileges.'

Carrick's face brightened. 'An interesting idea.' He drummed the fingers of one hand on the desk, his face in a frown as if pondering a difficult decision.

Niall waited, holding his impatience in check.

The drumming stopped and the hand clasped the one beside it. 'I'm called away to London on urgent business.'

Niall's stomach dipped. Would he then have no need of extra help? He stood silent, waiting for the axe to fall, wondering where he would go next. He certainly would not return to Dunross. Perhaps he'd find work in Edinburgh while he looked for a lawyer willing to take him on.

'I need someone to stand in my place during my absence. You seem like the man for the job.'

Niall felt his jaw drop. Carrick was jesting. Had to be. 'My lord—'

Carrick put up a hand. 'With Lady Jenna. She needs a firm hand. Someone to keep a close eye on her.'

'I don't think—'

'With my wife at my daughter's lying-in, there is no one else I can ask.'

He swallowed. 'I'm not sure I have the right qualifications for such a role, my lord. Lady Jenna is no schoolgirl.'

Carrick raised a hand. 'No, she's not. But as my closest relative presently on hand, you will do as well as anyone.' His last words stung. It was the same thing Ian had said about him being the teacher at the school.

'Relative is too strong a word, my lord.'

'Then you will do it because your chief commands it.'

And that was that. 'As you wish.' He winced at how grudging he sounded, but he had a strong feeling that Lady Jenna was not going to like this any better than he did.

Carrick rose and went for the bell. A footman appeared within moments. 'Fetch Lady Jenna,' Carrick said.

The footman disappeared.

'I'll grant you it is not ideal,' Carrick said, looking at Niall from under his brows. 'But her companion, Mrs Preston, is as useful as a knife with no blade. Gilvry, if you managed to get the Lady Jenna to agree to anything, you have my undying admiration. She is a determined young lady, as you will discover.' His eyes narrowed. 'And you'll not let me down or your brother can go hang next time he needs cargo space in one of my ships.'

Niall stiffened at the threat, but kept his face impassive. Carrick didn't really know him. But as Ian would attest, having taken on a task, he saw it through to the end. Which was part of why he'd stayed so long as teacher at the school.

The door opened. 'Cousin. You asked for me?'

Lady Jenna. Niall rose to his feet, turning to face her. His heart stilled. She looked more ethereal than she had on the road. Or was it the way the sunlight drifted through the window and set flames dancing in her hair that stole his breath? Or the way the emerald gown clung to her figure and skimmed the tops of her breasts? Or simply a case of unrequited lust? Ah, definitely not a thought he should be having when he was about to stand *in loco parentis* to the young woman. That really would betray Carrick's trust.

Her eyes widened as she took him in. She swallowed and looked at Lord Carrick, who had half risen and then sunk back down into his seat. 'I apologise. I did not realise you had company.'

'Lady Jenna,' Carrick said heartily—too heartily. 'I know you had the good fortune to meet Mr Gilvry on the road today. A fortunate occurrence for you, I understand. Since I must travel on business, he will stand in my place as your guardian during my absence. You will defer to his decisions as you would to mine.'

'What?' She stared at Niall in surprise before turning her gaze to Carrick. 'How can this be?'

Carrick frowned. 'He is a cousin on my mother's side. There is no one else.'

Her expression shuttered. She lifted her chin with a smile that chilled. 'I see you have made yourself indispensable already, Mr Gilvry. You are to be congratulated.'

The words had the ring of a compliment, but in truth he knew them to be an accusation. She assumed he had broken his promise to further his own ends. Anything he might say would likely only make things worse. So he did the only thing possible. He bowed as if he took her words at face value and had the doubtful pleasure of seeing hauteur in her expression and a healthy dose of dislike.

As if dismissing him from her thoughts, she turned to Carrick with a bright smile. 'I had no idea you were planning a journey, Cousin.'

Carrick raised a brow as if to ask why she should be privy to his plans. 'Since Mrs Preston is apparently indisposed at the moment, would you please make the necessary arrangements for Mr Gilvry to join us at dinner?' He glanced at Niall. 'The family dines at five. It will be an opportunity for us to become better acquainted before I leave. That will be all, Jenna.'

She stiffened at the dismissal, then dipped a curtsy. 'As you wish, my lord.' But the glance she shot at Niall from beneath her lowered lashes before she left in a soft swirl of fabric and light pattering steps was a far cry from the friendly glances she'd given him earlier. He felt the loss as the soft scent of something spicy lingered in the air. Complex, like her. All bright sharp edges underpinned by subtle femininity.

He didn't want the job of guardian. It was not what he had been offered. He had been hoping to learn things that would stand him and his family in good stead for the future. Matters of business. And perhaps even of the law. Things that might set his feet on the path to a better future.

'How did you hear of my meeting with Lady Jenna?' he asked.

'One of the lasses hired in from the town was on her way home when she saw a fight on the road and raised the alarm. By the time the message reached me, the pair of you were at the gate.' He gestured to the window. 'I watched ye come through.'

The muscles in his shoulders tightened. He eyed his chief warily. What else had the girl seen? Not their kiss, apparently, or Carrick would not be looking so calm. At least *that* he would keep to himself for both their sakes. 'What happens with regard to the position of under-secretary? Does Mr McDougall not require my services?'

It was McDougall, Carrick's secretary, he'd originally been employed to assist.

Carrick rubbed his hands together. 'I am sure Lady Jenna will take little time away from your other duties.'

Niall wasn't so sure about that, but he could see he'd been well and truly snared. Two duties for the price of one, when nursemaid to a wilful lass ought to be paid double. Rumour did not lie. Carrick was known to be a man who would not spend a shilling where he could make a bargain for a sixpence. He bowed his assent, as if he had a choice.

Carrick dismissed him with a flick of his fingers. 'I will see you at dinner, then. That is all.'

Chapter Two

Jenna raked the comb through her tangled curls, her eyes watering with the pain. 'He gave his word and he broke it. Why?'

'My lady.' Mary McDougall, her maid, grabbed unsuccessfully for the comb. 'I dinna ken who you are talking about.'

'That mealy-mouthed Scot who came to work with your father. He told Lord Carrick about the footpads when he swore he would not. Currying favour.' And now Lord Carrick would think her still the hoyden she had been when she first came under his care when her father died, instead of a responsible woman, ready to take up the reins of her own life.

'It seems to have worked, too. He is to dine with us tonight.' And replace Carrick as her guardian in his absence. How could he leave now, when he had promised to take her to Edinburgh?

It was as if he was deliberately dragging his feet on the issue of her finding a husband. He had agreed it was the right next step and had promised her a Season. Her estates, her people, had been left without a caring hand for far too long.

Braemuir. Her home. How she longed to see it again. To feel the comfort of knowing she was safe within its walls. She only had to close her eyes to see every inch of it. The grand staircase with the honours of her family going back for centuries. Her room at the back of the house overlooking the park and the hills beyond. The people in their little crofts. The gypsies who had come every year to help with the hay. And she had promised her father to do everything in her power to care for it the way he would have, had he lived.

Only she couldn't. Not without a husband. Carrick insisted she wed before he would give up his trusteeship. Females did not manage their own estates. Worse yet, there were debts incurred by her father to be paid. And no money to pay them. Leasing the estate these many years had not been enough to pay them off.

She handed the comb to the insistent Mary and stared unseeing at her reflection. Surely it wouldn't be too difficult to find a husband. She was no beauty, she knew that, but it wasn't a one-sided bargain. In exchange for paying off

the debts, her bridegroom would gain the title of
Baron Aleyne, which by ancient charter passed
through either the male or the female line. Not to
mention the ancient house and surrounding lands.

A fine house for children to grow up in.

She had promised her father she would not let
the family name die. Yet here she was, two years
beyond her age of majority and still unwed. Not
that she regretted these past two years caring for
her father's widowed sister during her illness.
The woman had been the mother she had never
known. She had taught her how to be the lady of
a house instead of a hoyden who liked to ride and
fish and all of the other things she'd learned from
her father. Jenna had managed Mrs Blackstone's
house almost entirely alone these past few years
and it galled her to be treated by Carrick as if she
did not have a brain in her head.

'It is Mr Gilvry you are meaning?' Mary
asked, pinning a stray lock of hair in place. 'A
handsome young man by all accounts.'

Ruggedly attractive and traitorous. The feeling
of betrayal writhed in her stomach anew. 'He's
only out for himself.'

'Is that right, then? You know so much about
him already?'

She knew more than she ought. The velvet feel
of his lips on hers. The hard strength of his body
inside his clothes. A tremor ran through her. She
pushed the sensations away.

'He is not worth discussing, though I am sure the lasses below stairs will find him charming enough.' Oh, my word, didn't she sound spiteful? Most unlike herself. She took a deep breath. 'That looks lovely, Mary. Thank you.'

The maid smiled. She picked up the dress from the end of the bed. 'May I put this on you, now? We should probably hurry, or you will be late.'

Lord Carrick hated tardiness and ruled his castle with a rod of iron.

The dress slipped over her head with a whisper of silk. The silver thread in the lace edge of the sleeves scratched up the length of her arms. Why was she doing this? Why had she asked Mary to put out her best evening gown instead of one of those she would normally wear for dinner *en famille*? Not for Mr high-and-mighty-you-shouldn't-be-riding-out-without-a-groom Gilvry, that was certain. Tonight her mission was to remind her cousin of his promise to take her to Edinburgh. She really could not afford another Season to pass her by.

Not after receiving a plea six months ago from Mr Hughes, the vicar at Braemuir. He had begged her to return home and take up her duties, before there was no one left on the land.

When she had told Carrick about Mr Hughes's concerns, he'd been insulted by her lack of trust in his administration. Times were changing, he'd told her. He'd also forbidden any further communication with the old vicar. However, when she pressed the issue, he had grudgingly agreed it was high time she found a husband to look after her affairs. Six months had passed and she seemed no closer to the married state.

She pressed her lips together and smoothed her gloves up her arms. She was determined to wait no longer. Especially in the light of what she assumed was another message from Mr Hughes waiting unread with the tinker in the market because of those wretched footpads.

If Mr Hughes's pleas had been urgent before, she could only imagine what they would be six months later.

Despite the urge to move, to pace, she remained still as Mary pinned her brooch on her gown—the pearls and diamonds her father had given her mother on their wedding day, with the family motto inscribed in the silver surround: *Family Before All.* Family meant the people on her estate. People she hadn't seen for years. It was a promise instilled into her from birth. A promise she had so far failed to keep.

Mary handed her a shawl. 'Will there be anything else, my lady?'

Jenna gazed at herself in the glass. Was she ready? Was she suitably armed for battle with her cousin and the traitorous Mr Gilvry? 'Quite ready.'

* * *

Two flights down and a draughty corridor brought her to the second-floor drawing room, in the suite of rooms set aside for the lord of the castle and his retinue. Such old-fashioned formality. Outside the great wooden door studded with iron, she squared her shoulders, pinned a smile to her lips and drew on the mantle of a woman aiming to please. The waiting footman opened the door and stepped back to his place like a man who did not exist.

Her cousin and Mr Gilvry were engaged in conversation beside the hearth. They turned at her entry. Once more, Jenna could not but be startled by Mr Gilvry's towering height, the lean length of him encased in well-fitting evening clothes, his youth and manly figure more apparent beside her portly cousin.

Freshly shaven, his face was all hard planes and sharp angles. He looked sterner than earlier in the day, more remote, as if he had donned armour to keep the world at bay. The face, undeniably handsome in a rugged kind of way, did not seek to set her at ease. And those broad shoulders were just too intimidatingly wide.

She blinked as she got a good look at his waistcoat. Instead of the usual discreet cream or other pastel shade worn by men these days, it was pale green, embroidered with delicate sprigs of heather. It demanded attention. On another man it might have looked effeminate. On him, it only served to emphasise his stark masculinity. Her stomach gave the same odd little jolt it had given when she first saw him on the road. Surprise. It could not be anything else.

The man clearly knew nothing of fashion.

She dipped a small curtsy, acknowledging their greeting.

Mrs Preston, on the other side of the hearth, looked up with a pained smile. She had an unnatural pallor. A peptic stomach again, no doubt. The widow held out a hand. 'Come, sit beside me, child.'

Dutifully, she did as requested.

The woman lived in fear of her cousin's opinion. Fear she would be turned off to fend for herself on the meagre funds left her by her husband if she did not appease Lord Carrick's every wish, though never by word or deed had he indicated he entertained any such thoughts.

'It is good to see you up and about again, ma'am,' Jenna said.

The lady shot a nervous glance at Carrick. 'How could I not, when we have a guest for dinner?'

'A member of the household and a relative, too,' Jenna said, giving Mr Gilvry a cool smile. Playing the great lady was a skill she had learned from Mrs Blackstone, and it would be as well to keep this young man at a distance. Put them back on a proper footing.

Mr Gilvry acknowledged her words with a slight incline of his head.

'Ratafia?' Carrick asked.

She nodded. 'Thank you.'

Her cousin served her with a glass of the icky stuff. She sipped at it, keeping her grimace of revulsion hidden. Oh, for a nice dram of whisky. But ladies did not drink whisky in public.

'Fine weather we are having for this time of year,' Mrs Preston said, filling the silence.

Gilvry raised a brow. Carrick sighed.

'Surprisingly fair,' Jenna said, trying not to smile at how the words echoed those she had exchanged with Mr Gilvry on the road. Better to recall nothing of their meeting.

'And are your rooms in the castle to your satisfaction, Mr Gilvry?' Jenna asked.

'Yes, thank you, my lady.'

'Oh, don't thank me. Mrs Preston organises all on behalf of Lord Carrick.'

His quizzical look said he was wondering if she'd had the ordering of it, she would have left a basket full of snakes in his room. Clearly the man had a sense of humour, even if he was a tattletale.

He bowed to Mrs Preston. 'Then I thank you, ma'am, for the excellent accommodations. To be truthful, I did not expect such lavish quarters.'

Too charming to be true. But it was working

on Mrs Preston, who fluttered her fan and looked pleased. 'You are welcome, Mr Gilvry, though nothing was undertaken without his lordship's instructions, I can assure you.'

Carrick waved off the compliment. 'How are things at Dunross, Gilvry? I understand your brother is making improvements to his lands. And how is dear Lady Selina? I really must find the time to visit.'

'My brother is well, my lord. As is his wife. I am sure they would be honoured by your company and that of the ladies, too, should they wish to accompany you.'

'I really would prefer to go to Edinburgh, as soon as it can be arranged,' Jenna said, giving her cousin a bright smile. 'As we discussed.'

Inwardly she winced as Carrick stiffened. Perhaps she should not have been quite so pointed. Carrick wouldn't like the insinuation he had not kept his word. Or it might make him stir his stumps. If he did not make it so difficult for her to have this conversation in private, she wouldn't be forced into this tactic.

A look of disgust flickered in Gilvry's eyes. His lip curled slightly. He was judging her again. Assuming her to be a woman with nothing but frippery pleasures on her mind. Well, she didn't give a hoot what he thought. Not about something so important. This was between her and Carrick.

Her cousin tugged at his collar. 'I have been

meaning to talk to you about that, Jenna.' He slid a look at Gilvry. Had they been discussing her behind her back? Heat flared through her, anger at the assumption that they, having her interests at heart, knew what was best.

'I am sorry to disappoint you, my dear, but I do not think it is going to be possible this year.'

Jenna's chest emptied of every gasp of air. This she had not expected. How was she to find a suitable husband if she never met anyone? 'But you promised.'

Carrick's face froze. Blast. She really had gone too far.

'Dinner is served, my lord,' the butler said from the doorway.

'We will discuss this later,' Carrick said smoothly.

Oh, no. He thought he was going to put her off yet again. She would not allow it. She had been the very soul of patience these past few months, but she wanted to go home. Surely Carrick could see how necessary it was? She'd told him often enough. Or perhaps that was the trouble. The more she pressed him, the more he resisted.

Naturally, while Carrick took Mrs Preston's arm, Mr Gilvry came forwards to escort her into dinner. As she placed her hand on his sleeve, she felt the heat of his body down her side and sensed the raw power of his arm beneath her fingers. Tingles shivered up her arm in reaction to that leashed strength. She recalled how casually he had faced those villains on the road and how safe he'd made her feel.

A foolish impression. The man was ruthless in pursuing his own ends. A tremble shuddered deep in her bones. If it was fear, it came all tangled up in an excitement she did not understand.

She lifted her chin and walked beside him steadily, outwardly calm, while inside her unruly blood ran hot. She was glad when he released her to pull back her chair so she could be seated. The relief, when he moved to the opposite side of the table, was tainted by a confusing feeling of loss.

As they talked of political matters of interest to Carrick and the court gossip that so entertained Mrs Preston, Jenna glanced at Mr Gilvry from beneath her lashes. What about him set her in such disarray? His darkness? His reserve, except for the odd flash of interest when he glanced her way? Every time he did that, she felt a surge of blood in her veins. And all the time her heart felt too high in her throat.

No. It wasn't he who had her feeling at sixes and sevens, it was Carrick's about-face on the visit to Edinburgh, and the strain of saying nothing of importance until the moment was right.

Somehow, she managed to chatter on about inanities, all the while aware of Gilvry's speculative glances.

What had Carrick said about her? Had he been

told she'd been brought up a hoyden by an indulgent father and spoiled by her lonely widowed aunt? It wasn't entirely true. Yes, she was determined to have her way, but she had to be. She had responsibilities. She'd learned what she needed to know about being the mistress of a house and it was time to put that learning into practice.

The servants brought in the last course: platters of sweetmeats and fruit. Now that the man had a full stomach, perhaps he'd be willing to listen to reason. She glanced at Mr Gilvry, who was gazing at her intently, with a look that made her toes want to curl inside her slippers.

She did not dare think about what that look meant. She plunged ahead with her question. 'Well, Cousin, will you explain why it is you're breaking your promise about taking me to Edinburgh?' she asked casually while peeling an apple.

Carrick reared back in his seat.

Mrs Preston shot him a worried glance. 'I really don't think this is the time or the place to discuss family business, dearest Jenna.'

'Why ever not?' she said, widening her eyes in innocent surprise. 'Mr Gilvry is family, is he not? At least as close to Lord Carrick as I am. Isn't that right, my lord?'

Carrick cast her a look of displeasure, but seemed to wrestle his emotions under control because his voice when he spoke was surprisingly mild. 'One can hardly refuse a request for a meeting when it comes from Lord Gordon.'

Mr Gilvry's eyes widened. He lowered his gaze to his plate as if he was trying to hide his reaction. But there was no mistaking it. He had been surprised by this announcement. If one of the most influential Scottish Dukes had called for a meeting, would the under-secretary not know about it?

'When?' she asked, unable to prevent the question from tripping from her tongue and trying to soften it into a more civil enquiry by adding, 'When do you leave?'

Carrick waved his fork. 'Tomorrow. By ship for Edinburgh and then on to London.'

London? The largest marriage mart in the world. An abundance of wealthy gentlemen ripe for the plucking like low-hanging fruit. Surely one of them would be suitable? He didn't have to be clever or handsome. He just had to be willing to spend his blunt on Braemuir in exchange for a title. 'Why don't Mrs Preston and I come with you?'

'Not possible, I am afraid,' he said, shaking his head. 'This is business. I will have no time for assemblies and balls. I plan to return home as quickly as I may, I assure you.'

Her hand clenched around her knife as she fought to control her disappointment. 'You agreed that it was necessary that I have a Season this year.'

The pained look on Carrick's face said she'd disturbed his digestion. He put down the grape he had been about to eat. 'I promised you would have an opportunity to find a husband. And so you shall.' His jaw thrust forwards and Mrs Preston sent Jenna a look of alarm. Mr Gilvry looked as if he wished the floor would open and swallow him up. Clearly she was pushing too hard.

She took a deep breath. Forced her rising anger down. 'Oh,' she said lightly. 'You are postponing. Now I understand. We will go to Edinburgh for the end of the Season, upon your return.'

It wasn't exactly what he had said, but it might be one way to pin him down. He twisted and turned like an eel in a net whenever she tried to get a straight answer.

Having sent her shot across his bow, now might be the wise time to retreat. 'Are you finished, Mrs Preston? If so, then perhaps we should leave the gentlemen to their port and adjourn to the drawing room for tea, where I hope we shall see them in a short while?' She cast both men an inviting smile.

Mrs Preston fussed with her shawl. 'Indeed. Indeed.'

Carrick grunted and half-rose to his feet.

Mr Gilvry stood and helped Mrs Preston from

her chair. More pouring on the charm. Trying to impress his lordship, she presumed.

She dipped a curtsy and departed feeling as if she might have won a minor skirmish.

'Did you know about this meeting with Gordon?' she asked Mrs Preston as they walked the corridor to the drawing room.

The older woman shook her head. 'I wish you would be less forthright with your cousin, dearest girl. More is accomplished with honey than with vinegar, you know.'

Was it? She'd tried both ways now. Being patient. Hurrying him. Nothing moved him. If his younger sons had been single gentlemen, she might have suspected him of wanting her lands and title for them. But they were married. And very advantageously, too. Was there more to these delays than the lack of time he always claimed? Ought she to be more suspicious? Certainly her estates were of no great import to him. He'd seemed barely aware of her existence while she was living with her aunt. If that dear lady hadn't died, he might never have remembered he had a ward.

In the oak-panelled drawing room, the tea tray was already set out on the table in front of the hearth. It only wanted the delivery of hot water. Not that water was ever very hot by the time it made its way up from the kitchen in its separate building in the bailey.

One of the joys of having a history to maintain.

She had her own history to worry about. A Baron Aleyne had lived at Braemuir since the Dark Ages—until her father died. It was her duty to rectify the lack. Daily, the responsibility felt heavier.

And yet there was comfort in it, too. The thought of returning to the home she loved. All she needed was a wedding and a child or two, boy or girl, to know she had done her duty, honoured her promise.

'Do sit down,' Mrs Preston said. 'All that pacing makes me feel quite bilious.'

She hadn't realised she was pacing. She stopped short, staring at Mrs Preston.

'What a charming young man Mr Gilvry is,' Mrs Preston said, picking up her embroidery. 'I had heard all the Gilvry men are as handsome as sin itself. Having seen this one, I can well believe it. Sadly, quite poverty-stricken, I understand.'

The kind of man she couldn't possibly conceive of marrying, even if he was the closest thing to an eligible bachelor she had met in months.

Surely Carrick wasn't thinking she would marry his poor relation? Without doubt, Mr Gilvry was young and attractive. Her heart gave a painful little hop. A reminder that it didn't do to become too attached to anyone. It was too hurtful when they left one alone.

No, she would need to be careful around Mr

Gilvry. He stirred up uncomfortable emotions she couldn't control. And Braemuir required a woman of sense if it was to prosper.

If only she could bring Carrick to see the urgency of the matter. But how?

The butler arrived with the hot water and set it on the tray. 'Will that be all, madam?'

'Yes, thank you,' the widow replied.

Jenna sat down opposite Mrs Preston and focused on the important issue of preparing tea. Or rather the important issue of how to ensure she would soon be pouring tea in her own drawing room at Braemuir.

Niall sipped at his port, though he would have preferred the traditional dram of whisky.

'Lady Jenna is a determined young woman,' Carrick muttered.

'She seems set on this trip to Edinburgh,' Niall responded in what he hoped were neutral tones. After all, this really was not his concern.

'Aye, and if my wife wasn't busy with my daughter, she would be there right at this moment. I certainly don't have the time.' Carrick stared into his wine as if it could provide answers.

Niall shrugged non-committally. The man just wanted to voice his frustration.

'No doubt about it. She needs a husband,' Carrick said moodily. 'A man worthy of her title.' He tossed off his glass and poured another. He grimaced. 'I've already had one dubious offer. A lowlander and a shopkeeper to boot.' He frowned. 'Now what was his name? Davidson? Drummond? I think that was it. Verra unpleasant. Not the sort of family her father would want inheriting his title.' He pinched the bridge of his nose between thumb and forefinger as if suffering a headache. 'And who knows what sort of man she'd end up with if I let Katy Preston take her to Edinburgh.'

Did he really want to discuss bridegrooms for the lady? Yet he couldn't help himself. 'You don't trust Lady Jenna to choose wisely for herself?' It was as close as he could get to an objection of his employer's high-handed dealings with the lass.

'I promised her father I would see her well settled before I had any idea of the weight of debt his father had left him. If he'd had more time, he might have managed to see himself clear, I suppose.' He shook his head and took another swallow of his drink. 'I gave him my word I would do my best by the lass and make sure the family fortunes were improved. And I will. I just wish he hadn't brought her up more like a son than a daughter. My wife could handle her, no doubt, but Mrs Preston...' He subsided into silence. 'She'll need a strong hand on the reins, I'm thinking.'

'She reminds me a bit of my youngest brother, Logan. The more you tell him "no", the more he insists on his own way.'

Carrick puffed out his cheeks. 'Wildness is a Gilvry family trait.' He gave Niall a sharp look. 'Except for you.'

As a child, Niall had sometimes wondered if the faeries had taken the real Gilvry son at birth and left him in its stead. A changeling. Pure nonsense, of course. His childish way of explaining why he never quite felt as if he belonged, why he preferred to read when his brothers wanted to rampage out of doors. 'I've had my moments,' he said, refusing to be thought any different to his brothers. And besides, while he might counsel caution, he always stood shoulder to shoulder beside them even if they did laugh at his occasional bouts of cowardice.

'Drew was the worst of ye,' Carrick said.

Niall stiffened. 'Drew is dead.'

'Let me down badly, too. He had letters of instruction for my agent in Boston. A position waiting for him. Instead he took off on some wild adventure.'

Niall frowned. This was the first he had heard about letters. 'Drew might have been a bit reckless, but he usually kept his word.'

'Not this time. He sloughed my task off to another, I know that. The letters arrived far too late to be of any use and cost me a great deal of money.'

Niall flushed at his sour tone. Carrick was famous for turning all his ventures into gain. He

did not like to lose a groat, but he was right—
Drew had been reckless and in this instance
clearly careless. 'I'm sorry to hear it.' Though
there was little he could do to rectify something
that had occurred so long ago. He had the feeling this was something Carrick would always
hold against the rest of the Gilvry clan. Particularly Ian.

Carrick gave Niall a glance sharp enough to
skewer him to his chair. 'You will not be following your brother's example and letting me down,
now will you?'

Niall returned the stare steadily. 'Not if I can
help it.'

Carrick chuckled. 'Aye, I know. Lady Jenna
willing.' He lifted his glass in a toast and swallowed deep. 'I can see you've a head on your
shoulders, young Niall.' He leaned back in his
chair, his eyes narrowed, his lips pursed. 'What
I don't understand is why you are willing to undertake the lowly position of under-secretary. I've
been giving it some thought since you arrived.
Was it Ian's idea?'

'No.' He hoped he didn't sound too defensive
as he recalled Ian's request for information. 'I
have my own plans.'

'What are they, then?'

'Once I earn enough money, I am going to Edinburgh to study law. A man can make a good
living as a lawyer. And it would help the clan.'

'Aye, help keep them out of gaol.'

Niall bristled. All right, so it might have been one of the things at the back of his mind, but that didn't mean he would admit it.

Carrick leaned forwards, twisting the glass in his hand between finger and thumb, sending ruby rainbows dancing across the table as the port reflected the light from the chandelier. 'My journey to London could not have come at a worse time.' He watched the port continue to swirl above his now-still fingers. 'I am relying on you to keep a close eye on the Lady Jenna. Her encounter with those footpads on the road has me worried. Why was she out of the castle without her groom?' He looked up. 'Did she say?'

Niall shook his head. 'I did not think it my place to ask.'

He gave Niall a sharp stare. 'I am making it your place. I want to know what mischief she is plotting. Who she is meeting. I want you to call a halt to any nonsense before she comes to harm. Do that for me and I'll consider myself in your debt.'

'I can only do my best, my lord.'

'Do it well and I'll see about recommending you to a solicitor of some standing in Edinburgh. My own.'

Niall's mouth dried. It was something he would never have expected, not given the strained relations between Carrick and the Gilvrys. The offer of the position of under-secretary had been a surprise as it was. 'Thank you, my lord. I will, of course, do everything I can—'

Carrick held up a hand to stop him with a nod of satisfaction. 'I'll tell you this, then. I've an idea in my head of a way to satisfy Lady Jenna without any of us traipsing off to Edinburgh.'

Niall raised a brow.

Carrick grinned. 'I don't want to say too much in case I cannot match deed to thought.' He hesitated, then leaned closer, touching a finger to the side of his nose. 'She will insist on a choice, but I've in mind a way to limit that choice to a few good prospects. I'll write to you with the details when I know I have the matter in hand. And I'll trust you to ensure all goes off without a hitch. In the meantime, you will make sure she does nothing to ruin her chances.'

Did he have to be so damned mysterious? Perhaps he feared he would tell Lady Jenna what was in store. 'You can trust me to do my duty.' The words sounded as stiff at he felt, but if the man thought he wasn't to be trusted, it was no wonder.

Carrick nodded and raised his glass towards Niall. 'To the women who plague us.'

Niall accepted the toast and swallowed what was left in his glass in one go. It was always better to down bad-tasting medicine in one go. He wasn't sure which tasted worse. The port. Or his bargain with respect to keeping an eye on the Lady Jenna.

Still, he'd be foolish to turn down such an opportunity to further his prospects and be of use to his clan. And no one ever called him a fool. His task didn't have to be difficult. Provided he made sure she didn't meet anyone beyond the castle walls, he would have nothing to report. But God help him, unless he managed to keep her within doors, it seemed he would be spending a great deal more time in her company.

Something inside him didn't exactly regret it.

And therein lay the danger.

Chapter Three

'Begging your pardon, Mr Gilvry, but the Lady Jenna sends her compliments and wonders if you have forgotten your appointment to ride out with her?'

Niall lifted his head and glanced at the clock on the shelf on the opposite wall and groaned. Damn. He hadn't realised how the time was passing.

The blotches of red on the young stable-lad's cheeks darkened the hundreds of freckles on his milk-white skin. 'She says if ye are no ready to go in ten minutes, she is leaving.' He ducked his head.

'Did she, now,' Niall said calmly. 'You can tell Lady Jenna she will not set a hoof outside of the castle without me. Then take a message to have the gate closed and not to be opened without my word.'

The boy fled.

Niall put down his pen and stuck his head through into McDougall's office-cum-bedroom next door. The secretary was so fat he had had a bed installed against the wall in his office to save himself the effort of walking to his assigned chamber. He must have heard the conversation because he shrugged resignedly, making his multiple chins wobble like a dish of blancmange. 'You have your orders.'

Niall met McDougall's small twinkling eyes with a rueful smile. 'I'll finish off entering the receipts when I get back.'

McDougall waved a pudgy hand in dismissal.

Niall shrugged into his jacket and strode out. To his chagrin, he'd anticipated riding out with Lady Jenna with far more pleasure than was seemly. And then he'd let the time slip away and given her the chance to take him to task.

He shook his head at himself for being eager to spend time with her. She was his charge. His burden. And his ticket to a new and brighter future. So long as he kept her under control.

He paused in the threshold of the outer door and glanced up at the sky. High clouds like brushstrokes of white across pale blue suggested the day ahead would be fine. At scarcely nine in the morning, the sun wasn't high enough to chase the shadows from the high-walled courtyard. The upper windows in the towers glinted gold amid grey stone walls.

Towers. He shuddered and thanked God he'd not been located in one of those upper rooms. The sound of metal striking stone brought his attention to Lady Jenna already mounted. Not the horse of the day he'd met her on the road. A high-spirited strawberry roan circled around and around as she waited to be off. She sat gracefully in the saddle in the middle of the hustle and bustle of servants about their business, controlling her skittish beast without apparent effort.

She had no need of sunlight to dazzle the beholder. Auburn curls peeking from beneath a blue and gold hat styled to look like a shako were flame-bright. The military-styled riding habit, also blue with gold trim, fitted her slender body so closely he could see the swell of her breasts and the deep curve of her waist—not something he should be noticing. Fortunately for him, her legs were well covered by her skirts.

Another horse was being led into the yard, saddled and ready to go. A magnificent black gelding, but from the way it rolled its eyes and snorted, it looked only half-broken. He glanced over at the gates and saw to his satisfaction that they were closed.

He sauntered across the cobbles to the stable-hand struggling to hold the animal beside the mounting block. 'This horse is for me?'

'He's a bit fresh, sir.' The young man grunted with the effort of holding the creature. 'Hasna' been out of the stall in a week. Normally he's no so wild.'

The black-haired blue-eyed Peter Campbell, Carrick's head groom and Niall's friend from school, emerged from the stables behind the lad. He hurried over. 'I'm sorry, Niall. I told her to have one of the others saddled, but she insisted on Midnight. She said if you were going to stand in Carrick's place, you might as well ride his horse.' Peter sent him a quizzical look that Niall pretended not to notice.

He sighed. So that was how it was to be. He glanced over at the Lady Jenna, who had dismounted and was now talking to one of the maids from the kitchens. Both women glanced his way and the Lady Jenna's laugh reached him. If she thought those kinds of feminine games could put a man who had taught schoolgirls out of countenance, she would be disappointed.

The horse was another matter. 'How is Midnight when he's not so fresh?' he asked Peter. They'd remained correspondents over the years, but until now their paths hadn't crossed.

Peter winced. 'He needs a strong hand. It's why he doesn't get out much. None of the lads can ride him when he's fresh and I rarely have the time. I get him out on the leading rein when I can.'

Niall studied the gelding. A beautiful specimen. Glossy black coat. Heavily muscled. He ran a hand down its nose and patted its neck. The animal didn't flinch or start and nor were there any signs of malice, just high spirits. Fortunately, while Ian was the only one of the Gilvrys who owned a horse, he'd been generous in sharing Beau as needed.

Niall took advantage of the mounting block and eased into the saddle. The feel of the animal beneath him and through his gloves, the trembling eagerness, warned him to be ready for anything. No doubt the Lady Jenna had hoped he would be thrown so she could look down her haughty wee nose at him.

'Let him go,' he said to the groom.

Midnight sprang forwards. Niall held the horse under tight control, guiding him to the gates. He signalled to the gatekeeper to open them. As they slid up, the animal tossed its head and fought him. Then finally they were passing under the arch and out beyond the bailey. The road wasn't empty, but there was room. He urged the animal into a controlled trot then a slow canter, feeling his gait, the way he responded to commands, the strength and the power. The animal was truly magnificent. Lady Jenna should never have ordered up such a fine beast as this without knowing his skill level. Not unless she wanted him to fall.

He was surprised she would be so petty. Still

angry with him about Carrick hearing about the footpads, no doubt.

He let the animal have its head, let him run for a good few minutes in the direction of town, then brought him to a halt and glanced around. The countryside was spectacular. He never ceased to feel awed by this country of his. The green hills. The mountains, faint smudges on the horizon. The streamers of mist rising up from the dense trees, sucked up by the sun. He frowned. One of those curling, twisting ribbons looked darker, more like…smoke from a fire.

The hairs on his nape rose to attention. He scanned the road behind him for his charge. She was coming towards him at a ladylike trot. She halted as he drew close and wheeled his horse to stand beside hers.

She slanted a glance at him from beneath the jaunty hat. 'I'm glad you finally managed to get him in hand.'

Unfair criticism. But three brothers made him immune to such jibes. 'Forgive me, my lady, but you will not be riding out today.'

Her eyes widened in surprise 'Why ever not?'

'I have changed my mind.'

She frowned at him. 'But I had an appointment.'

'You mentioned nothing of an appointment to me, my lady. Where is this appointment? With whom?'

She hesitated a fraction too long. 'With the seamstress. I have a riding habit on order.'

It was his turn to be surprised. And annoyed. 'What were you thinking? An unmarried woman of quality cannot go to a seamstress with a gentleman. Not if she values her reputation.'

He had visions of sitting in the dressmaker's front parlour while the Lady Jenna removed her clothing in a nearby changing room. He envisaged the seamstress taking her measurements, exposing her delectable curves, passing strings around her waist and breast and a plump little bottom he'd very recently cupped in his palm.

His blood thickened and heated and headed south. He shifted in the saddle to ease the discomfort. He caught a quirk of her mouth, a small secretive smile that had him wondering if she'd read his mind.

She cast him an arch look from beneath her lashes. 'I had not planned that you would accompany me inside. You were to wait for me.'

'On the pavement, like a lackey.' He couldn't think why the idea annoyed him so much, but it did. 'I am no a fool, my lady. You should have invited your chaperon to go along.'

'Mrs Preston isn't well this morning.'

'Well, then, you cannot go.'

'Oh, but—'

'No buts, Lady Jenna.' To make sure she understood, he grabbed her horse's reins and turned it around, heading back for the castle. He scanned the surrounding moors and the distant trees, but saw no reason for concern, so released her bridle and gestured for her to go ahead of him.

'Mr Gilvry, the seamstress is expecting me. I must have the final fitting today.'

How many riding habits did a woman need? The one she was wearing looked perfectly adequate to him. More than adequate. It fit her luscious figure like a second skin, hinting at the curves that he knew lay beneath it. He glanced at her face as she leaned towards him and saw genuine concern in her eyes. 'Please, Mr Gilvry.'

And he couldn't believe his urge to make her worry disappear. He gritted his teeth. Her safety was more important than making her happy.

As soon as they were back inside the castle walls, Niall leaped down and signalled to a lad to take his now-calm horse. A groom came forwards to help Lady Jenna down.

Peter left the young plump pretty girl he'd been chatting with and strode across the cobbles to join Niall. 'Is aught amiss?'

Niall glanced across at Lady Jenna descending from her mount and an idea flashed into his mind as if from nowhere. 'Is the carriage available? Lady Jenna has a mind to go shopping.' He lowered his voice. 'There are some ugly customers hanging about the road. It will be an opportunity for me to report them to the local authorities.

I'll need a weapon and a man who can handle the ribbons.'

Peter gave him a hard look. 'I'll drive. I've some bridles at the saddlemaker's for repair. They should be ready by now. I'll fetch the carriage.' He hurried off.

Niall caught Lady Jenna as she was about to go up the stairs into the keep. 'I have had an idea of how we can both accomplish our errands this morning.'

She looked up at him, surprise and curiosity reflected in her green, catlike eyes. 'And what is that, Mr Gilvry?'

'We will go to Wick in the carriage and take your maid.'

He gestured closer the young woman Peter had been talking to. 'It is Mary McDougall, isn't it?' She nodded.

'Are you willing to accompany your mistress to the seamstress in the carriage, Miss Mary, since Mrs Preston is indisposed?'

Mary looked thrilled. 'Yes, sir.'

Lady Jenna tilted her head as if trying to decide whether she would accept this as a peace offering or not. 'I didn't think you were the sort to change your mind, Mr Gilvry.'

'I am when it suits my purpose,' he said drily. 'I also have urgent business in Wick. This solution suits us both, I believe.'

For a moment he thought she might refuse.

It would be typical of a spoiled young miss to cut off her nose to spite her face. But even as he had the thought, she smiled at him prettily. 'Very well. Thank you.'

That seemed too easy. But since he could see nothing in her face beyond delight, he pushed the suspicion aside. 'Very good, then. The carriage should be ready at any moment.' He would not tell her about his suspicions with regard to the footpads. There was no need. She would be safe enough with him and Peter and it would only worry her. In his experience, worried females were inclined to be difficult.

As he expected, Peter had the carriage put to with quick efficiency and, with the two women safely shut up inside, Niall leaped up beside Peter on the box. The head groom accomplished the delicate manoeuvre through the gate with skill that spoke of long practice.

'What makes you think these men are out there?' Peter asked, once the carriage was on the road to town.

'I saw smoke from a campfire. It might have been nothing. A traveller. But the men I encountered a day or so ago were a dangerous lot.'

'No honest Scot would spend the night in the open with the hospitality of the castle so close. It wouldn't make sense.'

'My thoughts exactly. To make matters worse, the men were *Sassenachs*. Lady Jenna is not to take her horse out without my permission until we either have them under lock and key, or they have left the area.' At Peter's quizzical expression, he grinned. 'And it is me who will decide if they are gone.'

'I'll tell my men.'

Niall narrowed his eyes against the sun's glare and scanned the trees on the hillside.

Peter followed the direction of his gaze. 'Is the smoke still there?'

Niall shook his head. The faint blue haze he had noticed rising into the sky was no longer visible. But the sun was higher now and a light breeze had picked up. 'I plan to report them to the local militia. There is a company in town, is there not?'

'Aye. Under the command of a Lieutenant Dunstan.'

Niall groaned. Lieutenant Dunstan wasn't exactly a friend to the Gilvrys, although Niall had no reason to doubt that he would do his job and do it well. 'He is in charge?'

'Aye. Watching the coast for smugglers.'

'He is looking the wrong way, then.' Almost all the illicit whisky went overland.

Peter chuckled. 'Thank God.'

It took barely a half hour to reach the outskirts of town and Niall acknowledged to himself that he was glad to arrive at the first of the

stone cottages lining the road without incident.
Perhaps he was being overcautious. They passed
the White Rose Inn and, with the addition of two
small buds on its stem barely discernible, Niall
knew the picture on its sign for what it was—a
Jacobite's nod of allegiance to the King across
the water, and nothing to do with the white rose
of the House of York.

'You'll find Lieutenant Dunstan there,' Peter
said. 'He's been trying to recruit some of the local
lads.'

'Has he had any success?'

'One or two have taken the King's shilling.
They'll pass on his troop's movements to family
members engaged in the trade.'

'You would think the *Sassenachs* would have
figured it out by now.'

Peter grinned and pulled up in front of a small
bow-windowed shop in the centre of town. 'The
seamstress. I'll drop you here and continue on
to the livery.'

Niall jumped down.

Peter waved his whip in acknowledgement and
Niall could not help noticing how his friend's
gaze sought out Mary as she stepped down and
turned to help her mistress. Oh, yes, the poor sod
had it bad. Niall promised himself he would try
to help his cause with McDougall.

Lady Jenna swept by him regally with a small
incline of her head. He hoped that meant they had

achieved a truce. He followed the two women into the shop.

A woman of about fifty, modestly gowned and with a cap over her greying brown hair, hurried to greet them. 'Your ladyship!'

Was it his imagination, or did the woman sound surprised? He looked at the Lady Jenna, who was stripping off her gloves. 'I'm here about the riding habit we spoke of last time.'

The woman's face wreathed in smiles. 'But of course. Please. Take a seat while I prepare the dressing room.' She glanced doubtfully at Niall. 'Can I offer you refreshment, sir? Tea? Whisky?'

Hell, did she think he was some sort of *cicisbeo*? 'I'll no be staying. Her ladyship's maid will keep her company.' He looked at Jenna. 'How long do you think this will take?'

'No more than an hour, I shouldn't think.'

The seamstress nodded a confirmation.

'I will be coming back before the hour is up, then.'

'And where will you be going, Mr Gilvry?' Lady Jenna asked with deceptive sweetness.

'To the White Rose.'

'I should have guessed.'

'Yes, you should.' He bowed. 'In one hour, Lady Jenna. Do not leave here without me.'

'I will be waiting. Please do not imbibe so much that you lose track of the time.'

A jibe at his earlier tardiness, no doubt. His

ire rose. He forced himself to ignore the slur on his character and departed before he said something he would regret.

'What a handsome young gentleman he is, to be sure,' the seamstress said to Lady Jenna, taking her coat and hat.

If you liked arrogant men who ordered everything to suit them. Jenna sniffed.

The seamstress gestured for them to sit down. 'Give me a moment to prepare. My last customer left only a few moments ago and I wasn't expecting you.'

'I know. I am sorry for that.' She gave the woman a confident smile. 'While you are getting ready, I will run an errand.'

Mary stared at her. 'But Mr Gilvry said we were to stay here.'

Jenna gave her a reproving stare. 'And I said I would be here waiting for him when he got back.'

She turned to the seamstress. 'I am just popping down to the market. Is it all right if I use your back door for a shortcut?'

The woman looked a little startled. 'If that is your wish.'

'It is. Thank you. And, Mary, if Mr Gilvry should return before me, do keep him busy out here.' She gave the seamstress a bright smile. 'Please make sure the rear door remains unlocked.'

Not waiting for a reply, or for the argument clearly forming on Mary's tongue, she made her way to the back of the shop and slipped out into the filthy back alley, the kennels running with night slops and other matter. It would all find its way down to the sea eventually, but on a fine day like today it stank. Jenna tried to breathe as little as possible until she found herself out in the open and a few yards from the market square.

Having very little time to spare, she ignored the hawkers and farmers and kept a lookout for a tinker's stall. Ah, there, a colourful awning hung with pots and pans and a trestle piled with goods of every description. The stall owner's gypsy heritage showed in his olive skin and dark flashing eyes. A gold earring glinted in one ear. He'd been the one who had brought Mr Hughes's message to her before she left Mrs Blackstone's house. He came out from behind his counter to greet her with a quick sly smile and a flourishing bow. 'Lady Jenna. An honour to meet you again. What can I do for you today? A paper of pins, perhaps? A pot of rouge? Not that your pretty lips need enhancement.'

His point was obvious. No sale, no message. And good for him, too. 'I'll take some ribbons, if you please.' The gift would settle Mary's feathers, hopefully.

'How about a gift for a young man with hazel eyes?'

Her heart stilled as she pictured Niall as if the gypsy had conjured him up. His strong jaw. The firm lips that had lingered on hers with such warmth and tenderness. And the determined set to his chin when he'd refused to take her riding this morning. She jerked back from the image.

How could he know about Niall? And she certainly wasn't buying him a gift. She shook her head. 'Just the ribbons and the message.'

He put a hand to his heart. 'And there I was thinking you came for the pleasure of my company.' His eyes darkened. 'You are not the only one interested in people from Braemuir.'

A suspicion crossed her mind. She looked around her, but saw no sign of a tall handsome Scot. 'Who are you talking about?'

He shrugged

'A young man? Handsome in a rough kind of way.'

He raised a black brow. 'I can't say I noticed his looks. Indeed, I hardly noticed him at all. I was busy with a customer at the time.'

Why didn't she believe him? But it couldn't be Niall. He knew nothing of the message she had come to collect. And glad she was of that, or he would no doubt have told Lord Carrick about this, too.

She pulled out a small pouch of coins. 'How much for the ribbons and your services?'

'A shilling, if you please, my lady.'

No doubt Mr Hughes had also crossed his palm with silver, but she didn't argue. The man needed to make a living. She dug out the requested coin and held it out. He slipped a folded piece of paper into her hand. 'You have been sorely missed, Lady Jenna.'

A pang twisted her heart. She should have returned home long before this, but Mrs Blackstone had been so kind to her, she'd felt obliged to see her through her long illness. She would never regret that decision, but she could only hope it was not too late for Braemuir. It could not be. She would not allow it. 'I will be there very soon.'

'Mr Hughes will be pleased.'

She turned to leave and almost bumped her nose on the chest of a man standing right behind her.

She stepped back. Looking up, she instantly recognised his face and gasped. It was one of the brutes who had accosted her on the road. To her right, a knife appeared as if by magic in the gipsy's clever fingers. Oh, no. Was he in league with this thief?

Wildly, she glanced around for help. The gypsy backed away, his gaze fixed not on the footpad or on her, but on something behind her. Weak at the knees, she glanced over her shoulder to see another large figure looming towards her. Her breath left her chest in a rush of relief. 'Mr Gilvry.'

'Lady Jenna,' he said in disapproving tones. 'What the blazes are you doing here?'

Despite the anger in his tone, Jenna edged closer to his bulk, unconsciously seeking protection, while his gaze raked the footpad and a grim smile curved his lips. 'So. We meet again. There is someone here who would like a word with you.'

The man backed up a few steps, then turned and fled. The gypsy's knife disappeared as if by magic.

'Is this the man?' An officer in scarlet stepped up smartly, glaring at the gypsy who immediately melted into the crowds.

'Not him,' Niall said. 'Him.' He pointed to the retreating ruffian's back. 'Quick, man, he is getting away.'

The lieutenant gave Jenna a quick bow and hurried after his quarry.

Niall took hold of her arm and swung her around to face him. 'What is going on, Lady Jenna? Why are you not at the dressmaker's as you promised?'

A very real desire to have him put his arm around her and hold her close until her body stopped its cowardly tremble, took her by surprise. With difficulty, she forced herself to stand her ground and look him in the eye. 'I did not promise to stay there. I promised to be there when you got back.'

'Hair splitting.' He glanced around, frowning. 'Why were you meeting that criminal?'

Shocked, still shaking inside, she stared at him open-mouthed. 'I wasn't. He must have seen me and decided to finish off what he started.'

His eyes widened. He didn't believe her. She could see it in his tight expression. His mistrust hurt. Not that she cared about his opinion, one way or the other. She didn't dare. It would make her too vulnerable when she needed to be strong.

'An odd coincidence that you should both be here at the same time.'

He really didn't trust her. She felt miserable and angry all at once. 'Wick is a small place. Many people come to the market.' Somehow, though, she didn't feel as if this second meeting was by chance. Yet how could it be otherwise?

His gaze was fixed on the note still clutched in her hand, suspicion rampant in his expression. 'Then why are you here? And to whom are you writing?' he asked.

Dash it all, was she to have no privacy? 'It is none of your business. You are not my guardian or my gaoler.'

His mouth tightened. Disappointment filled his expression, as if he expected her to trust him when he did not trust her. 'Unfortunately I am, until Lord Carrick returns.' He stared at the letter and held out his hand.

Unfortunately. What did he mean, unfortunately? That really hurt. 'This is a private letter, addressed to me from a friend of my father's. It came via the tinker at this stall.'

Mr Gilvry's lips thinned. 'If it is all so innocent, why not simply send it by way of the post office?'

Why was he being so starchy? Surely he wasn't jealous of her letter from home? Not possible. He was simply doing his duty. So he thought. She drew herself up to her full height. Not very impressive beside him, but necessary to make her point. 'Again, it is none of your business.'

'It is, if the getting of it puts you in danger.'

Did that mean he really was worried about her? Her heart gave a cheerful little skip. 'How could I have guessed the man would be here and would risk an approach among so many people? Besides, I thought they must be far away by now, fearing the hue and cry.'

An odd look crossed his face: guilt. She frowned. 'Did you know they were still in the area?'

'I suspected it. I should have warned you.'

So it was guilt. 'Yes, you should have.'

He huffed out a breath. 'It would not have been necessary had you stayed where I left you.'

Now she felt guilty. 'Well, I am certainly glad you came along at the right time.'

He glanced around. 'Where is the tinker you came here to meet?'

She shook her head. 'I have no idea. He ran off when he saw you.'

Should she mention the gypsy's knife? She hesitated a moment too long and Mr Gilvry's face hardened as if he guessed she was holding something back. 'It is back to the dressmaker's with you, Lady Jenna. And then home to Carrick Castle.'

'Carrick is not my home.' She belonged to Braemuir. Heart and soul, though no one else seemed to understand her devotion.

He marched her though the crowds as if she was the criminal, not the man who had accosted her. And yet she did not mind the feel of his hand in the small of her back, the warmth of his large body, and the protection it offered. Should she say something about her suspicion that the man had sought her out? He had probably figured that out for himself.

As he hurried her along, she caught a glimpse of the gypsy. He was watching them with dark unfathomable eyes. She wondered if she should point him out to Mr Gilvry, but before she could do so, the man faded from sight. Besides, if Mr Hughes trusted him, she should too. The person she must not trust was Niall Gilvry.

When they got back to the seamstress's, Campbell already had the carriage waiting outside. He and Mary were deep in conversation at the horse's heads.

'Are you finished here?' Mr Gilvry asked Jenna, nodding towards the shop.

She mentally winced. 'Not quite.'

He sighed. 'Verra well, let us go in. Miss Mary, your presence is required.' He opened the door.

'You don't need to come with me.'

He gave her a look that spoke volumes. Anger. Frustration. And something hotter than either, though he was doing his best to damp it down.

An answering glow sparked in her own veins. Like a child playing near the fire, the closer she got to him, the more likely she was to burn. But there was something about him that made him hard to resist. And that made him dangerous.

With a shiver, she let him take her arm and escort her into the shop.

Chapter Four

Jenna couldn't sleep. After an hour or so of tossing and turning, she'd given up and had moved to the window seat to gaze out into the night. Was it simply by chance that ruffian had been there in the market place? One of them had said something on the road, and it only just now had returned to her. *You are sure this is the one?* The one what?

It wasn't only the ruffian intruding on her rest. She kept seeing Mr Gilvry, at first furious at her trickery, but then reaching for her, pulling her close, kissing her. Not a quick touch of his mouth, but something far more erotic, a melding that made her body burn with longing. The vision had sent her fleeing from her bed.

She glanced over at the tumbled bedcovers. Her mind was going around and around far too quickly for her ever to fall asleep.

She picked up the book she'd finished earlier. She could read it again. Or she could go to the library and choose another one. It might help her sleep. Something boring, like a treatise on sheep-raising. Or something a little more *risqué*, like a book of Gillray's cartoons. Except that would make her laugh and keep her awake.

No, something deadly dull was in order. She pulled on her robe, shoved her feet in her slippers, lit a new candle from the stub in the candlestick on her bedside table, and headed for the library.

She was surprised to see a glimmer of light spilling out into the hallway from the slightly open door. She frowned. Surely the butler would not have left candles alight before retiring for the night. It would be the height of folly indeed. But it must be so, because she was the only one who ever used the library in the evenings. Her cousin never had time for reading and Mrs Preston preferred the drawing room, where the light was better for her needlework.

Still, she could not help feeling that someone was there. Cautiously, she pushed the door wide.

At one of the tables, a man sat in his shirt-sleeves. The light from the candle fell on the book he was reading and cast half his face in shadow. She had no trouble recognising his broad shoulders, the large hand that turned the page, or the studious and handsome profile cast into planes and shadows. Mr Gilvry. An inner gladness bubbled in her veins. A glow of joy at the sight of him. A feeling like nothing she had ever experienced.

As if she actually liked the man.

How was this? Her breath stilled. Her heart sounded loud in her ears. It was as if she'd made some monumental discovery, but did not yet understand its import. But in her heart she knew what it was. Recognised the danger. A growing attachment. Something she could not afford. She owed it to her position to think with her head and not let her heart get in the way. To think logically, as a man would. She must stand on logic or fail those for whom she was responsible.

It left an empty space in her chest. A dark, cold fissure.

Resentment flowed in to fill it. At him, because he was here in a place she'd thought of as her own, surely, for no other reason. Was there nowhere she could go and not stumble over him? He might have saved her life—twice—but it did not give him the right to invade every corner of it. She turned to leave.

He must have heard the movement, because he looked up, then shot to his feet. 'My lady.'

Blast. Now she had no way to escape without acknowledging his presence. 'Mr Gilvry.' If she sounded stiff and haughty, it was because it was either that or sound breathless.

'Can I help you?' He sounded at a loss and his eyes widened as he took in her state of undress.

She clutched a hand to the silky fabric of the robe, drawing it tighter about her throat. 'What are you doing here, Mr Gilvry?'

'Lord Carrick bade me make free with his library before he left.' His glance travelled from her face down her body. It was a lingering glance that almost felt like a physical caress. Her nipples hardened. She glanced down and saw them jutting against the gown's light fabric. Heat rushed to her face.

It is the cold, she wanted to shout. She clung to what little of her dignity remained. 'I doubt that he expected you to come here in the middle of the night.'

Nor should she have come, wearing next to nothing. Yet she had come here so often when she couldn't sleep it had felt like a refuge. Not any longer, clearly.

'He suggested I come in the evening. After my duties.' He picked up his candle and the light of it threw his face into sharp relief. The smooth lean plane of his cheek, the hard uncompromising line of his jaw. The jut of a blade of a nose. He had a strong face. There was nothing soft about it at all, but it appealed to her sense of what a man ought to be. Strong. Unyielding.

A child's view of the world, her father would have said. Looks meant nothing. Liking meant nothing. It was power and wealth that counted if she wanted to do her duty.

'It did not occur to me that anyone else would have the same idea,' he continued, looking uncomfortable. 'It is the first opportunity I have had to take advantage of his offer.'

'Then I should not disturb you.' With a brief smile, she turned away.

He reached the door before her, blocking her exit. As solid a barrier as the mahogany door itself. He stood staring down at her with such intensity, she could not hold his gaze.

'Do not let my presence stand in the way of you finding a book.'

His virile body exuded heat and power. And the scent of bay and lemon. Physical. Overwhelming. She could hardly breathe as she noticed the dark crisp curly hair at the base of his throat where he had removed his cravat. He wore another of those bold-patterned waistcoats he favoured. Strawberries, this time, amid dark-green leaves on a cream background. She dragged her gaze from that impressively broad chest and the beat of his pulse at the base of his bared throat and let her eyes wander upwards. Up past the uncompromising chin to gaze in awe at his firmly carved mouth.

The burst of memory of those lips on hers caused a slow burn low in her abdomen. And when finally their eyes met, his eyelids drooped as if he knew exactly the direction of her thoughts. The air in the room became heavy, thick, unbreatheable.

She moistened her dry lips. 'I couldn't sleep.' Her voice was husky from the dryness in her throat and the rushed beating of her heart.

'I imagine not, after what almost happened today,' he murmured.

Not only that, but how could she admit that she couldn't sleep because of the way he intruded on her thoughts? The way she kept remembering the taste of him, the scent of the wild outdoors that clung to him. She couldn't, so she merely nodded.

He closed his eyes briefly. 'I felt sure the man in the market was going to carry you away. It makes me go cold every time I think of it.'

'Your arrival was timely,' she whispered, gazing up into his eyes, mesmerised by the heat she saw in their depths.

Slowly, his hand lifted to her shoulder, a light touch, but searing, and she welcomed the contact, the feeling of not being quite so alone as she had been since her father died. Though why his touch should have that effect, she didn't know. Perhaps because he'd stood alongside her in her hour of need.

His other hand cradled her cheek. Warm. Callused. Yet infinitely gentle. She held her breath, fearful and wanting. Revelling in his touch, when she knew she should push him away. And knowing she did not want to.

And then his head dipped and his mouth, velvet, warm, brushed her lips. A sweet gentle pressure, softly demanding.

Nothing like the awkward affair she'd initiated on the road, his lips melded with hers, moving, wooing, a finely honed assault. Little chills darted down her back. Her breathing became uneven, her heart an out-of-control thud against her ribs.

The even deep rise and fall of his chest brushed against her breasts in a tantalising caress. His tongue darted against the seam of her mouth, tiny thrilling little flicks telling her what he wanted, yet not demanding. Encouraging.

Inside, she shook with the rise of desire, pressing closer to the wonderful lean length of him, parting her lips and gasping in pleasurable shock as his tongue languorously swept her mouth, sliding against her tongue, tasting her as if she was some sort of honeyed treat.

Heat curled through her veins like smoke filling every corner of her being. Delicious heat. Bone-melting heat.

Her arms went up around his neck. Naturally they would, there being no other way to prevent a slow slide to the floor. His hands encircled her back, pulled her close between his strong thighs, then roamed down her hips and her bottom.

Now she could feel his heartbeat against her

chest, a strong steady rhythm, if a little fast. His breathing rasped in the silence, and felt warm on her ear. She could not suppress a small moan of pleasure at the delicious sensations rippling through her body.

He made a soft sound like a choked-off groan, and his tongue withdrew, his kisses dancing like butterflies over her mouth. Slowly he drew back, his eyes dark, his expression dazed.

And as he looked at her, she saw the moment he came to his senses. Saw the shock and the regret.

He stood there staring at her, looking so stiff and awkward as if he wasn't sure what to do with his hands, which a moment before had been roaming her body in a most intimate way. A strange urge to giggle pressed at her throat. She covered her lips with her fingers to hold it inside. To not let him see how foolish he made her feel inside. How foolishly, femininely weak. A fatal flaw.

'I beg your pardon,' he said stiffly, his expression distant, uncomfortable. 'I should not have let that happen.'

Nor should she. Not when her future was set. A tremor of cold shame shook her body.

He frowned. 'Come to the hearth, my lady, I will wake the fire for you before I leave.'

A firm hand on the small of her spine, a hand that permitted no resistance, ushered her to the sofa. As she sat, he knelt on one knee at the hearth, grimly raking the ashes and stirring the coals. So intense. So distant.

Shaking inside, she watched the way his strong competent hands with their long elegant fingers brought forth a blaze. The flames flickered over his strong features, casting dark shadows in the hollow of his eyes and warming the skin of his cheeks to bronze. A braw bonnie Scots warrior whom she must not think of as a man.

She took a deep breath, finding her courage, straightening her spine, lifting her chin. So she had made a fool of herself this night. No doubt she wasn't the first woman to let lust overcome reason, nor would she be the last. But she desperately did not want him to speak of this to anyone.

Mr Gilvry sat back on his heels, staring at the fire, lips so soft and pliant on hers only moments before, set in a thin straight line.

Disgust at her wantonness for encouraging his kiss, no doubt. For there wasn't a shred of doubt in her mind that she had wanted to feel his lips on hers, to experience the tingles that had stolen her breath the first time they kissed. Only this time had been very different. She now had no doubt of his experience in the art of kissing. He had taken command. Controlled her utterly.

He had made her feel weak. Vulnerable. When she was supposed to be strong. When the future of Braemuir rested on her shoulders. That was why she was trembling inside.

He glanced down at his hands where they rested on his thighs. His fist clenched so hard the knuckles showed white. 'I apologise for my lack of honour just now, my lady.' He shook his head, closing his eyes briefly, apparently as stunned by what had happened as she.

'Oh,' she breathed, surprised that he would take all the blame to himself, as if denying she had been an enthusiastic participant. She stared at him, at the anger she saw directed not at her, but at himself, unsure whether to accept the apology as just, or admit to some of the fault.

A muscle jumped in his jaw. 'I will leave Carrick first thing in the morning.'

It would be dishonourable to take advantage of his guilt. Yet it would be so much easier to remain in control if temptation did not stare her in the face every day. So very much easier. But she had been equally at fault. She gave him a haughty look. 'So you intend to leave me at the mercy of the ruffians who roam the roads hereabouts?'

He looked up at her then, his eyes shadowed. 'Lieutenant Dunstan has the matter in hand. He will find them and bring them to justice in a day or so.'

She arched a brow. 'And in the meantime?'

'You will stay within Carrick's walls. It is but

for a day or so. Dunstan will let you know when the thing is done.'

The note in his voice was both commanding and pleading. Asking her to be sensible, so he could leave with honour. But if he left, her cousin would not be pleased. She knew Carrick. He expected his orders to be followed without question. He would find a way to make this young man suffer for what he would see as his lack of loyalty. 'Then I am to hide out here in fear of my life? For days. Perhaps weeks.' She smiled. 'Ah, but there will be no one to tell me no, will there?' She flicked a dismissive hand. 'Fine. Go.'

He glared at her and pushed to his feet, looming over her, and once more she was very aware of him as a man. 'You are not so foolish as to ride out while those men are at large.'

'Of course not,' she said sweetly looking up at him. 'Not alone.'

He heaved a sigh. 'If you will not be sensible, then you give me no choice but to remain.' He gave her a hard look. 'And there will be no more sneaking off. I'll have your word on it.'

Relief flooded through her. To know he would stay. That he would stand between her and danger. It seemed cowardly, but it was sensible. Rational. 'You have my word.'

Suspicion lurked in his eyes, but he did not give her the lie. He merely nodded and sat down beside her on the sofa.

'Then I will have no more lies from you,' he said harshly. 'What was so important about the letter, that it must be delivered in secret?'

The odd note in his voice alerted her to something more going on than the question revealed. 'It was a letter from my home. Braemuir. My cousin Carrick prefers I not interfere in what he sees as his prerogative while he remains as my trustee. But they are my people, Mr Gilvry. It is my land. It is only right they should make their concerns known to me.'

'Who sent the letter?'

Her spine stiffened at the suspicion in his tone. 'The vicar.'

'He is a fine young man, no doubt.'

She frowned at the offhand way he passed his comment. It contained a note of jealousy. She opened her mouth to tell him that the Reverend Hughes was seventy if he was a day and married, but some devil inside her put other words on her tongue. 'He is indeed a fine man.'

Silence greeted her words. He leaned forwards, his elbows on thighs encased in skin-tight pantaloons, and clasped his hands together. She had a strong urge to rest her head against the strong right arm, to draw on his strength, even unburden her worries. The letter spoke of neglect and implored her to return and take up the reins as her father had intended. And so she would. As the wife of a husband who could set things to right.

Mr Gilvry was not that man, and to lean on him would be weakness.

If only she did not find Mr Gilvry so wickedly alluring or so serious and honourable, it would be easier to keep him at a distance.

He looked at her sideways. 'I gave my word to Carrick that I would stand in his stead with you until his return. So far, I have made a muckle of it. But that will change from today. There will be no more sneaking off. Or wandering the castle at night, putting yourself in harm's way. No more nonsense between us. Do I make myself clear?'

Nonsense meant kissing. And she certainly had no plan to repeat the experience, having demonstrated that she had no power to resist him. 'You are very clear, Mr Gilvry.'

He didn't look particularly comforted by her answer, but he nodded and pushed to his feet. 'Then I will leave you to the fire and your reading.' He gathered up the tomes he had been looking at and strode from the room.

Leaving her in command of the field of battle.

An ache filled her chest. Because she had the strong suspicion that while he had felt a twinge of jealousy over Mr Hughes, he had definitely enjoyed their kiss.

The thought made her feel warm all over.

Three days later, while Jenna sat reading and Mrs Preston worked at her embroidery, there was a decided rap on the door. Jenna looked up, knowing even before the door opened that it was Niall. Knew it from the way her heart rose in her throat, from the hum in her veins. The tingling awareness in her scalp. And there he was in the doorway.

For three days they had carefully avoided each other, making sure what had happened in the library could not possibly happen again. Heat crept up her face at the recollection. She met his steady gaze with calm indifference, despite the unsteady beat of her heart and that betraying blush.

'Good morning, Mr Gilvry,' Mrs Preston said. Her face held enquiry.

He bowed. 'Good morning, Mrs Preston. Lady Jenna. Letters have arrived from Lord Carrick.' He handed her a sealed note.

There was something about the way he spoke that gave her an odd feeling in the pit of her stomach, something dark in his eyes, as if whatever was in that note was not to his taste.

And he wasn't leaving. But then if it had been nothing but simple greetings, the butler would have delivered the note.

She broke the seal and unfolded the paper.

At first she did not quite believe what she was reading. Each word sent a different emotion careening though her. Surprise. Gladness. Worry. And, strangest of all, disappointment. She read again more slowly. Absorbing the full import of the words. Bridegrooms. Three of them, coming here. To woo her.

'Oh, my,' she said looking at Mr Gilvry, who stood hands behind his back, shoulders square, his face set in grim lines. 'You know what he says?'

He nodded. 'I also received a letter.'

'What is it, my dear?' Mrs Preston asked. 'You've gone quite pale.'

'It seems we are to have visitors.' Jenna got up, handed her the letter and went to the window, looking out across the countryside to a gleam of sea in the distance. Seeing, but not seeing.

This was what she had asked for. Not quite this. In her heart, she had hoped for a Season in Edinburgh. Balls. Dancing. Society. A rather childish dream, in light of Carrick's impatient admonishment to do her duty and select one of these men as a husband before his return in a week.

She had pressed him hard and this was his response.

A brisk determination of her future. At least he was letting her have her choice. Somewhat. A choice he controlled. Because he did not think her capable of making a sensible decision.

The thought rankled.

She turned back to the room and caught Niall looking at her with an expression on his face she could not read. He masked it quickly, so she wasn't sure, but she thought it might be regret.

He looked so handsome in the morning light, so clearly intent on his duty. If only he was…eligible. Her heart stumbled. How could this be? This funny little stab of pain in her chest. This foolish feeling of longing.

Because of their kiss.

Surely she had more sense.

A muscle jumped in his jaw. And while his gaze left hers to watch Mrs Preston as she read Lord Carrick's letter, about his mouth there was a hint of distaste.

Her spine stiffened at his disapproval. She glanced at Mrs Preston, who was still reading. 'An unusual way of proceeding, don't you think, ma'am?'

The older woman looked up, her eyes wide. 'I have never heard the like. But it is what you wanted.'

Her voice quavered with doubt. As if she expected Jenna to balk.

And on one level she wanted to. She wasn't sure she was ready. Not really. Yet this plan would have her back to Braemuir in weeks instead of the months it might take if she went to Edinburgh.

These men were all approved by her cousin. Handpicked. And, according to his letter, they were willing.

'I think it will serve my purpose.' It had to, despite a sudden feeling of panic.

'Then we must prepare,' Mrs Preston said, looking brighter. More animated than Jenna had ever seen her. 'Three bachelors arriving here at any moment to vie for your hand? Like a fairytale. I vow it is positively romantic.'

Terrifying, more like. 'Romance has nothing to do with it,' Jenna said a little more sharply than she intended, and Niall's gaze shot to her face as if seeking out her true emotions.

Emotions had no place in her choice of a husband. They could not, if she was to do her duty.

Even so, the constraints of her situation chafed. Made her less than charitable. 'Well, Mr Gilvry, how do you propose we entertain our guests?' She waved a hand. 'Have them read books, perhaps?'

He gave her a puzzled frown.

'It will be hard to amuse them, if I am not to leave the castle walls. Young men don't take kindly to being shut up all day as well as all evening.'

He stiffened, instantly picking up her oblique reference to his position as her gaoler. No lack of quickness of mind in Mr Gilvry. Something she admired about him. No. Not admired. Admiration had no place in their relationship. But she could respect him.

'There is safety in numbers,' he said coolly. 'I am sure something can be arranged.'

But she heard an underlying tension in his

voice. He was not as calm as he appeared, despite his refusal to rise to her challenge.

But then nor was she the slightest bit calm. Her pulse was beating far too fast. And she did not have time to think about her inner turmoil.

'We must prepare for our visitors at once, my dear Mrs Preston. Chambers. Musicians from Wick for dancing in the evening, perhaps.' These men must have the chance to show off all of their accomplishments so she could choose. 'My cousin gives me only a week to make my decision since he does not wish to bear the expense of entertaining these gentlemen for any extended period.' After a week, her cousin threatened to make the choice himself. That, she would not allow.

She turned to Niall. 'What can we offer them out of doors, Mr Gilvry?'

There was a harshness in his voice when he replied. A disapproval. 'Hunting, perhaps. Boating on the loch if the weather is fair. A visit to local points of interest.'

And he would accompany them. Of that she was sure. And glad. He would be her rock in what felt like an upcoming storm, much as he did not seem to like the idea. 'I am glad to see you rising to the occasion.'

'It is my job, my lady.'

That was all she was to him. A responsibility. What more had she expected? Had she thought he would try to talk her out of following her cousin's wishes? If she had, then clearly she was due for disappointment. 'You will let me know if you have other ideas.'

He bowed. 'I will give it my undivided attention.'

Sarcasm? Or just him being punctilious? Likely the latter. 'I am sure you will.' She gave him a brief smile—an apology of sorts—but received nothing but a steady glance in return.

Whatever his thoughts on this way of proceeding, he was not going to share. And it would do no good if he did. She was committed.

'Come, Mrs Preston, let us seek further information about these men from *Debrett's*.'

Niall left them to it and went to seek out Mc-Dougall, to see if he had any commands for him. 'I will have some time before these gentlemen arrive.'

McDougall sat slumped in his chair like a deflated pig's bladder after Niall had told him what was about to transpire. 'Aye. See if you can find a receipt for a pistol from Manton's in his lordship's office. They are dunning us, but Carrick says he paid them last time he was in London.'

'Where shall I look?'

'In his desk. He sometimes throws them in his right-hand drawer and then forgets to pass them on. Bring everything you find, if you wouldn't mind.'

Glad of something to do that would allow him to forget the prospect of entertaining young noblemen, Niall wended his way back up the stairs in the castle.

He hesitated outside Carrick's office, feeling a little uncomfortable about entering the man's private space. But if he trusted McDougall to read his mail, then he must have the authority for this, too.

He opened the door and went in. The desk dominated the small room, its walnut surface polished to a shine and completely bare.

A matching glass-fronted bookcase stood behind it, and tapestries of ancient hunting scenes covered the walls. A harmonious mix of old and new.

Niall crossed to the desk, pulled on the drawer on the right-hand side and it opened. As McDougall had said, it was full of scraps of papers itemising various purchases and reckonings from inns. They all looked like they'd been crumpled and stuffed in a pocket before ending up here.

He took them out one by one, smoothing them flat so he could carry them back to McDougall.

Near the bottom of the pile was a small brass-bound ledger with a clasp to lock it. It wasn't like any of the ones down in the office where he worked. He pulled it out to get to the rest of the drawer's contents.

It fell open as he put it down. He continued rescuing the papers and soon had a neat pile.

He went to put the ledger back in the drawer. A name caught his attention. Indeed, it leaped off the page. Tearny.

None of his business. He went to close it, glanced up at the open door, then could not help but read the entry. Tearny had been employed at Dunross on Carrick's recommendation. He had set fire to the distillery and then tried to kill Ian's wife. They had never got to the bottom of his motive, because Ian had killed him in self-defence. Ian had asked Niall to see what he could discover about the man's background while in Wick. One thing he hadn't expected was to find such large payments to the man from his chieftain.

The size of the number beside Tearny's name made him whistle under his breath. Why would Carrick have paid the man thirty pounds? The date was odd, too, falling a week after Tearny's death, and the first initial was wrong. Perhaps this was a different man altogether.

He flipped back through the pages. Other payments in varying amounts over several months had been made to J. Tearny, the land steward, in the months before his death. But Niall had seen Tearny's regular pay listed in the books held in McDougall's office. These were in addition to his salary. Beside each entry in the explanation column were annotations in capital letters as if it was some sort of code. He could not help but notice some had the initials IG and AG. Did the G stand for Gilvry and if so what service had Tearny performed that related to Ian and Andrew? He tried to recall the significance of the dates to see if there was a pattern.

He went back to the entry he'd first seen and looked at it again. This was E. Tearny. Who would that be? The man's widow, perhaps? Some sort of pension after the man's death? Why such a large sum? And no indication of where this Tearny might be found. He might find the name in the rent rolls in McDougall's office. He made a mental note to check.

There were many other entries in the ledger, some bearing the identifier "Braemuir" in the explanation column. Where had he heard of that?

Footsteps echoed on the stone stairs outside. He closed the book. Shoved it back in the desk and felt the heat of guilt scald his skin. He picked up the pile of papers.

'Mr Gilvry,' a soft voice said.

'Lady Jenna,' he replied with a bow. 'Just collecting some documents for Mr McDougall.'

'So I see. It is unusual to see the door open. My cousin usually keeps it locked when he is not here.'

'Mr McDougall gave me the key.'

'Oh,' she said. 'Of course.'

She stood staring at him, hesitating on the threshold, looking as if she wanted to say something but was having trouble choosing her words.

She looked pretty in her blue gown. He wanted to touch her, to feel her soft skin against his palm. Kiss her sweet lips and see if they tasted as good as he remembered. Damn it, they were alone. Something he had sworn he would ensure did not happen again.

He forced himself to look away. 'If you'll excuse me, I have to get these back to Mr. McDougall.' Brusque. Practically rude. His tongue, never silver at the best of times, turned into a blunt instrument around her. But then he wasn't a man with soft address tripping off his tongue, and the longer he stood here, the more likely he was to forget his vow. He bowed and she stepped back to let him pass and lock the door.

He ran down the stairs like the hounds of hell were on his heels. He would gladly have faced the hounds of hell, but the temptation of Lady Jenna was more than he wanted to risk.

And as his boots clattered on the stairs, he remembered where he had heard of Braemuir. It was the Lady Jenna's holding.

Chapter Five

Niall had been assigned a chamber in one of the towers beside the gatehouse. Each time he went anywhere near the window, he felt dizzy. He should have insisted on lodgings elsewhere, but that would have required an explanation, so he'd said nothing. It was bad enough being laughed at by his brothers without exposing himself to ridicule here.

Even standing far back from his window, he'd seen the cavalcade winding up the road from the town. Men on horses. Carriages piled to the roof with luggage. Outriders. Like a royal procession. He had hurried to inform Lady Jenna of their imminent arrival.

Now he stood with Lady Jenna on the steps to the entrance, waiting for the guests to come through the gates.

The men were three younger sons of Scottish nobility, all wealthy, and all apparently seeking the advancement of their ambitions by the purchase of a title. Could no one but him see how medieval this was? What sort of men were willing to endure being picked over like apples in a barrel when it was clear Lady Jenna was the real prize?

He froze, surprised by how angry he felt. All right, so he was attracted to the lass. He was a man. Likely half the men in the castle found her alluring. It didn't mean he cared who she decided to marry. His job was simply to keep her safe until she picked a husband. And if one of these bachelors tried anything untoward, Niall would ensure he'd wear his guts for garters, as Drew had liked to say.

The thought eased his tension until he turned his head to look at the lady in question. She wore a white gown of the finest muslin, like a virgin sacrifice, except the fluttering cherry-coloured ribbons on her straw bonnet and tied in little bows down the front of her gown added teasing touches of temptation. As did her rosy parted lips. Not a sacrifice at all. An eager participant.

This was exactly what she wanted.

Something ugly and dark twisted inside him. He wanted to hit something. To howl a protest. He recognised it for what it was: jealousy. He beat it back with a wry smile. He had no right to be jealous. So what if he had kissed her? Twice now. It was an error of judgement on both their parts. A mistake that would not be repeated.

As if sensing his regard, she glanced his way. It was then that he saw the shadows in the depths of her eyes. The anxiety. The knowledge that if she chose wrongly, the future would be bleak. In the second that their eyes met and locked, he vowed she would not be the only one taking a close look at these men and their worth.

And then they were coming through the gates. Three fine men whose horses pranced into the courtyard, gallant and dashing, proclaiming their status and wealth. The carriages would wait out on the road until the guests were safely inside. The servants in the courtyard sprang into action and Peter's grooms and stable hands were soon leading the mounts away.

With Mrs Preston at her side, Lady Jenna tripped lightly down the steps to greet the arrivals. Niall stationed himself behind her. The butler, waiting at the bottom of the steps, took each man's calling card and introduced them to Mrs Preston and Lady Jenna in turn. The men bowed politely.

'Welcome,' Lady Jenna said, her voice clear and steady. 'Welcome to Carrick Castle, gentlemen. Permit me to introduce Mr Niall Gilvry, who stands in Lord Carrick's place in his absence.'

The oldest man of the three, a Mr McBane, gave him a sharp look and shook Niall's hand firmly. He was of average height and build, his brown hair already receding, but his brown eyes were mild and intelligent. The other two followed suit. Mr Murray was a fair-haired man in his early twenties with bright blue eyes who no doubt considered himself a Corinthian, judging from his dress and his attempt to crush Niall's hand. Lastly, Mr Oswald, sandy-haired with sharp, almost foxy features and shirt-points starched to insurmountable points, offered a languid two-fingered touch.

'Shall we go inside?' Lady Jenna said. 'I expect you would care to refresh yourselves after your journey.'

The guests passed the servants standing on each side like soldiers on parade: the secretary, butler, the head groom, maids and footmen. Only McBane nodded an acknowledgement of their presence. He was a good few years older than the other two and a widower by all accounts, and the best of the bunch from Niall's first impression.

The other two were popinjays, one a sportsman and the other a dandy. But it was wrong to judge a man by appearance alone. Carrick must think any one of them would make a good husband and it was actions, not appearances, that counted.

Niall followed them in. It was his duty to show

them to their quarters and give them a brief explanation of the castle layout, so they could find their way to dinner in the dining room later.

A dinner where he would sit in place of her guardian. A role he would not shirk.

Almost over, dinner had gone perfectly smoothly. Not that Jenna had expected otherwise. The castle staff were a well-oiled machine. Conversation during the meal had allowed her to learn more about the characters of her suitors.

Mr Oswald, seated to her left, was the second son of an earl and a tulip of fashion. She suspected he might even be wearing a corset. Not that he creaked or anything, as she had heard about the Prince Regent, but she sensed an odd stiffness in his spine.

He also lisped very slightly, yet his blue eyes seemed to glimmer with humour at the oddest moments. 'My dear Lady Jenna,' he said, putting down his fork, 'when I learned I was to live in a castle, I must be honest, I had no idea what to expect. I am entirely gratified to discover there are no rushes on the floor, or dogs scrabbling for bones under the table.'

She couldn't help but laugh at his droll expression. 'We aim to please.'

'What are the plans for tomorrow?' Murray asked.

'Do you like to shoot, Mr Murray?' she asked.

'Rather,' Murray replied. 'I never travel without my own shotgun. Ordered it from Manton's to my exact specifications. I am an excellent shot. Bagged the most birds of anyone last time out.'

An excellent shot or a braggart. Time would prove which.

'At this time of year we have little to offer in the way of game birds,' Mr Gilvry said matter-of-factly. 'But if it is sport you want, there are hares and wood pigeons aplenty.' He had been silent for most of dinner, watching their guests with a grim intensity as if he would pounce on anyone who stepped out of line.

Jenna had smiled at him once or twice and received only a steady stare in return. Clearly, he was taking his position seriously.

'And you, Mr McBane?' she asked the gentleman seated beyond Murray, the oldest of the three gentlemen, a widower with three children according to the latest edition of *Debrett's Peerage*.

'I'm not averse to an afternoon with a gun, Lady Jenna,' he replied, shifting slightly to permit one of the footmen to refill his glass in a polite little gesture that suggested a kindly heart. 'A little variety in the kitchen is a good thing, I believe. I did not bring my shotgun, however.'

A man with a practical turn of mind, it seemed. 'Lord Carrick keeps guns for his guests.'

'I prefer my own,' Murray said, thrusting his

jaw forwards and looking around as if daring anyone to suggest he was wrong.

'Then we shall definitely have to see if we can provide you with some sport,' she said soothingly. 'If the weather remains fine. And once you have recovered from your journey.'

'I expect I could manage it in a day or so,' Mr Oswald said, 'provided we are not required to be in the field before noon.'

'You cannot be tired, Oswald,' Mr Murray scoffed. 'You didn't set foot from your cabin the whole time we were on board.'

'I loathe travelling by sea.'

'I'm a fine sailor,' Murray said. 'Never see me keeping below. I was able to put a line in, too. Caught a couple of cod. Had 'em for dinner.'

Did the man think of nothing but sport? Would he care about the land and the people at Braemuir, or only about its game?

'You gentlemen did not run into any trouble on the road from town?' Mr Gilvry asked. 'We've had trouble with footpads in the area.'

'Never saw a one,' Mr Murray said. 'Would have dealt with them soundly if I had.'

Mr Oswald gave a good imitation of a yawn. 'It might have alleviated some of the boredom.'

Mr McBane smiled at him cheerfully. 'I doubt any footpad would dare come anywhere near us with so many grooms and outriders as Oswald brought with him.'

'My dear fellow, a man must have his comforts,' Oswald said.

Mr Gilvry's mouth flattened. 'No doubt you are right.'

Whether he referred to the comforts Mr Oswald required or the size of the party putting off any villains, Jenna wasn't quite sure. Likely both, from the look on his face.

'I don't know if you gentlemen are interested in history, but there are a few sites not far from here worth visiting,' Mrs Preston said hesitantly. 'Some ruined castles. And standing stones.'

Mr Oswald unsuccessfully hid yet another yawn. Mr Murray frowned.

Mr McBane on the other hand brightened. 'Perhaps a picnic would be in order.'

'My thought exactly,' Jenna said. She was beginning to like this man, even if he was a little older than she had expected. He certainly seemed easier to please than the other two. But being easy to please could be a sign of lack of energy.

'And we could arrange a day of sailing up the coast,' she offered.

'With fishing,' Mr Murray said, looking more cheerful.

Mr Oswald shuddered. 'I'll vote for the picnic after all.'

Jenna couldn't help it—she laughed.

He grinned at her. 'And if there are enough of us, I would not be averse to an evening of cards.'

So that was where his preference lay. And if it was deep play he wanted, he was not the man for her. 'I am sure it can be arranged,' she said with a cool smile.

'You are a wonderful hostess, Lady Jenna,' he said with fervour. Oddly enough, she had the feeling he meant it.

The servants began to clear the last course.

'Shall we retire, dear, and leave these gentlemen to their dram?' Mrs Preston said, smiling brightly at the company. 'After such a long journey we do not expect your company in the drawing room this evening, but we shall not let you off so lightly again.'

The gentlemen rose and smiled their agreement.

To a chorus of goodnights, she and Mrs Preston left the room.

'They are all such handsome, eligible gentlemen,' Mrs Preston said as they walked along the corridor to their respective chambers. 'I have no idea how you will choose which one to marry.'

Jenna held back a hysterical laugh, a reaction to the panic she was feeling inside. 'Neither do I.'

She hadn't expected to know which of these men to choose at first sight, or to fall in love with. Indeed, that would be the last thing she wanted. She just hadn't expected to be left feeling quite so indifferent.

* * *

Niall paused outside the library door, bracing to steady himself, and checked his cravat and fastened his coat buttons. He'd been on his way to bed after too much of Lord Carrick's whisky. The other men had talked and he had listened. And drank. More than he should have. But not nearly enough to dampen the feeling of foreboding that had plagued him from the moment these men had arrived. A feeling that this role of watchdog was far more onerous than he could ever have imagined.

Being polite to men for whom he held a feeling of contempt. And, damn it, envy.

And now Lady Jenna had asked him to meet with her.

God help him, what on earth could she want at this time of the night? He hoped to hell she was wearing proper attire. His body tightened at the thought that she might not be. At the hope. The drink was making him stupid. The last thing he needed was any kind of entanglement with a woman he was supposed to be protecting as if she was his ward or his daughter.

He glowered at the door. He should just turn around and go to bed. See her in the morning, when his head was clear. But then, the footman who had caught him outside his chamber had said it was urgent.

Aware of that same footman watching in the

hallway, he knocked. When invited, he stepped into the room, deliberately leaving the door open. He remained standing, barely over the threshold. 'You sent for me, my lady.'

She was seated on the sofa, dressed in the rose-hued gown she'd worn at dinner tonight. A far more daring gown than the one she had worn to welcome their guests this afternoon. He'd had the strong urge to wrap her in a shawl when he'd first seen her in the drawing room where they had gathered before going into dinner. Especially after young Murray had openly ogled her breasts.

Though it was hard not to ogle—they were so bounteously displayed. But it had offended him the way Murray had looked at her: like a horse trader at a fair.

'I am sorry to interrupt your evening, Mr Gilvry,' she said, her voice brittle.

He dragged his gaze away from that lovely expanse of creamy flesh to gaze at her face. She looked anxious. Just as anxious as she'd looked this afternoon standing on the steps. Shouldn't she be happy? She'd got her wish. Her choice of a husband. The idea of it churned in his stomach, mixing with whisky and the coarse talk of men in their cups.

He narrowed his eyes, squinting at her to make sure she stayed properly in focus. 'How may I serve you, Lady Jenna?' He glanced around pointedly for her companion. 'The hour is late.'

She got up and paced to a small inlaid table on the other side of the room. She picked up the decanter. 'May I offer you a dram?'

Oh, yes, that was all he needed. More whisky. He already had so little defence against all that lovely exposed flesh. Another drink and he'd be trying to ravish her on the sofa. 'No, thank you, my lady.' Ha. That sounded polite enough.

She splashed some of the golden liquid into a tumbler and took a deep swallow. 'I find I am in need of some advice.' Her voice trembled a little.

The word tumbled through the molasses in his brain. 'Advice,' he echoed. He pressed his lips together, determined to say nothing more until she revealed what was on her mind.

'Perhaps it is more your opinion I am seeking. In my cousin's absence.'

His gut gave a nasty lurch and tossed his dinner upwards towards his throat. Suddenly, he wished he had not refused the whisky.

She gave him a quick glance and returned her gaze to her drink. 'I wondered…' She paused, swirling the liquid in the glass as if trying the words out in her head before actually saying them. Picking over them with care, if her frown was anything to go by.

His heart stilled. She was not going to ask him… No. Oh, no. 'It is not my place to offer an opinion,' he said swiftly, surprising himself at how easily the words formed on his tongue, when his tongue felt rather too large to fit behind his teeth.

'But you have formed one?'

'No.' He could see that answer was too blunt. Too cryptic. He got his thoughts in order. Spoke carefully. 'All of these gentlemen are approved of by your cousin. They must all be equally... equally...' What? Equally idiotic? Rich? Connected? He shrugged, lost for words. He did not like equivocating, but he would not give her his opinion. Because if she listened to him, she would be sending all of them back where they came from.

And not because there was anything wrong with them.

She stared at him. Her shoulders slumped. 'I see.' She swallowed hard. 'I thought it would be easy. I find I don't know how to choose,' she said huskily. 'And I only have a week. They are all perfectly pleasant, each in his own way. They are all of good family and suitably wealthy. But how can I be sure I understand their real characters in such a short time?'

Wealth. Was that all she cared about? What he wanted to say and what he should say were so diametrically opposed. He remained silent.

'What if I said I was leaning towards Mr McBane, then?'

A man nearly old enough to be her father. His mouth tightened.

'You don't like the idea?'

'I don't have an opinion, my lady,' he said woodenly.

'You perhaps prefer Mr Oswald?'

The man set his teeth on edge. 'No, I don't.'

'Then it is Mr. Murray you favour?'

'I favour none of them.' He cursed inwardly at the harshness in his voice. He gentled his tone, forced a smile that he had the feeling was more like a grimace. 'I mean, my lady, it is your decision.'

She finished her drink and turned away, looking towards the hearth, the fire dancing in her hair like flame and heat. And if he wasn't mistaken there was a slight tremble in those milky-white shoulders. 'You are of no more help than Mrs Preston,' she declared. 'I am sorry to have troubled you.'

The tone in her voice said she'd thought he'd let her down. For some reason she had expected him to have the key to choosing the right man. And damn him, he had the urge to offer help. But how?

He recalled words his grandfather had said to him and his brothers time and again. 'The true worth of a man can only be judged by his ordinary behaviour in extraordinary circumstances.' He winced as he realised he had spoken out loud. But it had been on his mind while listening to those three men brag and posture, jostling for position in the marriage horse race after she'd left them in the dining room, as if it was his decision as to which of them would be the winner. They clearly were thinking about themselves and not the woman for whom they vied.

She whirled to face him, her skirts belling around her tiny feet. 'What sort of circumstances?'

'How he accomplishes a difficult goal. Some worthy objective.'

Her head tilted. 'Oh. Like the fairy tale. The princess who set her suitors tasks so she could choose the right man to marry. Stealing gold from a dragon.'

He stared at her blankly. The molasses once more made it impossible to follow the twist and turn of her mind. He had thought they were talking about the men who had come to offer for her hand. 'There is no such thing as dragons.'

She frowned. 'I know. But something of that nature. Something that would test their mettle.'

He wished he'd never mentioned it. Because he remembered the circumstances surrounding those words spoken by his grandfather each spring with a feeling of nausea.

'What if we have each of them rescue me from some sort of danger?' she mused.

The hairs on his nape rose. 'What if they fail?'

Her eyes slowly focused on him, as if she had

been drawn back from somewhere far away. 'What did you say?'

'I said, if you are in danger and the man fails, what then?'

'Oh, you will be there to straighten everything out.'

'Me?' He felt as if a huge weight had landed on his shoulders.

'Yes. It is your idea.'

'It is not my idea to put you in danger.' He dragged through what had been a pleasant buzz in his mind and was now a poisonous fog, searching for something that would keep this under control. 'Test their dancing skills. Their intelligence. Their…I don't know…their competence with regard to putting food on the table. You suggested they go shooting. Pick the one who bags the most pigeons.'

She frowned. 'I don't care much about how they shoot, or dance, or ride. And my understanding is that most gentlemen do all these things very well.'

'Even Oswald?' He could not keep his lips from forming a smirk at the thought of that fussy gentleman doing anything that involved breaking a sweat.

'I think Mr Oswald has more to him than he lets on.'

'Then pick him,' Niall said and winced at the irritation in his voice.

She put her hands on her hips and looked at him, but she wasn't seeing him, she was seeing something else entirely. He wanted to move out of her line of sight. He did not like the way she was looking right through him. He remained still. Waiting for her to realise it was all nonsense. She wasn't brainless. She'd see it in a moment or two. And then he could crawl into his bed and try not to dream about kissing her and more.

She drifted to the sofa and sat down. 'What I want to know is,' she said softly, so softly it was almost a whisper, 'will they make decisions that are just and fair? Will they keep their word, no matter what the temptation? Will they deliver on a promise, no matter what? These are things I must know before I make a decision.'

He found himself dropping down to sit beside her, looking into stormy eyes and feeling as if he was sinking fast. 'Why? What does it matter? They are all wealthy. All well connected and all approved by Lord Carrick. Pick the one you like best.' And end his torture.

'But which one will be best for Braemuir.'

He frowned. 'I thought Braemuir was a house. And land.'

A tinge of red coloured her cheeks. Anger. Or passion. It lit her from the inside out as he gazed at her. 'You don't understand,' she said, twisting her hands in her lap. 'How could you? How could anyone? I love Braemuir. I grew up there and always knew it would be mine one day. Braemuir is who I am. What I am. The house. The land and its people. It has been neglected for too many years. The man I marry, the next Baron Aleyne, must be willing to invest in its future. And soon if it is to be saved. I must make the right choice.' She looked at him, her eyes full of fire. 'I promised my father.'

Passion indeed. A great responsibility for such a small delicate lass. Yet she had more determination than most men. And he certainly understood her sense of responsibility. But he could not see how he could help her make her choice.

'You definitely need to ask them to fight a dragon.'

She laughed then. A genuine laugh full of honesty that made his heart grow too large for his chest. 'I don't think there are any in these parts,' she said, still smiling, eyes sparkling with amusement. 'But I have only a week. And while I have a sense of each of them, I think you are right, you cannot really tell what someone is like until they are thrown into a situation out of their control. Mr Murray is handsome and energetic, but I wonder about his intelligence. Mr McBane is a true gentleman, mild of manner, kindly and yet seemingly lacks purpose. And Mr Oswald...'

'A man-milliner.'

'Beneath all that fussiness is a wicked sense of

humour and a great deal of cleverness. But I very much suspect he hides who he really is.'

Niall wasn't convinced. He'd met men like Oswald before. They cared only for the set of their coat and the height of their cravat and the latest gossip. But then a wealthy man didn't need to care for much else. Unless it was snaring a title.

'There is good and bad in all men, I suppose,' he said.

She nodded. 'Which is why the idea of a test is so appealing. Something that will make one of them stand out against the others. There has to be something we could devise.'

Or make them all look like idiots. The thought was a sharp bright light in his mind. A very tempting flash of brilliance.

To what end? She'd only have to start again. And Carrick would be as displeased with him as he would be with himself. He had been given a simple task and it did not involve endangering either Lady Jenna or her suitors.

On the other hand…

'What?' she asked.

He looked at her. Could she read his thoughts? He hesitated.

'Tell me,' she demanded.

The dark ugly thing inside him refused to be silenced. 'There was this annual competition between us Gilvry lads each spring. Our grandfather would give a prize for the one who collected the most eggs from the gulls on the cliffs.

'A test of daring.' She sounded disappointed.

'Not entirely. One year, while we were all climbing up the way, Drew tied a rope to a boulder and went down. He won easily.'

She frowned. 'What is your point?'

'Ian, my older brother, was furious.' He laughed as he remembered Ian's fury. 'He said it was cheating. By going down on a rope, he had two hands free, you see, whereas everyone else needed one hand to hang on to the rocks. My grandfather said there was nothing in the rules to say he had to climb upwards and gave him the prize.'

She wrinkled her small nose and he had a terrible urge to kiss the tip. He was leaning towards her with that very purpose in mind when she spoke. 'How does it fit our current situation?'

He halted the pursuit of her nose to think about the answer. 'My grandfather said it showed that in addition to courage, Drew had more than his fair share of wit. After that, we all went looking for other ways to win.' He could not help a foolish smile, recalling how Logan, to go one better than Drew, had paid a boy to lead his donkey slowly along the cliff face and collected more eggs in one hour than the rest of them had managed in a day. Grandfather had deducted the cost of the boy and the donkey out of the value of the prize.

'Did you ever win?'

That stopped him cold. Sobered him. Somewhat. 'Once.'

'How?'

'By climbing the cliffs at night. At night, the birds can't fly at you and try to knock you off the cliff.' And he hadn't been able to see how far it was to the ground. It was the only time he'd ever climbed higher than ten feet from the sand. There weren't many eggs at that level.

'They fly at you?' Her voice rose in a squeak. 'But wasn't it dangerous in the dark?'

It had been freeing. But he'd never told anyone that part, because his brothers would have laughed harder at him than usual. He had dreaded that contest every year. Loathed it. His grandfather had deemed it a foolish risk, given him a tongue-lashing as he gave him his prize.

'Are you suggesting we ask the gentlemen to collect eggs?'

'No. It was an example, that was all.'

She tilted her head. 'If it was good enough for your grandfather, I don't see why it shouldn't be good enough for me.'

He shook his head, trying to clear his thoughts, trying to imagine the gentlemen sitting around that table tonight scrambling up a cliff. A chuckle rose in his throat. 'They won't do it.' Hell, he'd barely done it himself. 'Better to find a dragon.'

She laughed again, shaking her head this time.

And he once more felt inordinately pleased. Beyond pleased, because when she smiled her whole face lit up. And for an instant the shadows were gone. And the way her mouth curved upwards at the corners when she smiled made him want to touch it with his tongue.

He forced himself not to look at her mouth. Or her chest. He gripped his hands on his knees and looked at the fire, watched the flames dancing. He'd like to dance with her. Hold her in his arms, whirl her around the room until she was giddy. Then he'd walk with her in a moonlit garden and kiss her senseless. 'You should hold a ball. Let the gentlemen court you properly.'

She turned a pretty shade of pink. 'We will talk more in the morning.'

When he was sober and careful. He turned to her, gazing into her eyes, losing himself. 'Jenna,' he breathed.

'Niall, please. You must go now.'

Because she knew he wanted to kiss her. And she didn't want it. Of course she didn't, any more than he did. He was cup-shot. Surely he'd be kissing any woman who came into his field of vision.

'We will discuss this in the morning, when you are more yourself.' The words were kindly meant, but it felt as if they cut a strip from his hide.

When was he ever himself around her? He pushed to his feet and looked down at her. The shadows in those green eyes clung there like mist among the hills. He wanted to hold her and tell her it would all be all right. That whichever of these men she chose, everything would be fine. Only how could he promise such a thing, when he was filled with doubt?

'Goodnight, Mr Gilvry.'

He bowed. 'Goodnight, my lady.' He felt proud when he managed to leave in a perfectly straight line. Almost as proud as he had when he won the egg contest. The need to win, the need to prove himself as good as his brothers, had pushed him beyond what made sense. When his mother had heard what he'd done, she'd declared an end to their annual contest.

His brothers had been furious that he had ruined their fun.

He'd been so utterly relieved. And then he'd felt like the worst kind of coward.

A cuckoo in the Gilvry nest was what he was. Undoubtedly.

Chapter Six

Mr Gilvry looked sterner than usual when he presented himself in the drawing room the next morning. 'Good morning, ladies,' he said with an abrupt bow. 'You wished to speak with me?'

Mrs Preston smiled at him vaguely. 'We were wondering about the entertainments for the gentlemen.'

His frown deepened. 'Given the weather, I would suggest a game of billiards, ma'am.'

The weather was abysmal. Rain rattled against the windowpanes and the wind was whistling down the chimney.

Jenna rose to her feet and went to look out at the dismal day. 'Do you think the weather will clear later, Mr Gilvry?'

'No, my lady.'

So brusque. Once again trying to put her at

a distance. But she needed his help. She stared out across the town to where the sea should be, now hidden in mist. 'Surely that is a patch of blue there on the horizon?'

As she had hoped, he came to stand beside her. Or rather, not quite beside her, a little back from the window. He barely glanced out. 'I see naught but rain clouds.'

'Have you thought any more about our idea from last night?' she asked in a low voice.

He gave her a startled look and glanced back at Mrs Preston, who was busy setting a stitch.

'She can't hear us over the noise of the rain,' Lady Jenna said softly.

His jaw hardened, giving his already grim expression an edge of sternness. 'I have not thought any more about it, my lady. Except to decide that it was and is a bad idea. I should never have mentioned it.'

She felt her spine stiffen. 'Why?'

'You are talking about three gentlemen. My grandfather didn't wake up one morning and say, there are the eggs and the cliff, have at it. We'd grown up collecting eggs. They were food for our table. Every boy in Dunross climbed those cliffs to feed his family. My grandfather simply added a bit of competition to it. A challenge. And the eggs we didn't need for our table, we gave to those less well off.'

'That is exactly what I want. A challenge.'

His mouth flattened. 'It is too dangerous. I'll have no part of such a fool's errand.'

'It won't be a contest of how many eggs they can collect. They would have only to bring back one. It would be how they set about getting that one.'

'One or a hundred, you could be sending one of those men to their deaths. I won't have that on my conscience. Nor should you.'

'It will not be on your conscience. It will be on mine.'

'I beg to differ. It is a stupid idea and I will not permit it.'

A spurt of anger went through her. Because she had not thought of the danger and knew he was right. She did not want him to be right. 'You would suggest a ball and dancing, I suppose.' Because that was all a woman needed. A man who danced well.

A faint tinge of colour stained his cheeks as he no doubt recalled his words of the night before. Though why it would make him blush she did not know. Or was it anger? Because his voice was harsh as he spoke. 'I also suggest you spend time talking to them. Get to know them that way.'

'I have only a week, Mr Gilvry.'

His mouth tightened. Disapproval. It was the expression she'd been seeing on his face since the first day they met. Either he was disapproving of her, or he was kissing her. She went hot at the wayward thought.

'Then the sooner you get started, Lady Jenna, the better,' he said in a low voice.

'Is something wrong?' Mrs Preston quavered from the other side of the room.

Jenna spun around, surprised that their discussion had roused the widow's suspicions. 'Just planning the week's entertainment.' She turned to Mr Gilvry with a bright smile. 'Mr Gilvry is adamant that we will not go riding today.'

'Indeed I am.'

'So billiards it is,' she added in a louder voice. 'I'll let the gentlemen know. They are expecting us in the library. Thank you so much for your help, Mr Gilvry. You may attend to your other duties.'

His normally cool expression held an edge of anger. 'With great pleasure, Lady Jenna.' He bowed stiffly and left, passing Mr McBane who was on his way in.

The gentlemen greeted each other. The urbane McBane raised his brows when he met Lady Jenna's gaze before greeting Mrs Preston. The man saw a great deal, Jenna decided. Perhaps he wasn't quite as lazy as he seemed.

Perhaps Mr Gilvry was right. She should talk to the gentlemen individually to learn more about their characters, rather than sending them on a fool's errand, as he had called it.

The idea that he thought her foolish was lowering. But he wasn't the one who would be bound to a man who would have all the power. She'd thought about it carefully. She needed a man who would listen to her opinions and be guided by her when it came to the matter of Braemuir. Braemuir had been in her family for generations. She loved it. The house. The park. The people. It was hers. And she would not let anyone ruin it.

She didn't want a weak man, exactly, but she did want one who was reasonable. One who would leave the running of Braemuir in her hands where it belonged.

'Lady Jenna,' Mr McBane murmured as he bowed over her hand. 'May I say how beautiful you look this morning with high colour in your cheeks and a sparkle in your eye?'

Oh, yes, he saw a great deal. And his voice held sympathy. She dipped a curtsy. 'You are very kind, sir.'

'Not at all. I speak only the truth. Such a surly young man, Mr Gilvry. And high-handed as a guardian, too, I shouldn't wonder.'

She smiled wryly. 'We were having a small disagreement as to how best to provide for your entertainment,' she said as lightly as she could manage. 'As you can see, the weather is being uncooperative for any outdoor activity.'

'I don't think you will find us hard to please, Lady Jenna. Your presence is all that is required.'

His eyes twinkled sympathetically. 'I do not envy you the task of choosing between us.'

He reminded her a bit of her father. Kindly and wise. 'It must be a rather uncomfortable situation for you, too, sir.'

'Somewhat,' he admitted. 'Come, sit down and tell me what Mr Gilvry has done to so displease you.'

Jenna felt his hand in the small of her back as he guided her to the sofa. She had the urge to pull away, but how could she? It would be rude when he was being so utterly charming. When she was settled, he sat down beside her, just as Niall—no, Mr Gilvry had done the other evening when they talked. It didn't feel nearly as...nice.

'It appears Mr Gilvry is somewhat strict in his notions,' Mr McBane was saying.

Unaccountably, she stiffened at the implied criticism. Surely he wasn't trying to drive a wedge between her and her guardian? 'Mr Gilvry is punctilious in the performance of his duties.'

'Which irks you, I think?'

It irked her that he was right. She let go a sigh. 'It was a small difference of opinion.'

'On the value of gulls' eggs.'

'You heard?'

'A few words when I was about to enter. You sounded angry and I was about to leave, when I realised Gilvry was about to depart.'

She shook her head. 'It was a nonsensical idea.'

'Is that what he told you? I gather Mr Gilvry is not always the most tactful of young men. I am somewhat surprised...well, never mind that. What is this idea of yours? And is there perhaps something I can do to assist?'

Surprised by what? 'Oh, no. Really. It is nothing.'

Something flickered across his face. Pain at her quick dismissal of his offer to help, perhaps? 'Then I must apologise for prying.'

And now she felt unkind. Perhaps even cruel. So she explained how she had discussed her difficulties with Mr Gilvry the previous evening and how they had joked about the fairy tale and he had talked about the contest between him and his brothers.

'And you thought the three of us should enter into such a contest.'

She coloured. 'It was a jest. A whim. As Mr Gilvry pointed out in the cold light of day. Far too dangerous.'

'You discussed this with him last evening. After dinner.'

She nodded and gazed down at her clasped hands. 'I became anxious that I would not make the right choice.'

He patted her hands, a kindly, almost avuncular gesture. 'You have a difficult task, my dear Lady Jenna. I do not envy you one bit.'

She lifted her gaze and found him smiling at

her with a great deal of understanding. 'Why are you here?' she asked. 'Why would you want to marry me? You have been married before. You are wealthy. You could have your choice of ladies, I assume.'

His eyes widened. 'A direct question deserves a direct answer. I cannot deny I have been thinking about a second marriage for some time now. I have three daughters in need of a mother. Your cousin suggested I throw my hat in the ring.' He pressed his lips together. 'I have to confess that, as a younger son, the idea of a title is almost as attractive as you are.' He gave her a rather regretful smile, but she could not fault him for his honesty.

'How old are your daughters?'

'All under the age of ten. They live at my home near Stirling. They are charming children, I assure you, but lacking a woman's guidance.'

That, she could understand. She had often felt the lack growing up in her father's house. Yet the thought of being mother to three when newly married felt rather daunting.

'Here you are, McBane,' said Mr Murray glowering from the doorway with Mr Oswald at his shoulder. 'Stealing a march on us while Oswald and I have been kicking our heels in the library.'

Heat rushed to her face at the accusation in his tone. As if he somehow thought they were doing something wrong. She rose to her feet. 'Thank you for waiting, gentlemen. I was wondering if you would care for a game of billiards, given that the weather is so uncooperative today. The table has been set up in the great hall.'

'Bravo,' Mr McBane said *sotto voce* as he stood up beside her.

'Will you join us, Lady Jenna?' Mr Oswald asked, his face bland.

'Indeed, I will,' she said.

'Capital idea,' Mr Murray said, rubbing his hands together. 'I like nothing better than a good game of billiards. Lady Jenna, you had best throw your lot in with me, if you want to win.'

Yes, spending time with these men was teaching her something about their characters. And they were all very different. She would have to approach this matter from a logical standpoint. Decide exactly what it was she needed in a husband. But at the moment, Mr McBane stood out.

There was a kindness about him, and wisdom. Nor did he seem like a man who would be foolish about money the way her father had been. He had let himself be persuaded into unwise investments, trusting where he should have looked into things more deeply, according to Carrick.

Would McBane be the sort to be more careful?

Niall had spent the day working beside Mc-Dougall in the office while Lady Jenna, chaperoned by Mrs Preston, played billiards with her suitors. Later, he heard from one of the servants, there had been great hilarity over shuttlecock and battledore played in the undercroft. By dinner time, Lady Jenna and her guests seemed very much at ease with one another and he was clearly the odd man out.

As the servants cleared away the last of the dinner dishes, he was racking his mind for an excuse to retire the moment the ladies left for the drawing room.

'Now, Lady Jenna,' Mr Oswald said, 'I do recall you offering an evening of cards.'

'So I did,' Lady Jenna replied. 'It is all arranged. The card tables should be ready and awaiting us in the drawing room the moment you gentlemen are ready.'

'Excellent,' Mr Oswald said. 'I hope the rest of you are prepared to lose your fortunes.'

'I doubt we shall play so deep as that,' Lady Jenna said firmly. 'You will join us, will you not, Mr Gilvry? We will need an even number and Mrs Preston does like to play.'

The older lady beamed. 'How kind of you to remember, Jenna.'

Both ladies were awaiting his answer. Did he actually have a choice? 'I shall be delighted.'

They repaired at once to the drawing room, the gentlemen apparently more than happy to give up their port for a chance to gamble.

Two card tables had been set up in the drawing room, and it was agreed that he would partner

Mrs Preston against Mr Oswald and Mr McBane in a game of piquet, while Lady Jenna played a hand of whist with Mr Murray.

A chance for her to get to know the man better. Cards would reveal the man's intelligence, or at least his ability to count.

Mrs Preston proved to be quite a good player, even though she played by instinct rather than calculation, and Niall easily made up for her occasional error with his skill in keeping track of the cards.

'This is dullness itself,' Mr Oswald said. 'A shilling a point? Let us raise it to a guinea.'

No one objected. The widow's eyes lit up as she eyed her winnings and calculated how much more they could be.

'A guinea it is,' McBane said casually and dealt the hand.

'Are you in, Gilvry?' Oswald asked.

Niall nodded. He would have to ensure luck continued to run their way. He certainly could not afford to lose the way these men could. He picked up his hand and glanced at his cards. Useless. He had to hope his partner had better than this or he would quickly find himself on Dun Street.

During the next hand, while Mrs Preston dithered over which card to lay, McBane leaned back in his chair. 'I understand you led an exciting youth, Mr Gilvry.'

Niall frowned at him. 'No more exciting than anyone else, I believe.'

'I understood your family to be engaged in the trade. I assumed you were part of it?'

'A free trader?' Murray said from the next table, his expression speculative. 'I wouldn't mind a few tuns of brandy.'

Lady Jenna's eyes widened in astonishment.

'I have nothing to do with smuggling brandy,' he said firmly.

'I thought smuggling was why your family set such great store on the climbing of cliffs,' McBane said blandly.

Niall felt his mouth dry as he heard Lady Jenna's indrawn gasp. He didn't look at her, but he knew she must have told McBane about their conversation. Their private conversation. He repressed a feeling of betrayal. There was no sense in denying it, despite the superior expression on McBane's face. 'We gathered eggs for food.'

'Very industrious,' Oswald said matter-of-factly.

Niall allowed himself a glance in Lady Jenna's direction. Her cheeks bloomed roses and she was focusing on her cards. Deliberately not looking at him. What else had she told McBane? He waved off the offer of burgundy from the footman. 'Your play, McBane.'

McBane put down a card. 'I understood it was some sort of contest.'

This time Niall managed to catch Lady Jenna's eye and she gave a little wince. An apology of sorts, he supposed. He stared at his cards without looking at them. 'Once a year, when I was growing up, my brothers and I competed to see who could gather the most gulls' eggs in a single day. My grandfather offered a prize.'

'And this time, the prize is a bride,' McBane said softly.

What the devil? Did McBane see him as a rival? He almost laughed out loud. What she needed was far beyond his means. Indeed, it was his duty to ensure she found a man who met some very exacting criteria.

'Mr Gilvry isn't competing,' Lady Jenna said. 'I mean, we are not having a contest.'

Mr Oswald picked up his glass and observed Niall over the rim. 'Were you planning on competing?'

Niall looked back at him steadily. 'There is no contest.'

'It sounds like a grand idea,' Mr Murray said. 'First one back with the most eggs in the morning wins the lady.'

'That wasn't it,' Niall began, then stopped at the triumphant gleam in Mr McBane's eye. The man was playing some sort of cat-and-mouse game. And he wasn't going to fall for it.

He looked at his cards, his face blank. He would be lucky if he held his own with this hand, provided Mrs Preston held the cards he thought she did, and played them well.

'What was the contest?' Mr Oswald asked idly, putting down a queen of hearts.

'One egg,' Lady Jenna said.

'The first one to bring back one egg?' Mr Murray sounded puzzled.

'The one whom I thought showed the most initiative in obtaining it would win,' she answered.

The furrowed brow Mr Murray sported said he was all at sea.

'Why?' Mr Oswald.

'It was a foolish notion,' Lady Jenna said, dropping her gaze to her cards. 'I had some idea that such a quest might...distinguish one from another since you are all such worthy and eligible gentlemen.'

'Oh, a quest,' Mr Murray said. He looked pleased with the idea. 'Like a knight in shining armour and a maiden in distress.'

One thing was clear—Murray, for all his good looks, was not of the highest intellect. So perhaps there was some benefit to this conversation. He just wished she hadn't discussed it with McBane. He looked at the widower, whose expression had settled into that of the mildest interest. Was that his purpose in this? To show Murray up as a dolt?

'Mr Gilvry refuses to countenance any such contest,' Jenna said as if to put an end to the matter.

'Really?' said Mr Oswald. 'I wonder why?'

What the hell did he mean by that? 'It is too dangerous,' Niall said. 'I advised Lady Jenna to spend time with each of you and then make up her mind.' Damn it all, now he was in the position of matchmaker.

'And will you be advising Lady Jenna on her choice?' Mr Oswald asked.

'No,' Niall said. 'My opinion is not relevant. Lord Carrick has deemed you all eligible. My only duty is to watch over Lady Jenna's safety in his absence.'

'And it is for Lady Jenna to choose,' McBane said. He smiled at his competitors. 'May the best man win.'

'He will,' Murray said, picking up his cards.

Damn it all. It seemed these men had picked up the gauntlet. He kept his face expressionless and focused all his attention on the cards. For once Mrs Preston played exceedingly well and they split the pot between them. McBane looked far from pleased and it was with difficulty that Niall resisted the temptation to show his triumph.

He rose from the table. 'If you will excuse me, gentlemen, ladies, I have an early start in the morning.'

'Ah, yes, your other duties. Secretary, isn't it?' McBane purred.

'Under-secretary,' Niall said. 'I bid you goodnight.' He strode from the room, knowing full well that McBane was itching for a chance to win his money back. Niall also knew that if he stayed, with Mrs Preston as a partner, it was almost guaranteed to happen. He'd be a fool to continue to play with men who dropped thousands in a night without blinking. And he wasn't a fool. Not about cards.

He'd been a fool to trust Lady Jenna to keep their conversation private.

He strode down the corridor, congratulating himself on having done his duty, and come out with some coin in his pocket. Mrs Preston would now have to do her duty and serve as chaperon for the rest of the evening.

The patter of hurried footsteps from behind had him turning around.

Lady Jenna, running after him.

His gut clenched and he strode back to meet her. 'Is something wrong?'

'The contest,' she said. 'I am sorry. I did not expect—'

'Why on earth did you tell McBane?'

'I didn't. He overheard us. I believe I have nipped the idea in the bud.'

He thought about the other men's reactions. 'Don't be surprised if you get a basket of eggs tomorrow from Murray.'

'Oh, do you think so?' She grimaced. 'I'll speak to him.'

'It would probably be best.'

They stood there staring at each other, the air warming and thickening despite the chill in the corridor. He wanted her. Drunk or sober, every time he was near her, he had the same desire: to take her to his bed and learn all of her secrets. If it had only been lust it wouldn't bother him so much. He had this feeling that he wanted to protect her from these men, and from herself. Which was why he had agreed to play cards when he should have refused. And had apparently earned McBane's enmity for winning.

Should he warn her against the man? Was it really his place? And could he really offer an unbiased opinion? Mentally he shook his head at himself. Clearly, he could not. 'Goodnight, Lady Jenna.'

He turned and strode away before he did something he would really regret. Like carrying her off to his room and ravishing her so that none of them could have her and she had to marry him.

Filled with self-disgust, he took himself to bed. Unfortunately, his body thought it was such a good idea that it plagued him with erotic dreams all night.

The storm blew itself out by morning. Which likely meant Lady Jenna would expect to go beyond the castle walls with her suitors trailing along. He'd looked into what might strike their fancy. As Mrs Preston had said, there were a couple of ruined castles nearby, some old standing stones. Or there was a river with good fishing. Or sailing, on the loch or the sea.

But first he paid a visit to Mr McDougall and found the secretary tut-tutting to himself.

'What is wrong?' Niall asked.

'This new land steward is an idiot,' McDougall muttered, not looking up. 'He either forgets to write down who paid, or he forgets to write down what they paid.'

Niall kept his body relaxed and his face mildly enquiring. 'Tearny used to be the land steward, did he not? Here and at Dunross.'

'Aye. And for all his faults, he never made these sort of mistakes.'

'Faults?'

'Aye. Disappearing for days on end. I brought it to the Carrick's attention, but he shrugged it off.'

'Perhaps he was engaged in Dunross business?'

'Perhaps,' McDougall said. He looked up. ''Twas a bad business. Your brother was lucky there were witnesses to the death or he might have found himself on the end of a rope.'

'Did Tearny have a family?'

'Oh, aye. A prolific man, our Mr Tearny.'

'I don't suppose you know where his widow lives? We heard she had returned to Ireland.'

'She did for a while, after his death, but she's back now, her and her parcel of brats.'

'Do you happen to know where she lives? Ian wants to offer her some aid since he feels responsible for her husband's death.' Perhaps his wife could say why her husband had been so set on causing Ian harm. And why Carrick had paid her husband so much money.

'Along the road, in the opposite direction to town.'

'Thanks.' The moment he had some free time he would talk to Mrs Tearny, but right now he had to organise Lady Jenna and her suitors.

Jenna stared from the smug Mr Oswald to the outraged Mr McBane and then back to the blue velvet-covered box in her hand containing a white conical-shaped egg. 'You are telling me that you agreed among you on this contest as a way of winning my hand?'

Both men nodded.

'Without my agreement?'

'You seemed pretty set on it yesterday, according to McBane here,' Oswald said. 'Sorry to get the jump on you, old chap.'

McBane glared at him. 'He cheated.'

'No more than you,' Oswald said with a small smile as he picked at a small piece of lint on his coat sleeve. 'Your man was grumbling about arising at five to go into town. When my man told me, I guessed why, so I had my man leave immediately.'

'And bought every damned egg to be had.'

'Bought them?' Jenna said.

'Naturally,' Oswald replied. 'You didn't expect me to go clambering up cliffs, surely?'

Jenna felt betrayed as well as foolish. 'And that was also your plan, Mr McBane?'

'Not quite. I planned to be first to bring you the one egg you wanted, my lady. And let the devil take the hindmost.'

She turned on Mr Oswald. 'What happened to the other eggs? The rest of those you bought?'

'I told my man to get rid of them, where McBane wouldn't find them.'

'He threw them away?'

Oswald shrugged.

Jenna smiled. 'You are to be congratulated. Your participation has given me great insight into your character, Mr Oswald.'

'So I win.'

He smiled his sly smile and Jenna wanted to hit him. 'You win your departure, sir. Any man who would deliberately destroy food is not a man I would wish to marry.'

McBane grinned. 'Sorry, old fellow. I forgot to mention the part about feeding the poor with what was left over.'

Oswald shot him a glare. 'I demand another chance. I was not given full information.'

Jenna got up and pulled the bell.

When she returned to her seat, she narrowed her eyes at McBane. 'You heard a lot more of my conversation than you revealed previously.'

'These stone walls carry sound in the strangest way.'

'I suppose it didn't occur to you not to listen to a private conversation?'

His ears turned red. As they should. 'Fair means or foul, Lady Jenna, I intend to win you.'

'And what of Mr Murray?'

'Off climbing the cliffs, I assume. Breaking his fool neck.'

'At least he is a sportsman,' she said. 'And you can't win, since you did not bring me an egg, Mr McBane. But don't bother rushing out to find one, because you still wouldn't win. I am looking for a man who will share my life, not go behind my back.'

'Oh, my dear girl,' Mrs Preston said from the other side of the hearth from where she had been watching the proceedings open-mouthed. 'Perhaps you should give this some thought.'

A footman arrived to see what was wanted. 'These gentlemen are leaving. Please inform Mr Gilvry to make the necessary arrangements.'

'Lady Jenna, don't be hasty,' McBane said smoothly. 'I was simply trying to give you want you wanted.'

'I think it is clear that I do not want either of you.'

Was she mistaken, or did Mr Oswald look relieved? It was hard to tell because he caught his expression when he realised she was looking at him and bowed deeply. 'May I say what a pleasure it has been, Lady Jenna. Should you ever change your mind...'

She gave him a hard smile. 'Don't hold your breath, Mr Oswald.'

McBane made a perfunctory bow and both men left.

She had never felt so relieved in her life. But now all she could think of was Mr Murray somewhere on the cliffs. Mr Gilvry was right. She did not want the guilt of any accident that might befall him.

After all, he was also her only remaining suitor.

She was shocked by her feeling of dismay.

But by dismissing the other two, she had in effect made her choice. All that was left was to tell him.

Chapter Seven

Niall arrived a few minutes later, looking concerned. 'You sent for me, Lady Jenna?'

'Oh, Mr Gilvry,' Mrs Preston said, dabbing theatrically at her eyes. 'Perhaps you can remonstrate with Lady Jenna. Lord Carrick is going to be so displeased. Nothing I can say will move her.'

'Can you wonder at it, ma'am?' Jenna said, trying to hold her temper in check.

'I spoke with McBane,' Mr Gilvry said. 'He explained what happened. He seemed quite irritated.'

'Whereas I imagine Mr Oswald is jumping for joy. I cannot deny I was completely taken in by the pair of them.'

'Mr McBane has such charming manners,' Mrs Preston wailed. 'And Mr Oswald. So personable and nice in his dress. Are you sure you want to send them away so soon?'

Mr Gilvry glanced around. 'Where is Murray?'

'I see McBane didn't tell you everything,' Jenna said, her jaw feeling tight. 'Mr Murray is off somewhere, climbing the cliffs.'

'Oh,' he said.

'Oh? Is that the best you can do?'

His brows drew down in a straight line. 'Do we have any idea where he went?'

She shook her head.

He heaved a sigh. 'I will have a word with his valet.'

'I'll come with you.'

'It won't be necessary.'

'Oh, I think it is. If anything happens to him, it will be my fault.' She strode past him and out of the door before Mrs Preston could add her objections to his.

'It would never have happened if I hadn't mentioned the contest to you,' Mr Gilvry said, easily catching her up.

'True,' she said. 'But then I might have made a terrible mistake. I liked Mr McBane. I was completely taken in.'

Mr Gilvry absorbed that information in silence.

She stopped and whirled around to face him.

'Well? Don't you have something to say? Something like I told you so?'

His expression held regret. 'No. There is nothing I can say at this moment that would make any sense. Come on, we need to hurry if we are going to find your Mr Murray before he breaks his neck.' He took the lead.

Her Mr Murray. Bridegroom by default. Not what she had expected when she started down this path. But having had him risk his life to win her, there was no way on earth she could turn him down if he should make her an offer.

Her chest felt tight, as if a weight had landed there, making it hard to breathe.

When she should be pleased the matter had been decided.

They discovered Mr Murray's valet in the kitchen polishing an already shiny pair of Hessians and drinking tea with Cook. Nobody raised an eyebrow at Mr Gilvry's entrance, but when they realised she was right behind him, there was a great deal of bobbing of heads and scurrying around.

'Plimpton,' Mr Gilvry said, 'can you spare me a few moments?'

The valet looked distinctly worried. He put down the boot and his brush and nodded.

'In the butler's pantry, if you don't mind. So we can be private.'

Now the man looked panicked. He followed them out of the kitchen and into the little room on the other side of the passage. Mr Gilvry closed the door behind them.

'I'll get straight to the point, Plimpton. Do you have any idea where we can find your master?'

'Mr Murray, sir?'

'Do you have another master?'

Plimpton flushed red. 'No, sir.'

'Plimpton,' Jenna said, gently, 'it is most urgent that we locate him. He might be in danger.'

The small man's eyes widened. 'He went out before it was light, miss. Seemed in high good humour, when he set off. Very pleased with himself.'

'So he did not tell you where he was going?' Gilvry asked.

'No, sir. But you could ask Jemmy, his groom.'

Niall raised a brow at Jenna and she nodded. 'Thank you, Plimpton. You have been most helpful.'

The man looked worried. 'You think he is in some sort of trouble, sir?'

'Hopefully, not.'

They left and headed for the stables. The place was in turmoil preparing for the departure of two of their guests. Niall pulled Campbell aside. 'Which one is Murray's groom?'

Campbell groaned. 'Don't tell me he is going, too.'

'No. Murray went out early this morning. We want to know where he went.'

Campbell looked surprised, but didn't question further. He scanned the stables. 'There in the corner, keeping out of the way. Good at that he is.' He stepped back as a coach began its wide turn into the courtyard, the coachman yelling orders and curses at the grooms at the horses' heads.

'Wait here,' Niall said to Jenna. 'I'll bring him outside. Better yet, wait for me in my office, we'll be out of the way there.'

Jenna nodded and, sidling around the coach, headed across the courtyard and into the secretary's domain. He looked up from his papers and huffed and puffed to his feet despite her signal that he should not rise. 'Good morning, my lady.'

'Good morning, Mr McDougall. How are you today?'

He wiped his red damp brow. 'Well, my lady.'

'I'm glad to hear it. Where is Mr Gilvry's desk?'

He pointed through a low doorway. 'Through there, my lady. But he is not here yet. Shall I have him sent for?'

'Not necessary. He is on his way.'

She wandered through the doorway and perched on a wooden chair, glancing around her at the ledgers and piles of papers. It wasn't exactly luxurious surroundings. She could not imagine working in here all day, confined to one place.

A few moments later, Mr Gilvry strode in accompanied by a rangy-looking individual in flashy bright-blue livery. Lank brown hair flopped over an extraordinarily high forehead. He paused when he saw Jenna, then stood straight-shouldered with his hands behind his back. 'How can I help you, sir, my lady?' He bowed.

'We are looking for Mr Murray,' Niall said. 'Do you have any idea where he was headed when he left here this morning?'

There was a lively interest in his eyes, but he shook his head. 'He asked me not to say, sir, should anyone enquire.'

Jenna felt a sense of relief. 'Then you do know.'

The man's eyes narrowed. 'Is there something wrong, my lady?'

'He may have put himself at risk for a rather nonsensical wager. I am hoping to stop it before he puts himself in danger.'

The man muttered something she did not quite catch. 'I beg your pardon?'

'He was more or less saying that you might be out of luck,' Niall said, grinning.

The man turned red. 'I beg your pardon, my lady. I've known Mr Murray since he was naught but a lad in short coats. I wasn't much older myself. And there's not much hope of stopping him once he has the bit between his teeth.'

'Nevertheless, I think we should at least try,' she said. 'Before any harm comes to him.'

'He was planning to hire a boat down at the quay. He's a good sailor, he is. Never met a boat he couldn't handle.' The man managed to look both proud and morose. 'I like to keep my feet on dry land.'

'Which is why he went alone,' Niall said.

The man looked embarrassed. 'Yes, sir. He said he'd leave the horse at the White Rose and find a boat in the harbour. He wanted to get down there before they set out for the day. I thought he was going fishing, but now I think on it, he would have taken the carriage and his gear. He never fishes without his own rods.'

'He had a different kind of catch in mind,' Niall said. 'That's all. Thank you for your help.'

The man nodded sharply and left.

'Let's hope that he told whoever rented him a boat which way he was headed.' Niall went to the hook beside the door and pulled down a greatcoat.

'I suppose we must start at the White Rose,' Jenna said, rising to her feet.

Niall shook his head. 'I think not, my lady. I could not ask for the carriage, not with all that going on out there.'

'Please, Niall. This is my fault. I swear I will obey your every command.'

A twinkle lit his eyes, a flash of amusement quickly quelled. 'Those footpads are still on the loose. I cannot guarantee your safety.' His gaze narrowed. 'You will give me your word to remain here. You will only make my job all the harder and the longer I stand here arguing, the longer it will take me to find Mr Murray.'

He was not going to give in. She could see the determination in his face. And he was right. The longer they argued, the more danger for Murray. She huffed out a breath. 'Very well. I give you my word. I will stay here as long as you promise to send word the moment you have news.'

He grabbed his hat from the desk. 'I will.' He gave her a long look. 'Don't worry. He will return safe and sound.'

His look said everything. *Trust me. Do not worry.* And to her surprise, she did. She let him usher her out of the door and watched him enter the stables to call for his horse. She felt an odd sense of longing. A wish that Mr Murray was more like him.

A disloyal thought about a man who would likely soon become her husband. It was wrong to wish things were different. She was Lady Jenna Aleyne and she would do her duty.

Chapter Eight

Jenna paced the library. Her tea tray, which the butler had delivered a few minutes before, sat untouched on the table beside a letter she had dashed off to Mr Hughes telling him to expect her very soon.

She stopped pacing and glanced out of the window in hopes of glimpsing a messenger from Wick. It was far too soon to expect word. Mr Gilvry hadn't been gone more than an hour. Still, she couldn't help hoping. She kept imagining poor Mr Murray lying injured at the base of a cliff with no one to help him and she wanted to murder Mr McBane all over again. And to think she'd actually preferred the man to the others.

The door opened behind her.

She spun around. Mr Gilvry. Alone. 'Is he with you?'

'No. He left on the tide this morning in a boat he hired from one of the fisherman. Him and a boy.'

Her heart sank to her feet. 'And he hasn't returned?'

His expression was grim. 'The tide won't fill the harbour for a good hour or more, but I found a man who has a boat anchored in deep water. He's going to search for him, first to the north, where we believe he went, and then south. He and his crew know these waters well. They will find him.'

'You didn't think you should go with them?'

'No. They know what they are about. I would only be in the way. I thought you would like to know what I discovered.'

'Oh, yes. Thank you.' She looked at him standing there so tall and confident and tried to feel better. 'I will never forgive myself if anything happens to him. Never.'

'It is more my fault than yours. If I had not told you about the contest, it would never have entered anyone's head to do anything so foolish.'

'No,' she said. 'Let us put blame where it is due. McBane set all this in motion quite deliberately.'

A small smile curved his lips, making him look more boyish, less stern. 'I agree. The man's a blasted troublemaker.'

'And I am well rid of him. Would you like

tea? You look as if you could use something to lift your spirits, and it is fresh. Unless you would prefer whisky?'

'Tea would be welcome. Thank you.'

She sat down, gesturing for him to take a seat. She poured tea into a cup. 'I suppose there is nothing more we can do.' She handed him his cup and poured her own.

'No. Mr Murray is a good sailor according to the man who hired out his boat. The boy he took with him knows the coast well and the seas are quite calm. He will either sail back on his own, or he will be found.'

She took a deep breath and smiled. 'Thank you for offering such comfort.'

He sipped at his tea. 'It is no more than the truth.'

'I think you are not a man to prevaricate.'

He set the cup in the saucer with a sharp clink of china. He pressed his lips together as he stared at the cup and saucer, so dainty in his large hands. 'I did not speak the truth when I told you about the contest.'

'I beg your pardon?'

He looked at her. 'Oh, there was a contest, all right. And my brothers looked forward to it every year.' He set the cup down on the table. 'I did not. I hated it. The cliffs around Dunross are verra high, Lady Jenna.' He inhaled a deep breath through his nose, the lines around his mouth deepening. 'It was the height of them, no the birds, that sent me climbing at night.'

'It worked, did it not?' she said brightly, not understanding the grimness in his voice.

'Aye, it worked. That once.'

'But you still don't like heights.'

He looked away as if ashamed to meet her gaze. 'I doubt Murray is so cowardly.'

He thought he was a coward. 'I don't think Mr Murray has the sense to be afraid of anything.' The words were out before she had thought about them. She'd only meant to comfort but, heavens help her, the words were probably true. She gave an uncomfortable laugh.

'And you will marry him?'

Was that regret she heard in his voice, or were her own feelings colouring her judgement? Her own longings that perhaps if things had been different... But they weren't. If Braemuir was to be saved, she needed to marry a man of wealth. She folded her hands in her lap. 'If he asks, I will say yes.'

'He'd be a fool if he didn't.' The resignation in his voice seemed at odds with the compliment.

She clasped her hands tighter. 'I will never forgive myself if he has come to harm.'

'Aye. Waiting is hard. It was the same when we were waiting for news of my brother, Drew. We were always hoping for the best, for my mother's sake, but in his case we feared the worst.'

The change of topic seemed welcome to both of them and so she followed his lead. 'What happened to him?'

'He went to America on family business. He went off on some adventure—so typical of Drew—and then we heard reports of his death. There was never any proof, but after a year with no word, it was clear he wasn't coming back.'

'How dreadful for your family.'

He looked at her then, sorrow on his face. 'He was our mother's favourite. She still blames my older brother, Ian, for his death. For sending him abroad. But I blame myself, too.'

'How could it be your fault?'

His mouth tightened. 'I put a foolish idea in his head.' He stood up. 'Full of ideas, I am. None of them good. Thank you for the tea, my lady. I think I will attend to some duties in the office while we wait for news.'

She wanted to ask him to stay but she could see that their conversation had brought back unpleasant memories. They all had those. Things they would sooner not recall. Which was why she was so anxious to return to Braemuir. She had let the memories of her father's sudden demise keep her away. It was time to face her ghosts. To return to the house she had loved as a child. Her home. Her true place in the world.

'You will let me know as soon as there is any news?'

'I will.'

The sound of a cart on the cobblestones in the courtyard below caused him to lift his head and listen.

Jenna ran to the window and looked down. 'Oh, it seems we will not have to wait after all.'

'Is it Murray?' he asked from where he was standing.

And she understood his reluctance to come to the window and look down. 'I believe it is. Please, stay. I asked the butler to bring him up here the moment he returned.'

Niall agreed with a nod and went to the hearth, leaning one elbow on the mantel as she returned to her seat. They were not required to wait long before a windblown and dishevelled Mr Murray was ushered in. His coat was torn, his neckcloth gone and there was a hole at the knee of his buckskins.

He gave a doleful sniffle as he bowed. 'Lady Jenna. Excuse my appearance.' He made straight for the fire, held out his hands to it for a moment, then turned his back on it. He sneezed and swiped at his nose with what looked like the remains of his neckcloth.

'Thank you for sending a boat to fetch me off,' he said. 'I holed the boat, bringing her in to the cove. On rocks below the surface.' His expression darkened. 'The lad I hired as a guide lied when he said he knew that part of the coast well.'

She rose and went to Mr Murray with a smile that felt a little too bright, a little too stiff. 'You don't know how glad I am to see you safe and well, Mr Murray.'

He took her hand in his. His fingers were freezing. 'Thank you, Lady Jenna. Sadly, it seems I failed. I caught nothing but a cold.'

Her heart gave a little thump of hope she did not quite understand as he stuffed a hand in his pocket, pulled out a soggy mess of cloth and held it out.

Disappointment filled his face. 'Your egg, my lady. I'm afraid it broke when the man Gilvry sent pitched me headfirst into the boat.'

She looked down at the sticky mess of shell and broken egg in what had once been a fine lawn handkerchief, then darted a glance at Mr Gilvry whose mouth was set in a straight line.

Her heart gave a painful twist. Regret. Sadness. Longing. A handful of painful feelings.

Somehow she managed to smile at the dejected man before her. 'The quest was to bring back an egg,' she said. 'There was no mention of it being whole, as I recall.'

Mr Murray looked as if he didn't quite believe her, then his face broke out in a charmingly boyish smile. 'You mean I won?'

'You completed the quest, Mr Murray.'

He glanced down at himself and back at her. 'I did, didn't I? Capital.' He took her hands in his. He went down on one knee. 'Lady Jenna, will—?'

Mr Gilvry made a sound of protest and turned his back. 'Do you not think you should wait until you are private, man?'

Mr Murray ignored him. 'Lady Jenna, will you do me the honour of becoming my wife?' He sneezed.

She snatched her hands back, looking down at his earnest expression, his reddened nose. For one mad moment she almost said no. She closed her eyes briefly. Swallowed and managed a smile. 'Thank you for the honour you do me, Mr Murray. Yes. I will.'

Once more he sneezed.

'I think a hot bath would be in order and a tisane,' Jenna said. 'Right away. Before you take a terrible chill.'

Mr Murray shuddered. 'Good Lord, yes.' He got to his feet and bowed. 'Thank you, Lady Jenna. You don't know how happy you have made me.' On those words he hurried to the door. 'We will talk, later. When I feel more the thing.'

'A mustard plaster sometimes works wonders,' she said as he disappeared.

There was an emptiness inside her. A coldness. She found she couldn't look at Niall, not with the way the coldness seemed to rise in her throat and threaten to choke her. She went to the desk and picked up the letter she had penned earlier. 'I wonder if you would mind delivering this note to the gypsy in the market, Mr Gilvry.' Her voice sounded as cold as she felt. 'I have a few words to add and it will be ready.'

'Certainly, my lady.'

There was something wrong with her vision. A blurring. She didn't understand it. Everything was just as she had desired. A wealthy bridegroom safely netted. A man she could manage quite easily, she thought. A wedding in the offing. She blinked the tears away and signed the note informing the vicar that she would soon be returning with a new lord of Braemuir. She folded the paper and pressed it with the seal provided. It would have looked more important with her father's seal, but that had been left at home, waiting for its new master.

She should be rejoicing that she had at last kept her promise to her father, instead of feeling like the egg in Mr Murray's handkerchief. Crushed. Annihilated.

She held out the letter. Heard his heavy tread as he crossed the room to take it, the creak of floorboards, the stomp of his boot heels.

'Lady Jenna,' he said quietly, 'Is something wrong? Is there anything I can do?'

She schooled her face into indifference and looked at him. 'Oh, no, Mr Gilvry. I think you have done everything possible.' She just wished there wasn't such a cold hard lump on her chest.

'I'm glad you think so,' he said in a low voice filled with pain.

And when she looked at his face she saw the same pain in his eyes. The pain of regret. Regret for the wild emotions that had flared between them that must not be? Something neither of them had wanted? It did not do to dwell on such a thought. 'Mr Murray is safely returned,' she said around the ache in her chest. 'And for that you will always have my gratitude.'

'You are welcome, my lady.' He bowed and took the letter.

The gypsy was in the process of packing up his goods when Niall arrived. 'Do you go back to Braemuir?' he asked.

'I do,' the gypsy said, his expression guarded.

Niall handed over the letter. 'Please give this to the vicar.' While the gipsy tucked the note into a pocket inside his coat, Niall idly poked through an assortment of hatpins on the table. 'And where do you go after that?' he asked.

The gypsy shrugged. 'Where the mood takes me.'

Surprising. He'd imagined him going from one market town to the next on a regular schedule. 'Your band is camped nearby?'

The gypsy stilled, his dark eyes unfathomable. 'Nearby. Yes.'

Gypsies. Always suspicious. He wasn't even

sure why he had asked. Some instinct told him this man travelled alone, which was highly unusual for his race. Not that it mattered. He'd been making conversation as a way to take his mind off Jenna's coldness. And off the regret like a lump of lead in his gut. He had no reason to feel regretful. He had done his duty. The fact that he thought Murray an idiot was immaterial. Lady Jenna had made her choice.

At least the man had acted with honour, which was more than could be said of the other two.

He picked up a silver pin that seemed to catch the light. At its head was a circle with the figure of a fairy enclosed. A pretty little thing. It reminded him of Jenna.

'A pound,' the gypsy said, shifting closer than was comfortable. 'Good silver, see?' He nipped it from Niall's grasp and scraped it with the tip of a knife that materialised in his hand. The scratch revealed nothing but silver beneath.

But what would she want with a paltry gift from him when she was marrying a man who could give her gold and jewels?

He pulled out a handful of coins. 'A shilling.'

'Two,' the gypsy said and exchanged the pin for the money.

It was probably made of brass and worth no more than a farthing or two. Niall stuck the pin into the lining of his coat and headed back to Carrick. Perhaps he would give the pin to her on her wedding day. Likely, he would not.

Niall! Thump. Thump.

Niall rolled on to his back and pressed a hand to his temple, seeking to ease the pounding in his head. But there was no ache. The yelling and the thumping must have been part of a dream. A dream that Lady Jenna was calling him. Hardly likely.

'Mr Gilvry. Niall.' More thumps on his door.

He shot up in bed, awake and alert. 'Jenna?'

'Open the door. I need your help.'

'All right. I'm coming. Give me a moment.' He fumbled around in the dark, found his pantaloons and pulled them on and then his shirt. He opened the door, blinking into the candle held in front of his face.

Lady Jenna stood before him fully dressed with a cloak over her arm and looking worried.

He watched her gaze take in his state of undress, the open collar of his shirt, his bare feet. The way she licked her lips and swallowed as if her mouth was dry gave him an intense feeling of satisfaction. What? Did she think he went to bed fully clothed?

'How can I be of service, my lady?' he said, intending every innuendo those words allowed.

Even by the light of the candle, he could see her turn pink at the purr in his voice.

She looked up at his face, then, and visibly pulled herself together. Anger flared in her eyes. 'The grooms refuse to let me take my horse without your permission.'

He let his gaze roam over her body before he answered. It wasn't nice. But then he wasn't feeling very charitable at this hour of the night. Hadn't been feeling charitable since her future husband had returned from his quest. 'And where would her ladyship be wanting to go in the middle of the night?' He straightened. 'Not thinking of eloping, are you?'

She waved him off with an imperious hand. 'A boy brought a message from one of Lord Carrick's tenants. Her youngest child is terribly ill. She is asking for help.'

'Why would she ask help from you?'

'Normally it would be Lady Carrick's charge, but in her absence it falls to me, since Mrs Preston is not mindful to leave her bed in the middle of the night.'

'If you want to help, send for the doctor.'

She shook her head. 'I doubt she can pay a physician's fee. It is a fever the boy described. I am sure a willow-bark tea is all that is required.'

It was the middle of the night, for heaven's sake. How urgent could it be? 'Where is the boy that brought the message? I want to question him.'

'They didn't let him in the gate. The gatekeeper sent one of the footmen to awaken Mary and it was she who brought me the message.'

'Then I'll speak to the gatekeeper, before we go haring off into the night.' He picked up the boots he had left outside his door for the boot-black and sat on his bed to finish dressing.

She hovered in the doorway. 'You'll take me, then?'

Damn her. When she looked at him like that with her eyes huge and imploring, he couldn't think straight. He stamped his feet into his boots. 'I'll decide once I speak to the man who received the message.' Messages got changed and embellished in the passing from one mouth to another. Likely it was all a storm in a teacup. But he wasn't going to say that to Lady Jenna. She'd think him unfeeling and cruel.

He shut the door in her face and finished dressing. When he opened it again she was pacing the corridor outside his chamber.

'Finally,' she said, as if he'd been hours instead of seconds, and led the way down the winding stairs to the courtyard.

Niall went straight to the old night porter, whose job it was to guard the gate, with Jenna hard on his heels. The man touched his forelock as they approached.

'Well, Gage,' Niall said. 'What exactly did this boy who brought a message for Lady Jenna say?'

The old man gave him a grin, revealing several missing teeth in the light over the door used to admit foot traffic. 'He said his sister was ill with a fever and begged her ladyship to come as soon as she might.'

'See,' Lady Jenna said, tugging on his arm. 'We have to go.'

'Did you recognise the boy?'

Gabe scratched at his stubbled chin. 'I did and I didn't.'

Niall glared at him.

The old man backed up a step. 'All the Tearny boys look the same. Red-haired like their mother.'

Niall stiffened. 'Tearny, you say.'

'Aye. Five of them, there are. This one was one of the older ones, I'm thinking. Michael or William.'

'Where is the boy now?'

'Ran home to his mother.'

'Mr Gilvry,' Lady Jenna said, 'Mrs Tearny is a sensible woman. She would not have sent for help if it was nothing.'

'Open the gate for me, Gage. I'll go for the doctor.'

He strode for the stables with Lady Jenna half running to keep pace.

'One of the grooms can come to Tearny's with me,' she said.

He stopped, staring down at her. 'What can you do if the child is seriously ill?'

She stared at him, drawing herself up tall. 'Are you doubting my skill?'

As he looked down into her face, he saw pride. Aye, she was a proud wee thing and who was he to crush that spirit? 'All right. We will go to the Tearnys' and one of the grooms can go for the doctor.' He had wanted to talk to the Tearny woman and this might be his chance.

She made a motion as if she would hug him, then stilled. 'Thank you,' she said instead. The note in her voice was heartfelt and he felt an odd warmth in his chest.

A groom met them at the stable door. Niall acknowledged his greeting. 'Sorry to turn you out at this time of day, man, but can you saddle horses for me and Lady Jenna and one for yourself?'

The man grinned. 'Her ladyship said she was going to get you out of bed. I took the liberty of saddling Midnight and Belle.'

Was there no one in this place who could stand up to her? 'Right.' He clapped the man on the shoulder. 'You need to ride to town for a doctor. Have him come out to the Tearnys' cottage. On my account.'

Damn. That would use up his winnings from the other night. Skinflint Carrick would never pay for a doctor whom Niall had bespoke.

'I'll go as soon as I see you and the lady mounted up.'

He brought out Belle and Midnight. Niall threw Lady Jenna up and, while the groom checked her straps, Niall settled on Midnight, who was snorting and blowing and eager to be off. By the time they were ready the gates were open.

Niall brought his horse alongside Jenna's mare. 'We'll have to take it slow. I'll not have you breaking your neck because your horse stumbled in a rut. Do you understand me?'

'Always so careful, aren't you, Mr Gilvry?' she said, but there was a smile on her face so he did not take offence.

'One of us has to be,' he replied, and set his horse into a walk.

They rode side by side, keeping to the middle of the road, letting the horses take their own path. Niall could feel Lady Jenna's urgency like a vibration in the air around her, but he was glad to see she kept her head and maintained a steady pace.

'Thank you for understanding my duty to Lord Carrick's tenants in his absence,' she said quietly.

He did understand. The same kind of duty had driven his older brother Ian for years. It still did. Only he was happy with the yoke of it now, because he shared it with Lady Selina and counted himself lucky.

The dark and the quiet, with nothing but the sound of the horses, made for an easy quiet between them. A sense of camaraderie. He did not recall feeling this comfortable with another person, not even with his brothers. Especially not with his brothers. There was always too much competition.

Camaraderie, he mocked himself. Was that what he was calling this attraction between them? He was far too aware of her as a woman to be a true friend. But he did like and respect her for living up to her responsibilities. Riding along beside her in the dark, it was tempting to wonder what might have happened between them if she was not Lady Aleyne of Braemuir, but an ordinary woman seeking an ordinary life with an ordinary husband.

He cut the thought off with impatience. He, too, had duties and responsibilities and they did not include dreaming about what might have been.

'The light up ahead is the Tearnys' house,' she said, interrupting his thoughts.

They drew closer, and the cottage took shape. A stone building with a peat roof and a couple of outbuildings. A house far superior to most of those in town. Tearny had indeed done his family proud. And they were clearly expected, because the front door opened long before they came close to the door. A woman stood in the doorway, looking anxious.

Niall dismounted, helped Lady Jenna down

and turned to secure the horses to a nearby post, while she hurried towards the woman.

Something hard pressed against his ribs. 'One sound and you're a dead man,' a voice said in a rough English voice he knew. Niall stiffened and looked towards the cottage in time to see the door close behind Lady Jenna. The weapon pressed against his ribs pulled away. Fists clenched, he turned to meet his attacker. Mistake, he thought, as he felt rather than saw a movement off to his right. Pain exploded at the back of his head. Big mistake. Black filled his vision.

In horror, Jenna stared at the man sitting in the armchair with a rifle pointed at her chest. The footpad who had accosted her on the road and again at the market in town. She looked at Mrs Tearny questioningly. 'What is going on here?'

The woman backed away, shaking her head.

'Well?' she said to the man with the rifle.

A cocky grin spread across his face. 'Third time lucky. The governor will be pleased.'

The words chilled her blood. 'What do you mean?'

'Full of questions, aren't you, milady Jenna?'

'What of the babe?'

'Sound asleep in its crib upstairs.'

'But—' She looked at the widow, who shook her head.

'There is no illness here, is there?'

'Nah.' He glared at Mrs Tearny. 'Upstairs you go with your brats. You aren't needed.'

'My son?' Mrs Tearny whispered.

'He'll be safe enough.'

What were they talking about? One thing was plain. She and Niall had been gulled. Jenna closed her eyes. Oh, good Lord, Niall would enter at any moment. She didn't know if he was armed, but she had no doubt he would not take kindly to having a rifle pointed at him. She glanced over her shoulder at the door, half-expecting him to come bursting in.

'You don't have to worry about your servant,' the man said with a smug grin. 'He's being well looked after outside.'

Dread filled her heart. 'If you've hurt him,' she said fiercely, 'I'll—'

The man pushed to his feet and loomed over her. 'You'll what?'

'I'll see you hung. My guardian, Lord Carrick—'

'Is away. And your bridegroom will no doubt pay a pretty penny to have you back.'

She swallowed. 'How do you know all this?'

'What, you think servants don't gossip? Turn around.'

'Why?'

He cocked his head on one side. 'Do it.'

When she didn't move he raised his hand as

if to strike her. She stared at him down her nose. 'You wouldn't dare.'

His face reddened. His hand curled into a fist. She braced herself for the blow.

Slowly he dropped his arm. 'The governor won't appreciate me damaging the goods he wants. But there's nothing to say I can't take a piece out of the fella that nigh broke my arm. I wouldn't mind seeing him with a few broken bones and a few bruises on that pretty face of his. Set the soldiers on us, he did.'

He stepped around her, keeping the rifle pointed at her chest. He opened the door. 'Jake!' he yelled.

'No,' she said, cringing at the thought of what they might do to Niall. 'I'll do as you say.'

The smug smile returned. 'Fancy him, do you? And you about to be married. I wonder what your groom would think of that?'

'Mr Gilvry is paid to guard my person.' And was here against his better judgement, too. 'I do not see why you would take out your spleen on a man doing his job.'

'And I've no time for arguifyin', so turn around like a good girl and we'll say no more.'

She didn't trust his word for a moment, but seeing that he held all the advantage, it seemed better to obey than risk them hurting Niall. She turned her back.

'Hands behind you.'

She complied and felt a moment of panic as he caught her hands in one of his. Then he passed a rope around her wrists and pulled it tight. She struggled to free her hands, but the rope didn't loosen. If anything, it felt tighter.

He grabbed her by the shoulder and pushed her outside the door and handed her off to another man waiting outside. The small cowardly one she remembered from the road.

'If you do this, you will be in terrible trouble,' she said to the little pipsqueak. 'Take me back to the castle and I will see you don't suffer.'

The man's eyes widened.

The man behind her swore and reached around to stuff a rag in her mouth. 'Don't listen to her, Pip, me lad. You'll swing same as me. Get her in that there wagon while I has a word with the missus, here. We don't want her runnin' to the castle neither.'

So Mrs Tearny wasn't their accomplice?

The man called Pip caught her by one arm in a hard grip, hustled her down the steps and around the back of the house. She looked desperately around for Niall but couldn't see him. Nor were their horses outside. Pip picked her up and tossed her into the back of a flat-bedded cart and threw something heavy and rough and smelling of mildew over her head. A sack, she guessed. More things piled on top. She couldn't breathe. She started to struggle. 'Lie still,' Pip said, 'or I'll hit you over the head like we did with the other'n.'

She stilled and breathed through her nose, turning her head to make it easier to draw breath in the small space beside her face while she processed what she'd heard. They'd hit Niall over the head? No wonder she hadn't seen him outside. Was he lying out there somewhere on the ground? Injured? But they'd sent for the doctor. He would find him. And then Niall would find her. She had absolutely no doubt he would come looking. None at all.

She could hear the low murmur of voices as the men came back to the wagon, felt it tip and jolt as they climbed aboard.

'You sit still, now,' said the voice of the man who was the leader of this band of outlaws.

A strange thing to say to one of his men. The cart jerked and then creaked and she had the sensation of moving. Where were they taking her? She shifted to ease the strain on her wrists and heard a soft groan from behind her. A groan of pain. There was someone else in the cart. Her stomach fell away as she realised who it must be. Niall. He wasn't going to come looking for her because he was here, in the cart. And hurt.

Their only hope now was Mrs Tearny. No doubt she'd been paid to keep quiet about what had happened. Which meant there was no hope at all.

Niall groaned again. Carefully, Jenna inched backwards, feeling with fingers that were already throbbing from the tight bindings around her wrists. Finally she felt something warm against her fingertips. Niall. It had to be. Though what part of him it might be, she wasn't sure. But there was fabric and she gave it a tug, hoping to get his attention.

She felt him shift. She didn't dare make a noise, in case Pip made good his threat. She backed up again. She could hear him breathing. Heavily. Did that mean he was still unconscious? They must have hit him dreadfully hard. She found some more cloth and tugged on it again. The breathing stilled for a second. A smiled curved her lips. They hadn't taken the slightest bit of notice of his groans and moans. She gave a pretty good imitation of the sounds he had made seconds before.

Something pressed up along the length of her back. 'Jenna?' he whispered in her ear.

Hearing him say her name made a hot lump fill the back of her throat. Tears welled in her eyes. Tears. Now. Not what she wanted. She sniffed, unable to make a sound or breathe terribly well with all that moisture clogging her throat.

He groaned again and this time it sounded full of anger and self-recrimination. 'Are you all right?'

She shook her head. But of course he couldn't see any more than she could.

'Jenna,' he said. 'Are you hurt?'

'Shut up back there,' the bandits' leader said. 'Or you'll take another nap.'

She tugged on his clothing in warning. He seemed to understand because he slid closer to her, his breath warming her nape, his chest against her back, his legs curving under her. When he didn't touch her with his hands, she guessed he must also be tied with his hands behind his back. She reached back with one foot and ran it up and down his leg in a silent message. He drew in a swift hiss of a breath.

The sound sent little chills running across her breasts. Thrilling little chills. So thrilling, she felt her breathing shallow and her pulse race. And she was having enough trouble breathing as it was.

She took a deep breath through her nose and inhaled something that tickled unbearably. She sneezed. Once. Twice. Her body jerking against his.

'Och, you are killing me,' he breathed softly, and pressed his hot mouth to a tender spot beneath her ear.

She moaned with the pleasure of it. And the pain of being unable to breathe, or speak.

'One tug for yes, two for no,' he breathed into her ear.

She tugged. Again that indrawn breath.

'Are you hurt?'

Two tugs.

'Thank God. Gagged?'

She nodded, then remembering, tugged once.

He drew back a little and she could feel his lips exploring the back of her head and some-times puffs of air as he spat out hanks of her hair. It made her want to giggle. She must be light-headed for lack of air.

He closed the distance and once more whis-pered softly. 'I can't find what they have tied around your mouth.'

Oh, so that's what he was doing. Two tugs.

'Bastards,' he said.

They lay still for a moment, rocking against each other with every movement of the cart, her bum in his lap. He huffed out a breath and rolled on his back.

She made a small sound of protest.

He rolled back. 'You don't understand. This is driving me mad.'

She didn't understand and she didn't care. She needed to feel him right there at her back, solid and warm and comforting. She reached for his clothing with her fingertips and found it, along with something hard pressing into her hand.

'Oh, God,' he breathed. 'Stop.'

And then she had an insight, a flash of un-derstanding as to what she was touching. Heat flooded her face. She immediately ceased her ex-ploration and gave a little sob of embarrassment.

'It's not your fault,' he said.

Not her fault. Of course this was her fault. But for her, he would not be here.

She lay still, trying not to bump against him. Trying not to wonder what would happen next. Trying not to think of anything at all. Even so, she could not deny that the knowledge that he was right there with her, at her back, warm and solid, made her feel a great deal better than she had when she thought she was completely alone.

The journey continued hour after hour. She knew it was a long time because they had stopped on several occasions. Once she had jerked awake because the cart had stopped and someone got off. She'd been surprised to realise she had actually fallen asleep. The second time they had stopped there had been other voices just beyond the cart. And a lad crying, begging to be allowed to go home. She had the feeling it was daylight. The darkness beneath whatever was covering her was a little less dense. And she could feel Niall moving at her back, small subtle movements.

'Trying to get the ropes undone,' he muttered as if he sensed her interest.

And then the men were back on the cart and they were moving again.

Her stomach felt hollow. If it was daylight, it was hours since she'd had any food. Where on earth could these men be taking them? They'd talked about asking for a ransom, but how would they get it if they'd gone so far from Carrick Castle?

Then everything changed. The steady creak and rock of the cart turned into a nightmare of jolts and the crack of a whip at the animal pulling the vehicle. It tilted so much she felt herself sliding forwards. Her head hit something solid. Niall cursed as he slid into her, knocking what little breath she had from her body. The men didn't notice.

'Damn you,' Niall yelled. 'I'm crushing her.'

Someone pulled off the covering and Jenna closed her eyes, dazzled by daylight and blue sky. But she could breathe. And above her she could see gulls wheeling on the breeze and smell the salt and seaweed in the air. And then there was Niall, looking down at her face. 'The devil take you,' he said over his shoulder. 'She's suffocating.'

'Shut your mouth,' the leader said.

'She does look a bit blue,' Pip said. 'There's no one to hear her shout, Fred.'

'All right. Take out the gag. But watch she don't bite you.'

Scrawny little Pip leaned over the back, while Fred pointed a pistol at Niall. 'Move back.'

Niall struggled clear and Pip pulled the rag from her mouth. And finally air filled her lungs. Her mouth was as dry as dust and her throat hurt, but she could at last take a deep breath. She looked at Niall. 'Thank you.'

He grinned. 'You are welcome, my lady.'

'Shut up, the pair of you,' Fred said, 'or I'll put it back.'

Niall raised a brow and shook his head. He looked so cheerful she had the feeling he must have worked his bonds free and was just awaiting the chance to break free. She shifted to see where they were going and was surprised to see not only the three men on the front of the wagon, but a red-haired boy staring back at her over his shoulder.

'William Tearny?' she said. She glared at him. 'You should be ashamed of yourself, throwing your lot in with these thieves after all Lord Carrick has done for your family.'

The boy cringed.

'That's it, miss,' Jake said. 'You tell the little prig.' He clipped the boy about the ear with a large hand. 'Needs a lesson in manners, 'e does.'

The boy pressed a hand to his head and sniffled, but said nothing in reply.

At that moment, the cart turned a corner and halted at the mouth of a small bay. Bobbing on the swell was a small boat. Alarmed, she looked at Niall. He frowned.

'Where are you taking us?' she asked.

'Somewhere you will never be found,' Fred answered with a malicious grin. 'Until I says so.'

He brought the cart to a stop. 'Now you can either go into the boat on your own two legs, or you can go on as cargo. Seems like Jake knows the way of putting a man to sleep.'

Jenna swallowed the dryness remaining in her mouth. 'I'd rather walk.'

'Me, too,' Niall said. 'But you'll have to untie our ankles.'

'Shackle him up, Pip, then cut the ropes.'

Niall's shoulders tensed. Jenna made herself sit upright, forcing herself to be ready for whatever came next.

Pip climbed over into the bed of the cart and pulled out a handful of shackles and chains from beneath the sacks in one corner. Niall kicked him behind the knees. Pip pitched forwards, dropping the gun trying to break his fall. Niall grabbed it and turned on his back, aiming at Fred.

The other man, Jake, stared at him, mouth agape. Fred grabbed Jenna by the hair and pulled her tight against his chest, then pressed a pistol against her temple.

Niall brought the gun to bear on him.

'Looks like we got a bit of a puzzle,' Fred said, his chest rising and falling at her back. 'I don't care if you shoot Pip, but shoot me and the lady dies. Of course you will probably save your own neck.'

Niall grimaced and threw the pistol down. 'You can't blame a man for trying.'

Fred pushed her away from him and she fell headlong into the bottom of the cart, banging her nose. She felt something warm trickling onto her lip. A coppery taste on her tongue.

Niall surged towards Fred, rage on his face.

'No,' she cried out. Too late. Jake hit him with a belaying spike. He collapsed in a heap. Fred stepped into the back of the cart and kicked him in the torso, hard. Then he glared at Jenna. 'I've got a good mind to toss him into the ocean.'

The Tearny boy hunched deeper into his coat and turned his face away.

'No,' Jenna cried out. 'I'll do whatever you want.'

Fred looked at her with that malicious grin. 'He was right, then. You do have a soft spot for the lad.'

Who was right? She didn't dare ask.

'Give her that there writing stuff, Jake. What's under the seat.' He grabbed Jenna by the arm and pulled her down from the back of the cart and set her on her feet. He pointed to a rock. 'Sit there and write.' He leered at her. 'And don't try to cheat. Pip there, he knows how to read.'

Pip, busy putting chains on Niall's unconscious form, looked up and nodded.

Jenna sat down and took the pencil and paper. Fred paced before her. 'This is what you say...'

Chapter Nine

Damnation, he was cold. Niall reached out for the covers, felt a sharp pain in his chest and heard the clanking of chains. What the…? He cracked open his eyelids and met Jenna's worried gaze.

Oh, yes. They'd been abducted. He frowned as the events of the past few hours flooded back. His temples began a steady throb.

'Thank goodness,' she said. 'I was beginning to think you were never going to wake.'

Trying to look less fragile than he felt, he pulled himself upright. Agony. Lancing through his chest. He couldn't stop the grunt of pain, or from pressing one hand to his ribs. He swallowed a curse.

'He kicked you,' Jenna said. 'After they knocked you out.'

'Sounds like something they would do,' he

said, trying to breathe slowly and evenly in what appeared to be the dying rays of the sun stabbing the shadows of a rocky cavern. He looked her over. Her face was pale. A trickle of blood had dried beneath her nose and her hair was falling around her face and down her back in a glorious tangled mass of burnished gold and copper, but her expression showed only anger.

'Are you all right?' he asked.

She nodded and held up her hands. 'I'd be a whole lot better if I wasn't tied up. Apparently, they only had one set of shackles and they thought you deserved them.'

He glanced down. Chained hand and foot, like a criminal. Slowly he eased himself into a sitting position and looked around him at the sandy floor and rock walls. Beyond the entrance he saw an endless sea and heard the sound of the waves. 'Do you know where we are?'

She shook her head. 'Not far from where we boarded the boat since we were not at sea for very long. I have no idea which direction they took. They covered us in tarpaulins again.' She wrinkled her little red nose and shook her hair out of her eyes. 'And now all I can smell is fish.'

It was the least of their worries. 'What happened after they knocked me out?'

'They made me write a letter to Carrick telling him I was safe and to await further instructions. Fred, Jake and the boy went off to deliver it. They said they will be back before morning to take us to our destination,' she said bitterly.

Something about what she had said didn't make sense. 'Are you telling me they did not demand a ransom?'

'Not in the letter I wrote. From what I overheard, they are to take us to the person who is behind all of this. In the note, they threatened to kill me if anyone tried to follow them. I suppose that is Pip's task, if they don't return.'

'There is something very odd about all of this. What on earth can they be after, if it is not money? Although I suppose we are lucky they didn't ask for a fortune and then dump us both overboard.'

Her eyes widened and her face grew paler. 'Perhaps they aren't after money. Or they know Carrick won't pay up until he is sure they mean business. If at all.' She bit her lip and winced. Now he looked at her mouth. He could see it was split. Fury rose in his veins, hot and angry. Anger at himself for scaring her and fury at these *Sassenachs* who held them captive. He clenched his fists and the chains chinked unpleasantly. 'Carrick will pay up. How could he not? And they know he will go after them, if we are not returned whole and well.' Or her, anyway. He was of no value, except perhaps as a means to ensure her cooperation. But why not demand the money right away?

'If only we could escape before they come back,' she said, looking around.

He looked at his shackles and her ropes. 'I certainly think I can untie you. You can go for help when it gets dark.'

She grimaced. 'They left Pip as a guard down on the beach. We might be able to go up the cliff.' She looked at him with sympathy. 'Though from what I saw they are rather high and quite sheer.'

Of course they were. His stomach slid unpleasantly sideways. It wasn't the only such cove along this shore. There was one very like it near Dunross. The cave there had been carved out by a river and its tunnel led up to the headland. This one was barely worthy of the name 'cave'. It edged only a few feet into the rock and had no back door.

Feeling like the worst kind of coward, he took a deep breath. 'We should look at all the options before attempting anything.'

She nodded her agreement matter-of-factly. 'Before we can do anything, we have to get you out of those chains.'

'Perhaps we can undo the lock with a hairpin. I think I still have a couple left.' She moved closer. 'Can you look and see?'

Her hair was a mass of curls, and thick and soft despite the tangles. The colour of autumn leaves, russets and reds and browns. He wanted to feel it slide through his fingers and see it spread over

white pillows. Hell, why could he not remember
the woman was betrothed to another man? Forcing himself to feel nothing, he fumbled through
the silken mass and found two finely worked
tortoiseshell pins. He set one down between his
knees and worked the other one into the padlock at his ankles. 'Let's see, shall we?' he said,
trying to keep positive. Not that he knew much
about picking locks. It wasn't something he'd ever
needed to learn. 'I need to get a look at the lay
of the land before it gets dark.' Hopefully, there
would be another option to climbing those cliffs.
The pin snapped the moment he twisted it.

'Oh, no,' she said. 'Why don't you cut my
ropes with this?' She held out a sharp-edged
shell. 'Then I can help pick the lock.'

'It would be better not to cut the rope. We
might need its full length if we do have to climb,
but I am not ready to give up on these irons.' He
eased the second hairpin into the padlock.

The sun was sinking fast. If he did not get
these chains off, he was going to have to find their
way out of here blind. The second pin snapped.
He cursed. He could not walk in these chains, let
alone scramble over rocks, or swim. 'That's it,
then. You will have to go alone. Come back for
me when you find help.' He grasped her arm. 'But
be careful who you trust. The best thing to do is
find your way back to Carrick Castle.'

Her eyes widened in horror. 'I can't leave you here.'

'You must. Come closer and I will see if I can undo these knots.'

She shifted closer, holding out her wrists. 'Oh, if only I had worn my steel pins this morning.'

Steel pins might have helped. 'You should have guessed we would need them,' he said, grinning at her worried face.

She made a half-hearted attempt at a smile. Hell, the woman was brave. As tough as any Highland lass he had ever met, despite her tiny stature. Perhaps tougher.

Steel pins would have indeed been handy, but a knife in his boot would have been better. Not that they would have let him keep it. He lifted her small hands and set them on his knee so he could get at the knots. Small hands, delicate fingers, wrists rubbed raw. He wanted to kill Fred and his men for hurting his little faery.

Faery. Damn it all. He had a pin: the silver one he'd bought from the gypsy. He put his hand inside his pocket and pulled it out. 'Let me try this first.' He inserted it into the lock, jiggled it, felt it bite and pushed harder. The shackle fell open at his feet.

'Oh,' Jenna said. 'You did it.'

'Shhh.' He unlocked the one at his wrists and put the pin back in his pocket. 'Now let me have a look at those ropes.' The knot was tight and firm, but easy to untie and he now had about three feet of good strong rope. Not nearly enough for climbing.

'Now to check out our avenues of escape.' Please let there be some other way besides those cliffs. 'Wait here.'

She nodded and stayed still while he edged towards the mouth of the cave.

Down on the beach their guard sat cross-legged on the sand beside a fire. Good. The light from the flames would make it hard for him to see much in the shadows as long as he did nothing to attract his attention.

He stood with his back against the rocks and scanned the cove.

It was little more than an inlet and surrounded on all three sides by cliffs at least sixty feet high. It was low tide and the waves crashing against the base of each headland made escape that way impossible. Behind the cave, the cliffs were jagged at the base, with lots of hand and footholds. Higher up they were sheer, except for a narrow vertical fissure that ended very close to the top.

Not a terribly difficult climb for someone with experience, but for a man who suffered from vertigo it was nigh impossible. Yet there wasn't a choice.

His stomach churned as he looked up. His head spun. Well, it would be dark when they went up.

The only thing in his favour. Carefully, he re-treated back into the cave.

'Can we do it?' she asked breathlessly.

'Oh, aye. No trouble at all,' he said and swallowed his bile. 'But we will need to do something about that skirt of yours.'

'Perhaps I can cut it shorter.'

He unknotted his cravat and handed it to her. 'Tie this around your waist and loop up your skirts the way the lasses do when digging for cockles.'

She nodded. 'When do we go?'

'When it is fully dark.'

'Then there is nothing to do but wait.'

'Aye.' He stretched out on the sandy floor and she dropped down beside him. He felt her shiver. 'Cold?'

'A little.'

'Put your cloak over both of us and lie close. Two are always warmer than one under the covers.'

'I suppose you speak from experience.' Her voice was warm and teasing in the growing dark. He forced himself to remember how afraid she must be. How this was bravery on her part. How he had to keep her at a distance.

'Many experiences.'

'Oh.' A sound filled with embarrassment, but still she covered him with her cloak, then slipped beneath it, hard up against his side. He had an urge to roll over and enclose her within his arms. To warm her with kisses. He gritted his teeth and stayed where he was. 'Better?'

'Yes.' She snuggled closer, making his heart beat a little too fast. No, a lot too fast.

'I was so glad you were there with me in that cart,' she whispered. 'I was terrified. When I heard your voice, I was so relieved.'

'I was of little use.' As little as he had been at the Tearnys' cottage. He'd let his guard down. Never imagined that a scurvy bunch of ruffians would come up with such a devious scheme. Even now, he could not quite believe it. 'I'm going to make Fred and his lads wish they had never been born, when we get back to Carrick.' *If* they got back to Carrick. The thought of climbing the cliff was his worst nightmare come true. Thank God it would be dark when they made the attempt.

'I wonder what Mr Murray is going to make of all this?'

Murray. Now there was a thought. No doubt if he was here he'd be shinning up the rocks and enjoying himself. 'He'll be glad to see you brought back, safe and sound.'

'I expect you are right.'

She didn't sound hopeful.

'He can't blame you for being abducted.'

'No. But people talk. They make assumptions... I will have spent two nights unchaperoned. He might not be so pleased to marry a woman whose virtue is in doubt.'

'A man worth marrying won't listen to un-founded gossip.'

She didn't reply. In the dark, he had no way of telling if his words had the desired effect. Not that he cared about Murray. But from the tension in her body, he could tell she did. And with good reason. Her future was at stake.

If they managed to escape in one piece.

Better not to think about what might happen. It was like worrying about cards one hadn't yet been dealt. It didn't help. In fact, if he thought about the climb, his teeth might start to chatter.

'Tell me about your home,' he murmured. 'About Braemuir.'

'Oh,' she said on a sigh and he felt her relax right away. 'I haven't been there for years.'

'But you remember it.'

'Of course. I grew up there. It was just me and Father, after Mother died.' There was a long pause and he thought she wouldn't say any more, but then she did and there was a smile in her voice, heart-stopping joy, and he wished he could see her face.

'It is not a large estate, compared to Lord Carrick's holding. A small park in a glen surrounded by hills. Everything is so green in the summer. And the winters are so fierce sometimes the road to the village is impassable for days.'

'And you didna' mind being cut off?'

'It was more of an adventure. Father and I used to hunt, though there was always plenty of food in the larder and wood and peat for the fires. Enough for a few days, anyway.'

Pretty much the way they survived at Dunross when the weather turned bad. 'Has your family lived there long?'

'There have been Aleynes at Braemuir for centuries. The current house was built for my mother's grandfather by the Scottish architect James Smith. They kept the great hall and built the new house around it. I loved it as a child. Hearing the stories of my ancestors from my father. Seeing their portraits and collections. He spent hours with me, teaching me everything he knew.'

'It is a rare father who spends so much time with a daughter.' His own father had spent little or no time with his younger sons.

'He planned to marry again, once he was done grieving my mother. It took a long time. But finally he felt he was ready. The night before he was to depart for Edinburgh, he collapsed. Apoplexy, the doctor said.'

'And now you are to carry on where he left off.'

'Yes. I've been gone a long time, but I've never forgotten my promise to my father to do my best for Braemuir.' Her voice lowered into a whisper. 'It was too soon, when he died. I wasn't ready.'

Damn. Now he'd stirred up unhappy memories. 'I'm sorry.'

'But I am ready now. My aunt, Mrs Blackstone, taught me all I need to fulfil my duty.'

It sounded like a cold future. 'So you will be pleased to go home at last?'

'I will. Braemuir needs its own lord again, though Lord Carrick has been assiduous in his role as trustee.'

Had he? Niall recalled the entries in that damned private ledger. Payments listed as coming from Braemuir. He had no idea of their legitimacy. Nor should he have seen them.

'And what about you?' she asked. 'Do you love your home?'

'Ours is a slightly different tale, I am afraid, though it ends well enough. The Gilvrys lost Dunross Keep after '45.'

'You picked the losing side.'

'Aye, like many Highlanders, we joined forces with the Bonnie Prince. After that, a *Sassesnach* lord took our lands. My great-grandfather fled to France, but a cousin remained close by Dunross and warded his son, my grandfather. The Gilvrys spent all their money and time trying to regain the land and the keep, until they were practically beggars.'

'But you did get it back?'

'Aye. My oldest brother finally married the

English lord's daughter. He seems happy about it, too.'

'To your surprise?'

'Aye, well, we all thought he'd tricked her into marrying him so he could get our lands back. It turned out they'd cared for each other for years. They just couldna' see how to make it work, the two families hating each other as they did.'

'It sounds romantic,' she whispered with a sigh. Perhaps she was wishing Murray was here instead of him. And although her sweet form was pressed against him so sweetly and his body was raging with lust, he held himself rigid. Because if he didn't he might just be tempted to kiss her again. And he was supposed to be keeping her safe.

He hadn't done a particularly good job of it so far, but tonight he would not let her down no matter how high those damned cliffs.

And she trusted him to do just that. Protect her from these men and whoever was behind them. The thought split something open inside him and a great surge of tenderness bubbled up through the crack. She made him want to give her the moon and to protect her for ever and always.

He touched his lips to her hair, a gesture of comfort, nothing more, and she lifted her face and pressed her lips to his.

A small breathy touch. A searing flare to the dry tinder of his will. He turned on his side and wooed her lips. She tasted of hope and despair and trust and woman. And he didn't care that she smelled faintly of fish—they both did. She also smelled of heather and roses.

He teased her lips to hear her sigh. He tasted the dark depths of her mouth and her body turned inwards, her small perfect breast pressing against his chest. It was worth the pain just to feel her against him. He was burning. Hard as the rock beneath him.

It was bliss. It was hell. She shifted. Pain shot through his chest. He drew in a sharp breath and she stilled.

'Oh. Did I hurt you? I'm sorry.'

Sorry? Dazed, he held her a little away from him. If they continued down this path she would be very sorry indeed. She was engaged to another man. A man who could give her everything she needed most.

Never had he wanted a woman the way he wanted this one. And here she was, ready and willing. If it was any other woman, he wouldn't give it a moment's thought. But this was Jenna. And he could not take the chance that what they might do at the edge of fear would ruin her life. She was innocent. He was not.

He drew back. 'No more, understand.'

'What if tomorrow we are dead?' She snuggled closer, her body half on his, her hands sliding around his nape.

His heart thundered in his chest. His blood pulsed in his veins. A celebration of the gift he was offered. Just one more kiss. Then he'd stop. But he wouldn't. If he kissed her again, he'd lose what little control he had left.

It was his fault she was in danger. And soon they had a cliff to climb. The cold inside him expanded until he wanted to shudder like a cowering dog. The thought of those cliffs. The height of them. His mouth dried. His throat closed. His limbs turned to water just thinking about them. But he could not let her see his cowardice. 'In a few hours we will be back at Carrick Castle and this will all seem like a dream.'

It was with a feeling of pride that he threw back the cloak and stood up, with a groan at the pain across his ribs. A feeling of having fought a devil within him and won. Her little sound of protest struck low in his gut, but he ignored it. 'It's time. Get ready.' His voice sounded harsh and that was just as well, because she moved to obey.

He heard the rustle of her skirts as he walked softly to the mouth of the cave and let his eyes adjust to the light from the stars twinkling in between patches of cloud. Down on the beach, Pip was slumped beside the fire. Asleep. Poor wee lad. He'd had a hard day. Niall smiled a grim smile. He'd help him sleep a little longer.

Soundlessly, he climbed carefully across the rocks to the beach. Pip didn't stir as he approached the fire. He picked up a piece of drift-wood and hit the sleeping lad above the ear. He collapsed with a gentle sigh. Tit for tat.

Niall searched through his clothes, took the pistol and his knife, then checked his pockets and found powder and balls in a waterproof package within. The pistol would come in handy when they made it to the top of the cliff.

When. Now there was positive thinking.

He glanced down and saw something much more valuable than a pistol: a long length of rope. He coiled it and slung it over his shoulder. By the time he got back to the cave, Jenna was stand-ing at the entrance, waiting. Her skirts tucked up above her sensible boots revealed the white gleam of stockings.

He tied one end of his rope around his waist and the other around hers. It was how Ian had taken him up the cliffs the very first time. The day he had discovered he was terrified of heights. His brother thought to help him get over his fear. It hadn't worked. Better not to think of that now.

The first part of the climb went relatively eas-ily. The rocks were more like stepping stones and Jenna kept pace. And just as the dark had helped him the last time he'd climbed a cliff, it helped him now. He kept his gaze fixed ahead, looking for the next handhold, the next place to step. Until they came to the crevice. This was the part he'd been dreading most. And now, up close, with the sky directly above, he could see it leaned out-wards. Could it get any worse?

Keeping himself flat against the cliff wall, he risked a glance down to the beach to the glow of the fire where he'd left Pip. No movement. God, it was such a long way down. His head spun. His knees weakened. He grabbed at the rock face and pressed his forehead to cold granite.

He'd reached his limit.

The point at which he could neither go up or go down. No. He could go down. He could do that. As long as he went slowly and didn't look.

'Is something wrong?' Jenna whispered from behind him. 'Is it your ribs?'

'Aye.' He certainly wasn't going to tell her he was afraid to move.

Bile rose in his throat. And anger. At his in-ability to conquer his fear. At his cowardice.

He didn't understand it. It was irrational.

He swallowed. This wasn't about him. It was about getting Jenna to safety. Back in her be-trothed's arms. Oh, now there was an incentive to spur him on. He took a deep breath. He didn't have a choice. He had to do this. Once more he leaned back to look up the crevice. It was about fifteen feet, from here to the ledge. Nothing, Logan would call it. 'Stay here. When I tug on the rope be prepared for me to lift you.'

'Wh-where are you going?'

'Up,' he said. 'Just do it, Jenna. Please.'

He didn't wait for her answer, just went to the spot where the rock face split apart. He'd seen his brothers do this countless times, put their back to one side of a crevice and shimmy upwards using hands and feet. He took a deep breath, pressed his back to the rough rock and one hand flat behind him, one foot high against the opposite wall and pushed up. Just like walking up a wall, Logan had crowed the first time he did it. And it wasn't that hard at the start, where the sides were close. Right foot, left hand, push. Left foot, right hand, push. But the distance was widening, and he was so high above the beach. He panted for breath, sweating so hard the hand supporting him slid on the rock, his stomach falling away in dizzying spirals.

It was happening again. He couldn't do it.

He leaned his head back against the wall and closed his eyes to stop the world spinning. Trembles shook his body. He could not do this. It was not fair that he should have to do this. Frozen, his arms and legs rigid, he felt like a block of ice.

Breathe. His grandfather's voice came back to him, just the same as when the old man had come to help him down that first time. Breathe? He could scarcely take a breath at all. Besides, breathing hurt because Fred had kicked him.

Take it one step at a time, the voice said.

All right for you to say. You are not the one forty feet up.

He had to do this. For Jenna's sake. He took one shaky breath. And another. Slowly his stomach settled in one place. He opened his eyes and glanced up quickly. He could see the top of the crevice. The edge of the ledge. All he had to do was get there and have solid ground beneath him. One step at a time. Don't think about anything else.

He moved one hand and one foot, just an inch or two and pushed. And then again. Three more times and he was up on the ledge, his body and cheek pressed hard against the blessedly flat rock and his ribs jabbing at him. A most welcome pain.

Now he had to pull Jenna up. Slowly he got to his feet and pressed his back against the rock wall. He squeezed his eyes closed and opened them, then looked down.

He could see her, a darker shadow against the rocks. He fixed the rope over his shoulder. 'Ready?'

'Yes.'

He braced his feet apart and began to pull her up. The brave lass used her hands and feet on the rock face, making it easier to ignore the pain in his chest. And finally he had her up beside him. He leaned against the rock, panting.

'That was interesting,' she said, her voice a few inches from his face.

Anger filled him. Anger at how relaxed she sounded, at how easily she'd accomplished something that had just about made him insane. So angry he climbed the last few feet without thinking. He flung himself over the cliff edge to land on his knees. He rolled clear, leaped to his feet, walking backwards, holding the rope taut until she followed him over and was clear of the edge.

'We did it,' she cried.

'Hush. Do you want Pip to hear us?' He bent over, hands on his knees, waiting for his gut to stop churning and his teeth not to chatter.

Finally, he took a deep breath and straightened. 'Yes, we did it,' he whispered. 'But we have a long way to go before we are safe.' He pulled her towards him, seeing her shape as a dark shadow against the starlit sky, feeling her warmth when she stood in front of him, the gleam of bare slender legs beneath her tucked-up skirts. His hands shaking badly, he fumbled with the knots to get them untied.

'Can I help?'

He stiffened at the sympathy in her voice. 'I can manage.' He certainly wasn't going to tell her he wanted nothing more than to lay flat on the ground in utter relief.

'It was amazing the way you climbed up there,' she said.

Sarcasm. It had to be. She knew he didn't like heights and no doubt she'd seen his panic. His fear. Now she'd seen his cowardice in action. At last the knot came undone. He stepped clear. 'Hurry and straighten yourself,' he said brusquely. 'I hit our friend Pip pretty hard, but he's no doubt had worse and who knows how soon he'll awake. We need to be as far from here as possible before the sun comes up and the others return.'

'Perhaps they will think we swam,' she said, shaking out her skirts.

He forced himself to turn away. 'Perhaps.'

'Perhaps,' she mimicked. 'Can't you at least be happy we've escaped?'

'I'll celebrate when I am sure we have.' He hated that he sounded so grim in the face of her joy, but until his stomach returned to its normal place and his head stopped spinning, he was not going to be in the mood for cheerful conversation. And he certainly didn't want her sympathy.

Chapter Ten

Poor Niall. Clearly, he hadn't yet recovered from the climb. She didn't dare offer comfort in case he took offence. She'd also been terrified, climbing up that cliff in the dark. Only the knowledge he was ahead of her, holding the rope, had given her the courage to follow. For a while, at the bottom of the fissure, she'd been sure she wasn't going to make it. Thank goodness he knew what he was doing. She breathed a sigh of relief. With that awful climb behind them, all they had to do was get back to Carrick.

She wasn't exactly looking forward to going back to the castle. There was sure to be an uproar. Her cousin would be furious when he learned what had happened and she very much feared he would blame Niall. Well, he needn't worry she would let him shoulder the blame or suffer the consequences.

Since there was nothing to be done about it at this moment, she strode along beside him, or at least he strode and she had to keep breaking into a run to keep up. She was just about to ask him to slow down when she saw a soft red glow up ahead. Niall must have seen it, too, because he grabbed her arm and pulled her to the ground.

Her heart sank. 'They left a guard up here, too?'

Niall hissed at her to hush.

'We could just go around,' she whispered.

Niall hushed her again and she knelt on the rough grass, listening to her heart beat hard in her ears.

Niall turned to her. 'Whoever it is has a horse. I can hear it.'

She listened. She could hear it, too. The odd jingle and a whooffly sound horses made at night.

'So?' she replied.

'So a horse will get us back to Carrick faster than we can walk.'

'Will he sell it to us?'

'I don't have any money.'

'Nor me.'

'We will have to steal it.' He grabbed her shoulders. 'Stay close. We'll work our way around the fire and try to walk it away without them noticing.'

'And if they do notice?'

'I have a pistol.'

A pistol was better than money in some circumstances.

Slowly they circled around the fire, towards the direction of the horse. As they drew closer, the flames revealed a wagon closed in by an arch of canvas and its owner relaxed against one wheel.

Oh, blast. The horse was still in the traces, munching on the contents of a nosebag. Niall must have noticed, too, because he stopped.

The owner of the wagon seemed to be looking straight at them. Which was impossible, because they were in the shadows on the opposite side of the fire. There was something familiar about the man.

The gypsy from the market. She clapped a hand over her mouth to muffle her gasp of shock.

She heard the click of Niall cocking the pistol and winced. They were going to have to steal the horse at gunpoint.

'Come to the fire,' a dark voice said. 'I have been expecting you.'

'We want only your horse,' Niall said, standing up. 'You will be compensated. Later.'

Surprised, Jenna stood up beside him.

'It's me or them,' the Gypsy said, still casually relaxed against the wheel of his wagon.

'We just want the horse,' Niall said tersely. 'And we will be on our way.'

'And you will be dead by the end of the day.'

Niall stiffened.

'I knew you would never accept my help,' he continued. 'Not at first, at least.'

'What?' Jenna said.

'Lady Jenna. Will you have more sense than your swain and join me by the fire?'

Niall growled low in his throat. A warning that she should not move.

She remained at his side. 'Are you part of this?' she asked. 'Part of this abduction?'

'No.'

'Then how did you know where to find us?' Niall said, holding her arm as if he feared she would step into a trap.

The gypsy shrugged. 'I dreamed it.' He flashed a smile, a white gleam in the darkness. A smile that suddenly seemed familiar. The image of tents and the fires and women weaving baskets and men making pots after they finished working in the fields filled her mind. Her father had gone there once to see their leader and taken her with him.

Niall snorted.

'I remember you now,' Jenna said. 'Your band camps near Braemuir in the summer.'

'Used to camp,' he said. 'Things have changed.'

'Niall, if Mr Hughes trusts this man enough to send him with a letter, then so should we.'

'What do you fear, *chavvi*?'

Niall nodded, but kept her behind him as he

stepped into the circle of dim light cast by the fire, still pointing his pistol.

The gypsy gestured at it. 'The powder is wet.'

To Jenna's surprise, Niall gave a short laugh. 'I know it. But how did you?'

The gypsy touched the side of his nose. 'I smell.'

Niall let go of her and shook his head. 'Will you lend us your horse?'

'No, *chavvi*, but I will carry you where you need to go. We must hurry, my friend, if you do not wish to be caught again.'

Jenna looked up at Niall.

The gypsy leaped to his feet and poured water on the fire. 'Into the wagon with you, where you will be safe. I travel the lanes and no one takes notice, except to spit and cross themselves. We will be gone from here before they discover your absence.'

'Thank you,' Jenna said.

Niall gazed down at his pistol and back at the gypsy. 'Betray us, gypsy, and you will pay with your life.'

The gypsy grinned. 'My name is Sean.'

Niall put his pistol in his waistband and stuck out a hand. 'Niall Gilvry. And this is—'

'The Lady Jenna.' He bowed. 'Now into the cart with you.'

Niall helped Jenna up onto the cart's bed and she crawled through a small gap between the boxes and sacks that filled the cart to the top of its canvas roof. She found herself in a roomy space, with something soft beneath her knees. A moment later the space was lit by a lantern, passed to her by Niall.

'He says there's a hook there somewhere,' Niall muttered, crawling in beside her. He looked around. 'Well, this is luxury.'

And it was. A mattress took up the width of the floor, one end of it littered with embroidered pillows. There was a small carved chest at the head and behind it more baskets and crates.

The cart began to move.

'You like my bedroom?' Sean asked from the other side of the canvass.

'It's wonderful,' Jenna said. 'I thought gypsies lived in tents.'

'Not when I'm on the road and alone. A bender takes time to put up, so I make my tent in the cart. Be quiet, now. In case someone comes along.'

Silence reigned. Only the sound of hooves and creaking wood broke the silence.

'As I thought.' Sean's sharp whisper came through the canvas. 'Dowse the light and keep quiet. Someone is coming.'

The man seemed to have some sort of sixth sense. Niall blew out the lamp and felt Jenna tremble as she grabbed at his arm. 'It's all right,' he whispered and reached beneath the pillows for the pistol.

The wagon slowed.

'Stay quiet,' Sean whispered again. 'Say nothing.'

Scarcely daring to breathe, Niall listened to the sound of approaching hooves. Several horses by the sound of jangling bridles.

Jenna gripped his hand tightly. He gave her a comforting squeeze.

'Where are you going, tinker?' a clipped English voice asked. A familiar voice.

Lieutenant Dunstan? Well, that was a surprise. Should they declare their presence? Have him escort them home. Or trust the gypsy and stay hidden. *Bide your time. Learn the lie of the land.* He'd been too trusting already this night.

'Along this road,' Sean said. 'To the next village.'

'Have you seen anyone?'

'Only a selkie and a hobgoblin or two.'

'Don't play games, gypsy. If I search that wagon of yours, I am sure to find something to give me cause to take you to gaol.'

'I have nothing to hide,' Sean said. 'What are you seeking?'

'A band of cut-throats who've been seen in these parts.'

No mention of him and Jenna? Had he not received news of their abduction? It seemed very odd. But not necessarily a bad thing. Perhaps with this man's help, he could have Jenna returned with no one the wiser. Her reputation would certainly be ruined if this young aristocrat found them snuggled up in the blankets together.

'I've seen no man on this road tonight apart from yourself, your honour.'

The absolute truth. The gypsy hadn't seen him on this road. Only on the cliffs. Niall gave a little shake of his head at the impudence.

'Sergeant, look in the back of the wagon,' Dunstan said.

He felt Jenna take a deep breath as if to call out. 'Wait,' he whispered close to her ear. And was glad when she did as he asked.

'Be my guest,' Sean said calmly and jumped down.

They heard the canvas pulled back and someone poking around. A clatter and a curse. A clang. 'Ouch.'

'Mind that pot,' Sean said. 'Look what you have done. It is dented. You will pay for the damage.'

'Look what *I've* done,' a gruff voice said in disgust. 'That pot near brained me.'

'Well, Sergeant?' Dunstan asked.

'There's naught back here but rubbish,' the disgruntled sergeant said. 'And I've a lump on me head as big as an egg.'

'I've some unguent for that,' Sean said. 'Let me sell you a jar. Made by my grandmother. I'll let you have it cheap.' More sounds of things being moved around.

'Get away,' the sergeant said. 'I want none of your heathen potions. Nothing back here, sir.'

The wagon tilted at the front where Sean must have climbed up on the box.

'There are three men,' Dunstan said. 'Rough-looking English sailors. Send word if you see them and there will be silver crossing your palm, gypsy.'

'Thank you, your honour. Very generous of you.'

The voice of the sergeant called his men to order and the troop passed them at a trot. Sean set the wagon in motion and the sounds were soon out of earshot.

Niall let go a sigh of relief.

'We must be close to the castle,' Jenna said.

'How far do we have to go, Sean?' Niall asked in a low murmur when he was sure they must be out of earshot of the soldiers.

'Far enough,' the quiet voice came back. 'I expect you are hungry.'

Niall's stomach growled agreement.

'Starving,' Jenna agreed.

The wagon stopped and once more they felt him get down from his perch. There was the sound of things being moved and then a lantern appeared, followed by Sean's face. 'We are safe enough now.' He handed Niall a spill. 'You can relight the lantern.'

Niall did so. Sean handed him a small bundle. 'You will find food and drink in here. Not much, but it's the best I can do. Then you will sleep.'

'What about you?' Niall asked. 'Do you not need sleep?'

'I slept all day,' Sean said. 'Waiting for you.' He backed out.

'How did he know?' Jenna whispered.

'He dreamed it,' Niall said and grinned.

Oh, how she loved it when he smiled. He looked boyish and wicked. What would she have done if he had not been with her when those men had taken her captive? She shuddered inwardly at the thought.

Niall shook his head in disgust. His beard was rough and dark, his eyes shadowed by blue circles and there were smudges of dirt on his cheek and forehead. He was lovely.

'Don't,' he said softly.

She frowned a question.

'Don't look at me that way. It's my fault we are in this fix. What's in that bundle?'

She opened it up to reveal hunks of bread, neatly cut wedges of cheese and a clay flagon. 'It seems that our rescuer has thought of everything.'

Niall grunted as if the thought did not please him. She portioned out the bread and cheese between them and they munched hungrily. She wished she could say something to make him feel better about what had happened, about them being caught unawares by their abductors, but she had the feeling that speaking of it would only darken his mood. And in the meantime, it seemed they would get back to Carrick Castle without much harm being done.

'Why didn't we reveal ourselves to the lieutenant?' she asked.

'He didn't seem aware of our absence. Someone at the castle must have decided to keep it a secret. It seems to me it would be better for all concerned if no one knew you'd been missing for two nights.'

Mr Murray wouldn't like it, he meant. He was right.

Mr Gilvry picked up the flask and drew the cork. He swallowed some of the liquid and made a face and held it out to her. 'Mead.'

She took a sip. It was sweet and deliciously cold. 'I like it.' She drank her fill and handed it back.

He drained what was left. 'Not too bad when you get used to it,' he admitted. He pulled out his pistol, inspected it, then set about the task of reloading.

She watched him for a moment or two.

'You don't think we should trust him,' she whispered, jerking her thumb towards the front of the wagon.

'I don't think we should trust anyone right at this moment.'

'Who do you think is behind all of this?'

He stopped polishing the barrel of the pistol and looked at her. 'I wish I knew. If I did I would sort him out.'

'Fred said something about the governor when we were in Mrs Tearny's house—I didn't know what he meant then. He must have meant the man he is working for.'

'Someone he's afraid of?'

She nodded. 'Yes. I think you are right. What about McBane? A man prepared to cheat might be prepared to take it further.'

'He might.' He frowned. 'But they accosted you on the road long before McBane came on the scene. Carrick did mention in passing that he had turned down an offer from one suitor who hadn't taken it well. I can't recall the name of the man. Do you?'

Shock, then anger, rippled through her. 'He said nothing about another offer.' She huffed out a breath. 'How dare he refuse a proposal without consulting me?'

Niall raised a brow. 'I expect he thought it for the best.'

'Everyone seems to think they know what is best for me. I wish they would ask my opinion.'

He dropped his gaze to the pistol and carefully poured powder in the pan.

What? Did he think she had no brain? Carrick certainly did. 'I would have listened to his opinion, you know.'

He smiled, but did not look up, his large hands easing the small ball down the barrel and ramming it home. 'Aye. And then done just as you wished.'

She laughed. 'You know me too well.'

He did look up, then, and heat blazed in his eyes. An answering flush ran through her body. Attraction. Desire. All the things she must not feel for this man. She turned her face away.

'You are as courageous as any man I know,' he said softly. 'You have been through a great deal these past few hours. Most women would be having a fit of hysterics.'

He thought her too much of a hoyden. 'I could faint, if it would please you better,' she said somewhat bitterly.

'No. I beg you do not.'

She couldn't help chuckling at his horrified expression. Perhaps he did not think her too hoydenish after all, but she wasn't entirely without feminine arts. Careful not to shower crumbs on the bedcovers, she folded the napkin and put it back on the chest beside a silver-backed hand mirror. She picked it up and peeked at her reflection. 'Oh, heavens, my hair. What a mess. Now that is enough to make me faint.'

He laughed. 'You look lovely.'

'No need for sarcasm.'

He sobered. 'I mean it. You look like a creature of the glens. Wild and beautiful.'

She threaded her fingers through a hank of hair, pulling at the tangles. 'I see what you mean about wild. It will take days to get these knots out.' She wrinkled her nose. 'And the smell of fish.'

'I can't smell it,' he said.

She leaned forwards and held out a handful. 'Surely you can.'

He sniffed. 'I can only smell you. And you smell of heather and roses.'

Her insides curled pleasurably. She batted her lashes just to prove she knew he was joking. 'Flatterer.'

He smiled. And the sensations inside her only intensified. She felt restless. On edge. Because she wanted to touch him. She wanted him to kiss her. She wanted to feel him against her. She could feel her hands itching to reach out to him.

To give herself something to do with those wanton fingers, she sat back against a cushion and worked at the knots, one strand at a time.

He tucked his weapon under a pillow. 'Sean,' he called out.

'Yes, Mr Gilvry.'

'Do you happen to have a comb among your wares?'

'I thought you would never ask. The penny

combs are in a basket at the foot of the bed. You can leave the penny in its place.'

Niall grimaced. 'I'll have to owe you.'

'Then consider it a gift,' the gypsy said.

Niall tossed Jenna a comb and she began work on her hair. Soon her eyes were watering and she was hissing in pain.

He came around behind her on his knees and took the comb from her hand. 'Let me.'

Surprised, she looked back over her shoulder. 'Playing lady's maid now as well as knight in shining armour?'

'Hardly that. But I can't bear to see you cry.'

She laughed. How did he know how to make her laugh when she ought to be worried? He took the comb from her hand. 'I promise to be gentle.'

Braced for the pain she knew was inevitable, she gave him her back, squaring her shoulders, only to be surprised by his gentle, skilful touch. She relaxed, leaning back on her elbows, and enjoyed the sensual pleasure of the feel of his fingers amid her hair. Her limbs turned languid, her eyelids drooped and a strange kind of tension built inside her. Yearning laced with desire.

Sensations she had no business feeling.

The rhythmic stroking was interspersed with small shiver-making touches as he teased out the knots and his knuckles occasionally brushed her nape or her scalp. She felt herself drift. She yawned.

'You get some sleep,' Niall said. He yawned, too. 'I can barely keep my eyes open,' he muttered.

At the suggestion, she closed her eyes as if they were weighted by lead. She leaned back, yawned again and closed her eyes. The last thing she heard was Niall organising the cushions to act as a barrier between them. He reached up to put out the lamp. She gave a little shiver and put a hand out. 'Leave the light. Lately, I have spent too much time in the dark.'

He nodded. 'You have been verra brave, Lady Jenna. Now relax and I will see you safe.'

Yes. She believed he would. With him beside her she could relax.

Niall came awake with a start. Or rather became aware of a raging arousal. It took a moment for the rocking motion and sounds of hoofs and wheels to make him realise where he was. Damn. He'd fallen asleep when he had intended to keep watch. How long had they been travelling? The lantern had gone out and no light showed through the canvas. Perhaps he'd only dozed?

With Jenna snuggled up against him, he wasn't sure how long he could stand the torture.

Short of leaving the protection of the canvas and sitting up in front with Sean, which would wake her, he didn't see any way to end it. Carefully, he tucked a pillow under her cheek and eased his shoulder and his leg out from beneath her. Breath held, he shifted until his body was at the very edge of the mattress. Moments later, she was once more pressed up hard against him, one leg draped over his knee, her hand very close to…

Hellfire. He gently lifted her arm away.

'What?' she mumbled.

'You are crowding me,' he said. 'Roll over.' Back to back, he just might be able to survive.

In agony, he waited for her to break the contact 'I'm cold,' she murmured.

He was burning up.

He sat up and found the quilt at the bottom of the bed where one of them must have kicked it off and pulled it over her. 'Better?'

'I dreamed we were back on the other cart,' she said in a small voice. 'When I thought I was all alone with those men. I was terrified.'

'You are safe now.' At least he hoped so. He felt under the pillow for his pistol. He breathed a sigh of relief. 'Go back to sleep.'

She was silent for a good few heartbeats and he started to relax, to think he had come off pretty well. 'I can't sleep. Every time I close my eyes, I see them.'

Damn. Damn the men. And damn him for his surge of lust at the sound of her voice.

'Will you hold me? Just until I fall asleep?'

Inwardly he cursed long and hard as he put an arm beneath her and drew her close. He felt a shudder ripple through her body. She had been so strong, so courageous—he hadn't realised she was also afraid. He was such a dolt.

'Will you kiss me?' she whispered.

His blood roared to life, blistering hot, racing south. It was all he could do not to groan at the pleasurable pain of it. 'Jenna, I don't think that is wise.'

'When you kiss me, every bad thought goes out of my head,' she said.

And every thought out of his. A very dangerous thing, because he tended to forget he was supposed to be a gentleman, not a schoolboy with a bad case of lust. Only it went far deeper than lust, because he wanted to possess her, not just physically. He wanted more, so much more. He could not believe he was so utterly full of desire for this woman who reminded him of a faery.

Had been since the first time they kissed. All right, now he'd admitted it. But it didn't mean he could do anything about it.

'Jenna,' he groaned, 'we can't. You are perfectly safe.'

'Hmmph,' she said and turned her back to him. He let go a sigh of relief and lay staring up into the dark, listening to the sound of her breathing, until he was sure she had fallen back to sleep. He just wasn't sure he would be able to resist the temptation to pull her into the cradle of his body to keep her warm.

* * *

Jenna's stomach felt hollow. Hungry. As a hunter. And then another more urgent need required attention. It was still dark. She sat up, realising the wagon had stopped. Oh, had they arrived? Beside her she felt Niall move.

'Are we here?' he said in a low voice.

'We must be.'

'Sean?' Niall said.

The now-familiar sound of things moving at the back of the cart. 'Out you come,' Sean said.

Jenna squeezed through the opening he had made and he held her hand as she jumped down. She looked around her expecting to see the castle, nearby or in the distance. Nothing but heather in the light of the rising sun. Right now she didn't care. She made straight for the nearest gorse bush. Taking care of business was the only thing on her mind.

As she crouched behind her bush, she could hear the low rumble of male voices and then silence.

When she returned to the wagon, Sean waved to a clump of gorse on the other side of the wagon. 'He'll be back in a moment.' He busied himself making a fire.

Jenna frowned. It seemed to be getting darker, not lighter. She looked at the horizon. There weren't any clouds and the sun was definitely sinking. 'What time is it?'

'Sunset.'

Sunset was about nine. In the evening. 'It can't be,' she said. 'That means—'

'It means we slept for half of a night and all of a day,' Niall said, striding towards them, sounding hugely irritated.

'Then why aren't we at Carrick?'

'If we were ever heading towards Carrick,' Niall said, his grim expression caught in the dying rays of the sun as he stared hard at Sean, who had got his fire started and was hanging a pot on a tripod.

'Sean?' Jenna said. 'Where are we?'

The gypsy looked up. 'We are farther from Carrick than we are from Braemuir.'

She wanted to shake him. To put her hands around his neck and choke him. 'What are you talking about?'

Niall put his hands on his hips. 'What the blue blazes is going on here, Sean? You were supposed to return us to Carrick, not drag us halfway across Scotland.'

The gypsy spat into the fire and muttered something under his breath. 'Please do not dishonour my hearth with your curses.'

Niall glared at him. 'Answer me, man.'

Sean shrugged and looked at Jenna, his dark eyes glinting. 'She is needed at Braemuir.'

'I was on my way. Soon. With a husband. I said so in my letter.'

'Ah, the husband.' His gaze slid to Niall and back to her. 'I heard about the test. Did you choose wisely?'

She gasped. 'How could you have heard?'

'Servants' gossip spreads like ripples in a pond.'

'If you heard about it, why have us abducted?' Niall threw at him.

'I had no hand in your abduction.'

'What do you call this?' Niall looked ready to throttle the man who sat so calmly beside the fire as if all was well with the world.

'I call it helping a friend.' He raised a brow. 'There is a burn yonder,' he went on as if the air wasn't crackling with outrage. 'You will wash before dinner, *chavvis*, yes?'

'You are a scoundrel,' Jenna said. She looked at Niall. 'But I don't think he is with them. I really don't.'

Niall shook his head and took a deep breath. 'All right. So we will take your word for it. But that doesn't mean to say I trust you.'

The gypsy flashed them a smile and held out two chips of soap and what looked like a bundle of washing. 'Clean clothes,' he said at Jenna's look of enquiry. 'Drying rags. You will need to wash what you have on. It stinks of fish. *Chummer*,' he said, insistently pointing to a rise beyond which she assumed there must be a stream. 'Or not eat.'

'I'm starving,' Niall said, 'and filthy. I see no reason not to do as he asks.' He took Jenna's hand and led her through the heather.

When they were out of earshot of the camp, he turned to her. 'We could make a run for it, right now.'

So that was why he had given in so easily. 'I know it sounds strange, but I don't think he means us any harm. Mr Hughes would never have sent him had it been otherwise. We should give him the benefit of the doubt.'

He looked grim. 'I tend to agree, but I would hate to be wrong. Under the circumstances, I plan to watch him very carefully from now on, I can assure you.'

They continued on to what turned out to be a shallow, fast-flowing burn. Niall emptied the bundle onto the ground. As Sean had said, there were rags for drying and clothes for both of them. A blouse and kirtle with petticoats for her, and shirt and trousers for him. She stared at the stream. 'It looks cold.'

'Something I'm used to,' Niall said and removed his shirt. A beautiful chest and shoulders of carved muscle and bone and sinew. Jenna could not stop from watching the slow unveiling. When he began to unbutton his breeches she gasped.

'Turn your back,' he said tersely. 'If I'm going to feel clean, I must needs wash all of me.'

Reluctantly she did as he asked, but risked a peek as he pulled off his boots and peeled the buckskin fabric down his legs. The flanks and rear end bared to her view were hard and firm. So unlike her own soft curves. Her body gave a little pulse of pleasure. She turned her gaze away, shocked at the delicious needy sensation.

She heard him splash into the water and gasp. 'Hell, that is cold,' he said.

She risked another peek over her shoulder. The dying sun made his beautiful torso glow with warm light. Her fingers tingled with longing to touch those beautiful shoulders, smooth her hands over the expanse of his back.

And when he climbed up the bank, her body clenched at the beautiful sight. The mat of hair on his chest glistening with drops of water, the wide expanse of delineated ribs, the ridges of muscled stomach, the slender hips and his male part, nested deep in black curls. So much smaller than she recalled it from her exploring fingers in the dark of that horrid cart.

He picked up a towel, rubbing at his body, his legs, his back, his behind and finally that part of him that she found so fascinating.

He glanced around, caught her looking and shook his head at her. 'Jenna,' he said reprovingly, turning away, but not before she saw that part begin to swell, jutting away from his body, as if it had a life all of its own.

She flushed hot all the way to the roots of her hair, shocked by her fascination, her wantonness, and averted her gaze.

'It is your turn to bathe, you know,' Niall said. 'Come on, out of that gown and into the water.'

The thought made her shiver. The thought of being free of the smell of fish... She undid the fastenings of her habit and shirt and let them fall to the ground. 'You will have to untie the laces of my stays, I seem to have a knot.'

'As always, I am at your service.' His words, while spoken matter-of-factly, strummed a chord low in her belly. A deep visceral reaction.

A startling response. A moment later he was tugging at the laces, slowly exposing her back to the cool evening breeze. Every time his warm fingers touched her chilly skin, shivers danced across her shoulders and her breasts. Little thrills that tightened her insides. Unnatural heat flashed through her body. A head-to-toe blush.

Most unnerving. Cold water suddenly seemed like a very good idea.

'All done,' he said, moving away and picking up a towel to dry his hair. 'In you go.'

She let the stays fall to the ground and then untied her petticoat and dropped it, too.

She sat down on the bank to remove her shoes and stockings, then with the bar of soap in hand, she dipped a toe in the water.

'Ugh. It's freezing.'

'The longer you dither, the harder it gets.' His back was firmly turned away. No peeking for him. Clearly a woman's nakedness held no novelty.

'You speak from experience,' she said, staring at the swiftly rushing water, bracing herself to brave the cold.

'I can tell you that my older brothers never let me linger.' On those words, he came up behind her and picked her up with his hands at her waist and stepped down into the water as if she weighed no more than a feather.

'Hurry up,' he said, 'or we'll have Sean coming to find out what is taking so long.'

His words had her scrubbing at her arms and legs, working the lather up through the fabric of her chemise, using his shoulder to balance on one foot as needed, while he kept his gaze averted. 'I wish I could wash my hair.'

'Do it. I'll hold you.'

She glanced at the rushing water. She'd trusted him with her life—this was nothing by comparison. He took her under the arms and lowered her into the water. It wasn't quite as cold as she'd first thought. Working quickly, she lathered until her scalp felt clean. He helped her rinse out the soap, one large hand supporting her back, while the other rubbed and squeezed until her hair squeaked.

'Enough,' she said.

He lifted her up and set her on the bank. She wasn't a big woman, even so, he lifted her as if she weighed no more than a child. Yet he treated her so gently. He did not make her feel weak, or helpless. Just... Just cared for.

She swallowed the lump in her throat and forced herself to concentrate on drying herself.

'You must take this off,' he said, plucking at the chemise.

He was right. It was clinging, wet and cold, to her skin. She could not put clothes over it.

'Here, let me.' He took it by the hem and she lifted her arms above her head, and he swept it away. She covered herself with her hands, but he wasn't looking—he was using one of the rags to pat her back dry while she rubbed at her front. In less than a moment or two she was glowing all over.

'Here,' he said, passing the blouse and skirt. 'Put these on. We will dry your hair at the fire.'

While he dressed, she slipped into the full skirts and laced bodice fashionable a century ago. Clothing she'd seen on poor village women all her life, although these seemed more brightly co-loured. She dried her hair as best she could with one of the rags. When she was done, she saw that he had gathered their clothes and was washing them in the stream. She joined him.

'They can dry by the fire,' he said, looking up.

She knelt to help, scrubbing at her gown and

petticoats with the soap and rinsing them clean. Side by side on the bank of the stream, she felt like a peasant woman with her man. It felt strange, yet oddly familiar. As if this was where she belonged. She wrung out her clothes and laid them on the bank, then sat back on her heels and looked up at the sky, purple on the horizon, black velvet overhead and sprinkled with stars. Never had she seen a more beautiful night.

'That should do it,' Niall said, rising to his feet, gathering up their clothing into the bundle. 'Let's go. I am starving.' He took her hand and they walked back towards the fire.

Never in her life had she felt so free. Like a wild creature. Part of the landscape. Free of obligation and duty. High in the sky, Venus winked and twinkled at her as if enjoying the joke.

A laugh bubbled up. She held up her arms to the sky and twirled, set free by the life pulsing in her blood, caring for nothing but the moment. 'Let us never go back,' she cried. 'We could live with the gypsies. Wander the Highlands, doing just as we pleased.'

'Jenna,' he whispered. He caught her and held her close, inhaling deeply as if he could breathe her right into his body. 'You are so beautiful. You have no idea how much I am tempted.'

The longing in his voice was painful to hear. It tugged at her heart, when she was not supposed to have one. Not if she was going to do her duty.

She reached up and stroked his cheek, feeling bristles rough and rasping against her palm. An exotic roughness. 'Oh, why can't we be two ordinary people, no one depending on us, no responsibilities, just Niall and Jenna?'

'Oh, lass, it would still all be there waiting for us.'

An insistent clanging made them jump guiltily apart. 'Sean,' Niall muttered.

She laughed. 'Getting impatient by the sound of it.'

'Aye, and my stomach is nigh to touching my backbone, I'm so hungry. It scarcely remembers we ate bread and cheese last night.'

He took her hand and they ran through the heather, the scent of it rising up around her, mingling with the clean scent of soap and night.

Sean looked up at their approach. 'Dinner is ready.' He gestured for them to sit and they stared in wonder at the meat roasting on skewers over the fire and the aroma of coffee brewing.

'Where did this come from?' Niall asked.

'While you slept, I hunted a little,' Sean said, his eyes crinkling at the corners.

'Ah, yes,' Niall said. 'Sleeping. I want a word with you about that.'

'It smells wonderful,' Jenna said, preferring to keep the peace until they had eaten.

'Everything smells wonderful to hungry children,' Sean said,

'I'm no child,' Niall growled, but not in an angry way.

'Is it not children who play in the stream instead of washing?'

Niall bristled. 'You had no business—'

'I heard you laughing.'

Grunting his displeasure, Niall hung their wet clothes over nearby gorse bushes. 'You hear too much,' he said.

Sean chuckled. 'Eat. Then we talk.'

Niall sat beside Jenna. 'Promise me this, Sean. That if we eat this meal we will not find ourselves sleeping night and day.'

'There is no need,' the gypsy said, flashing his grin. He handed them each a skewer and a slice of bread sprinkled with salt.

Jenna stared at him, opened her mouth to speak, then closed it around a morsel of meat. So delicious. Eat first. Talk later.

Chapter Eleven

Replete with food but far from content, Niall sat with a tin mug of coffee warming his hands and Jenna leaning against him. He eyed the gypsy across the fire. 'I thank you for your hospitality, Sean. But I am still wondering how you found us.'

'*Gadjo*, he is always suspicious. I told you, I had a dream.' At Niall's glare, he opened his hands wide, his face somewhat bemused. 'I can't explain it. Between waking and sleeping, things come to me. I have learned never to ignore them.'

'That's rubbish,' Niall shot back.

A knife appeared in the gypsy's hand, flickering red steel twisting and turning in his quick clever fingers. 'Do you give me the lie, Mr Gilvry?'

Niall cursed himself for not keeping his pistol

with him. No doubt he would find it gone from where he had left it under his pillow.

Jenna put a calming hand on his arm. 'Stop it, Niall. Please, Sean, won't you tell us what you know?'

The knife disappeared. 'I overheard them talking in the barn at auld Tam's tavern. He serves me a dram as long as I stay out of the taproom.'

That Niall did believe. Dreams were something else entirely. 'What did you hear?'

'They were angry. Complaining about not being paid until the job was complete.'

'Paid by whom?' Niall asked.

'They did not speak his name.'

'What else?' Jenna asked.

'They spoke of Tearny's widow being far enough out of town. Of a lad to deliver a note.' He glanced at Niall. 'So I followed them. Not close. But close enough to guess where they were going when they took the boat.'

'I'm grateful for it,' Jenna said.

'I am, too,' Niall said. 'I just don't understand why you didn't take us back to the castle.'

The gypsy shrugged.

Impatience ripped through Niall at his apparent indifference. 'Tomorrow we go to Carrick.'

'Then you go on foot,' Sean said.

'If necessary.' Niall narrowed his eyes. 'Perhaps I'll help myself to your horse.'

The knife was back, still this time, balanced on the tips of strong fingers. 'You can try.'

'Will you kill me for it?' Niall let his lip curl.

'No. Feel free. Try to lead her one foot from where she stands.'

He should have guessed the man would train his animal to follow only one master.

'So then we must walk.'

'You must. The Lady Jenna comes with me.'

Jenna looked at Niall, then at the gypsy. 'It was wrong of you to mislead us, Sean. If Mr Gilvry says we must return to Carrick, that is what we must do.'

'It is not safe for her in the castle,' Sean said.

'Don't tell me,' Niall said bitterly. 'You saw it in a dream.'

The gypsy's face split in a grin and the knife disappeared. 'You learn fast, *gadjo*.'

'Not fast enough, I am thinking.'

'Mr Hughes is expecting you,' Sean said as if it would clinch the argument.

'Ah, another of the Lady Jenna's suitors.'

'Sean,' Jenna said, shaking her head at him. She pressed her lips together and looked down at her hands. 'Whatever Mr Gilvry decides is what we will do. He has my best interests at heart.'

Longing filled her voice, but she had signified her trust in him. And didn't he feel like a fraud. He'd done nothing but endanger her life. By being stubborn about not going to Braemuir, he might be risking it further, if there really was danger at Carrick. *If* there was. He just did not trust this man who owed no one allegiance but his band.

'How soon can we leave?' he asked Sean.

'When the moon comes up. The tracks are hard to follow in full dark.'

'What tracks?' Niall said, looking around.

'Ancient pathways only the *fowki* can see.' He rose nimbly to his feet and went to the cart. He returned with a fiddle. 'While we wait, we will have some music.'

He sat cross-legged before the fire and began to play a haunting tune that filled the air with sadness. It made Niall think of Drew and his mother's mourning. Jenna sighed and by the light of the fire, he could see she was also thinking sad thoughts.

All at once, he felt a dreadful foreboding—as if what he had decided was wrong. What the hell was wrong with him? 'This is dreary.'

Jenna felt Niall's restlessness, his impatience. He was right. The music was too mournful. It made her long to go home with painful intensity. As the last notes died away, she clapped. 'How about something more cheerful, Sean?'

He bowed his head over his bow and began a merry tune that started her toes tapping and her hands clapping time.

Niall looked into her face and smiled. 'Would you care to dance with me, Lady Jenna?'

'I'd love to.'

He stood up and helped her to her feet. He looked over at Sean. 'I don't suppose you've a waltz in your repertoire, do you?'

The music changed instantly to the strains of the popular dance. Niall took her in his arms. He smelled like smoke and night-time as he waltzed her around the fire. His arms were strong and she had no fear of falling despite the rough ground.

'I had no idea you were so accomplished, Mr Gilvry,' she said, laughing up at him, the stars spinning above her head, the firelight glinting in his eyes. 'You dance delightfully.'

'You are too kind, Lady Jenna. You dance like a wee wicked faery.'

Wicked. Her breath caught in her throat. Yes, it was wicked to be held in his arms while they danced in firelight. But tonight she wasn't Lady Jenna, she was just a wild gypsy girl without a care in the world. Tomorrow she would return to her duties and responsibilities.

The tempo of the music increased and the dance became a wild whirling romp. Quite shocking and dangerous, until they were both laughing so hard, they had to beg Sean to stop.

'You dance like true gypsies,' Sean said, grinning at them, but he slowed the tempo to a gentle crawl.

A gypsy. If only she was. It would be wonderful to lead a life without obligations, with the freedom to wander the hills. She clung to Niall's hand, closing her eyes, letting the music drift over and through her, carrying her along on a gentle river of sweet-flowing sound. After a very long time, she realised the music had stopped and she was swaying in Niall's embrace to the rhythm of his heart, their feet barely moving, their breaths mingling, their bodies touching. A waltz no hostess would ever approve of.

And she didn't care. She leaned her cheek on his chest and felt his chin drop to the top of her head, and both of his hands come to rest on her back, stroking and caressing.

Her limbs felt liquid. Her blood hot. She tipped her face up for his kiss and his mouth took hers, his tongue stroking hers and plunging deep, and inside her was a great deep tremble of longing and desire.

She cupped his face in her hands, feeling the hard planes of his cheekbones, the strong set of his jaw. 'Niall,' she breathed at long last.

He raised his head, glancing to the place by the fire. 'It seems we are alone.'

'Yes,' she whispered.

'Jenna…' He shook his head. 'We—'

She touched a finger to his lips, felt the warmth of his skin, of his whisper of breath. 'Don't say it. Tonight I am just me, Jenna, a gypsy woman, and her lover carried away by wild music beneath the stars. With no tomorrow to worry about.'

He groaned. 'You are sure about this?'

'Very sure.'

He swept her up in his arms and carried her into the cart, somehow manoeuvring around the baskets and boxes to lay her down on the mattress where the lantern cast the tiny space with its jewel-tone cushions in warm light. She gazed up at his face and saw the strain and the desire and she smiled up at him and held out her hand, catching his to bring him down beside her.

Slowly, he took her mouth, feeling the warmth and the velvet softness and tasting salt from her tears. She parted her lips, opening to his tongue, offering her mouth like a gift from the gods. And he took the gift and slid his tongue along hers, silken, slippery heat. His heart banged against his ribs, blood roared in his ears and gentleness was forgotten as she wrapped her arms around his neck and arched into him, pressing against his length. Even through the thickness of their clothes he could feel the soft swells of her body crushed against his, and the jab of pain from his ribs was nothing compared to the pleasure of holding her as she plundered his mouth with her tongue, taking what she wanted with wild abandon.

As they kissed, he unlaced her bodice and loosened the ribbon at the neck of her blouse, hoping she would tell him no, praying she would not. She did not. He lifted himself on his arms to look down on her. He had seen her naked at the stream, like a wood nymph, shy and wary. Now she lay abandoned on the cushions, her limbs relaxed, her green eyes heavy lidded and her mouth red and ripe and sultry with passion.

No woman had ever looked so tempting. His gaze took in her shape beneath the cotton blouse and shift. She was lovely. A small woman, beautifully formed with swells and dips in all the right places.

Slowly he ran a finger along the edge of the cotton garment, dipping it into the valley of her breasts and his body tightened as her breath hitched and her small white teeth caught her full bottom lip. What wouldn't he give to feel that mouth on him.

His shaft hardened and strained against the fabric of his trousers.

He cupped one hand to her breast, felt the swell of it in his palm and felt her arch against him. His Jenna. His? No, and nor could he take what could never be his. But there was one gift he could give her. He cursed his weakness and broke the kiss, intending to stop this before things went too far.

'Don't stop,' she said with a pout of rosy lips. 'You make me feel warm, from the inside out.'

And he was lost. 'I am yours to command, my lady.'

This was not about him. Could not be.

He raised his gaze from her small high bosom

to her face and saw she was smiling nervously, licking her lips with anticipation and fear. But it was courage he saw shining in her eyes, amid the desire. She put him to shame.

He took a deep breath. 'I cannot be the ruin of you Jenna, but...' he swallowed '...it would be my honour to bring you great pleasure.'

Honour. He was going to die of honour. Please God she said no. No, he wanted her to say yes. He wanted to be the one to have her die in his arms. To die of pleasure.

A pulse beat wildly at the base of her throat. 'I am not sure I take your meaning.' Her voice shook. But not with fear. She feared nothing.

'It is not something I can describe, my sweet lady, but believe me, I can bring you more pleasure than you can imagine.'

A crease formed between her brows. 'And I would not be ruined?'

'No.' Though it killed him to know she would afterwards belong to another.

She swallowed. 'I think it might be wise,' she whispered.

Wise? Nothing about this was wise. But nothing could stop what was about to happen. Not him. Not her. Whatever had happened tonight, out there in the dark, dancing under the stars, it was some form of gypsy magic and no mortal man could resist it.

He kissed her mouth and once more she melted

beneath his touch. When, breathless and aching, he finally pulled away, she pressed her palm to his cheek. 'Yes,' she said. 'Please.'

He almost groaned out loud. He must be a glutton for punishment. First a cliff and then this, but he'd made a promise and he would keep it.

Slowly he pressed a trail of kisses along her jaw, then below her ear to the music of her indrawn gasp of breath and, finally, to the rise of her breast. With quick fingers he unlaced her stays and weighed one full round breast in his hand. He drew the nipple into his mouth, suckling.

She gasped with shock.

He stopped, thinking he had gone too far.

'No,' she moaned. 'Don't stop. Not now.'

A passionate woman, his Jenna, he thought with a smile as he paid attention to her other sweet mound of flesh, while his hand slipped up her calf to her knee, to the silken flesh of her thigh. She parted her legs as if she instinctively knew what was wanted.

He smoothed his hand up her leg, pushing up the hem of her shift, while his tongue teased her nipple and she writhed beneath him. His shaft was so hard it hurt. He longed to free it from the confines of his trousers, to press his hard flesh into her soft wet heat. Yet he had promised he would not ruin her.

He rose up and knelt between her knees, look-

ing down at her loveliness, the rise of her delicious breasts, the swell of her hips, the wanton
parting of her legs revealing the rosy pink flesh
of her sex in its nest of auburn curls. His breath
caught in his throat at the beauty of her, then he
leaned forwards and trailed kisses down her belly,
feeling the velvet skin beneath his lips, and with
one hand lifted her softly rounded bottom.

The sweet sweet flesh in his palm of a woman
made of the bright steel of courage.

He trailed a finger through the tight curls and
gently parted the delicate folds of her flesh.

'Oh, my,' she said breathlessly. 'That feels—'

He kissed her, right there, tasting the honey
of her desire and the heat of her need for fulfilment. He dipped his tongue between the folds
and heard her cry out, teased her little nub of
pleasure with his teeth and felt her body turn to
liquid, and sucked.

She shattered in a helpless series of little
whimpers and cries that broke his heart, even as
he was filled with a fierce kind of joy and reached
inside his trousers to bring himself to release before he collapsed next to her.

He lay there, exhausted, bliss-numbed. He was
a cur. The lowest of the low, to take advantage of
her innocence. Gypsy magic it was not. It was
lust, pure and simple. His only comfort was that
he had not gone too far. Never would he regret
giving her the gift of pleasure even if he did have

a sense of cold dread that he brought it at the cost of his honour.

If he told the truth, to him it had been a thing of wonder. Too soul-shattering for regret.

But he must not let base urges overcome him again.

And with that in mind, since Braemuir was closer than Carrick, they would go there.

The next morning, Niall plodded along beside the cart, Jenna marching alongside him in her jaunty red skirts and black bodice, and he in a drab waistcoat and a bright blue neckerchief in the open neck of his shirt, looking for all the world like a family of gypsies on the move.

Clearly taken with her part, Jenna had tied a red kerchief over her bright auburn hair. It didn't take away from her beauty one bit. But it was apparent from the moment they awoke that they were back in the proper places. She was formal to the point of stiff whenever she spoke to him.

She must really regret what had happened the previous night. Not him. Not one bit. He did regret the loss of what had been a burgeoning friendship. No, it was more than friendship, but that was all he would dare acknowledge, even to himself.

Last night they had become two different people, a man and a woman under the stars, without a care in the world. Today, they were real people, not those wild footloose folk of their imaginations.

He should never have kissed her, let alone made love to her. Even if he hadna' taken her in the full sense of the word, he'd led her down a path to carnal knowledge no innocent should experience before her marriage.

A vision of her in her bridegroom's arms made his anger rise higher because, after last night, he could not get past the desire to possess her again and again and again. He wasn't sure he would ever get her out of his blood.

He felt sick with anger at his failure. He was supposed to be protecting her, not taking advantage of her to assuage his own desires.

Lady Jenna stumbled over a clump of heather. Wherever this mysterious gypsy track was supposed to be, Niall could not see it. The ground was as rough at their feet as it was all around them.

He glowered at Sean, lounging on the driver's seat. 'Let Lady Jenna ride beside you.'

'Gypsy lasses walk. We don't want to draw attention to ourselves now, do we?'

Niall glanced around pointedly at the empty landscape of rolling hills covered in heather and gorse. 'All these people will notice, I suppose.'

'I am quite capable of walking, Mr Gilvry,' Jenna said with her wee faery hauteur.

'You are lucky he is not making you go barefoot, which is also what most gypsy lasses do,' he grumbled.

'Gypsy men, too,' Sean said, grinning wickedly.

Niall caught the hint of a smile on her face, a sparkle in her eyes. He crushed the urge to grin back. It was better they kept their distance.

They crested a hill and a wide glen opened up before them, rolling meadows in the flat plain at the bottom and stands of pines on its craggy hillsides.

'Do you see it?' Jenna said. Speaking without being spoken to for the first time that day. 'Braemuir.'

Nestled against one of the hillsides was a three-storey stone house. 'It's a grand house,' Niall said gruffly, his gut twisting at just how grand it was, with its magnificent stone façade and formal gardens. What had he expected? A hovel, or something in between, like the house where he was born, where he and his brothers had shared a bed? This was the house of a nobleman. It looked just as she had described.

They started downhill and the house was lost to view behind the undulating land and the trees.

Jenna was looking around her eagerly. 'I used to ride these hills with my father,' she said. She frowned. 'But there were houses. Crofts. Tenants.' She looked around. 'Or perhaps I misremember.'

'The crofts were in the way of the sheep,' Sean said.

'But those were my father's people...' She bit her lip. 'I should never have left.'

'A fourteen-year-old girl running Braemuir?' Sean's voice was without rancour.

Jenna shook her head. 'I should have been told. Your people should have been allowed to camp the way they did in my father's time.'

The gypsy shook his head. 'There was no work for us. No fields of crops. We moved on as we always do.'

'Did you?' she asked, looking at him directly.

'Most did,' he said.

Another evasion. Niall glared at the gypsy, but it didn't do the slightest bit of good.

Jenna subsided into silence, clearly busy with her own thoughts. Niall didn't feel he had the right to intrude. He was her escort again, little more than a servant even though Carrick had named him guardian.

A guardian doing his proper duty would have made their predicament known to Lieutenant Dustan. He deserved a whipping for that piece of foolishness.

'Where are you taking us?' Jenna finally asked.

'We go to Mr Hughes. He is expecting you.'

'Is he? Oh, I am so looking forward to seeing him.' A flush glowed on her cheeks.

Something sharp stabbed at Niall's chest. Jealousy. He beat it back. 'Is there a post office in the village? We need to get word to Lord Carrick and Mrs Preston before they are driven mad with worry.'

'There is a post office in the next town,' Sean said.

Of course it would be in the next town. 'Then while you are renewing your acquaintance with Mr Hughes, I'll be going there.' No doubt on foot. A thought occurred to him. 'I assume there is some sort of female presence at Mr Hughes's house. A chaperon for the Lady Jenna.'

'Mrs Hughes,' Jenna said with a teasing twinkle in her eyes.

All this while she'd let him think... He felt as light-hearted as a condemned man given a reprieve. It didn't make any sense to feel anything at all, but he grinned at her all the same.

The Kirk was the first thing they came to, and beyond it a few cottages lined the lane. A bend in the road obscured what lay ahead. 'The entrance to Braemuir is further along,' Jenna said wistfully.

Sean drew up outside the house beside the church. 'I will leave you here.' He handed Jenna a bundle. 'Here are your own clothes. Give my regards to the vicar.'

'Won't you come in and have a cup of tea?' she asked. 'A rest?'

'Other business is calling, but thank you.' He touched his hat, turned the wagon around and headed back the way they had come.

Jenna looked after him with a frown. 'Surely he didn't think Mr Hughes wouldn't make him welcome?'

'I have no clue what that man thinks,' Niall said, and he wasn't going to guess. He gestured her to go ahead of him up the garden path.

She glanced longingly down the road. 'We could go up to Braemuir. Just for a quick peek.' There was longing in her voice and her face.

'We can hardly go visiting, dressed as we are,' he said, taking in her gypsy clothes and the thick plait hanging all the way down her back to her hips. 'It might be wise to send a note.'

She sighed. 'You are right, of course. We might not be welcome even then.'

'They will no doubt be honoured you wish to visit.'

Seemingly satisfied, she headed through the gate and up to the front door of the two-storey stone house. Before they could knock, it opened.

An elderly gentleman, his thinning white hair a halo around his head, came rushing out. 'Jenna,' he said. He stopped short as if collecting himself. 'My lady. Look at you, all grown up and just as beautiful as your mother.'

Jenna laughed and opened her arms. 'Mr Hughes, you haven't changed a bit.'

Niall held out a hand. 'Mr Hughes. Niall Gilvry, at your service.'

The older man turned to greet him, but even as he shook his hand, he was looking puzzled. 'Lady Jenna,' he said in a querulous voice, 'where is your maid? Your lady companion? Do not tell me that mad gypsy brought only the two of you?'

'That mad gypsy saved our lives,' Jenna said. 'Can we go inside, so I can tell you all about it?'

'Oh, indeed. Indeed. Mrs Hughes has the kettle on the hob. It only wanted you to arrive for tea.'

Jenna turned to Niall, her face alight with mischief. 'Mrs Hughes always has the kettle on the hob for tea.'

'This way. This way,' Mr Hughes said, ushering them in. 'Straight into the parlour, my dear. You surely remember the way.'

The news relayed by Mr Hughes was not good. At least half of the people in the village had left. Most of the crofters had been put off the land by the lessee and their houses torn down. Apparently with Lord Carrick's permission. 'Where did they go?' she asked the vicar.

'Some to America. Some south to find work.'

There was a cold feeling in the pit of her belly. 'I can't believe you didn't write sooner to let me know.'

The older man's face took on a pinched expression. 'I wrote. Your cousin required me to desist at once. My interference was unwelcome.'

Her chest tightened painfully at the hurt in his voice. 'He never mentioned you had written.' She put down her teacup, afraid she would spill her tea she was shaking so badly. With anger. 'He had no right to keep your letters from me.'

The old cleric shook his head. 'I gather the lease on the land is due up in a month and there is talk of renewal. I thought I should give it one more try.' He rubbed his hands on his thighs, looking embarrassed. 'I thought to go around Lord Carrick by way of Sean. I wanted you to see for yourself what is happening here. I hoped that once you did, you would care again. The way your father did. The way you did when he was alive.'

'I do care. I have always cared. I just...' Her heart ached so badly she couldn't speak. But she had to be honest with him, with herself. 'But with Father gone, I just couldn't quite face it to begin with. Not on my own.'

'Aye, lass. I can understand it. You were always close to your father.'

'It was just so sudden. Such a shock.' Her eyes started to burn and she stared at her clenched hands in her lap.

'I know. I know. But we must accept God's

will for us, ye ken. But it is time you came back and took up where your father left off.'

'I would very much like to visit the house if you think the tenant would be amenable.'

His eyebrows climbed his forehead. 'There is no one there but the mice.'

Confused, she gazed at his sorrowful face. 'You mean he is away at present?'

He shook his head. 'No one has lived there since the day you left.'

'But that isn't possible. The land is farmed. I saw sheep.'

'Whoever leased the estate from your uncle, turned around and sublet the land to Mr Drummond in the next glen. It is his sheep you see in the pastures.'

'The house is empty?'

'Aye. The servants all paid off and long gone.'

'But my father's horses. His cattle.'

He stared at her sadly, shaking his head. 'Gone. Sold off to pay your father's debts. I think Carrick did all he could to make sure you didn't lose the house or any more land.'

Niall shifted. He had been silent throughout her conversation, but when she looked at him, there was a strange expression on his face. 'What is it?'

He grimaced. 'Something I saw. In Carrick's account book. Not the one in the office where I worked, but in his desk drawer.' His cheekbones tinged red. 'I was sent to find some receipts by McDougall beneath a ledger. I glanced through it.'

'What did you see?'

'It was a private accounting. I believe it showed payments to him personally on Braemuir's account.'

'I don't understand.'

He got up and went to the window, looking out with his hands behind his back. He turned and squared his shoulders. 'I can't say I do, either. Perhaps we need to find out who leased the land in the first place.'

'The land agent Lord Carrick assigned to find a tenant might be able to assist you.'

She sieved through her memory and recalled a slender youngish man with dark hair and eyes. 'Mr Stuart? Is he still here?'

'Stuart left shortly after you did.' Mr Hughes said. 'It was Carrick's man, Tearny, I believe was his name.'

Her eyes widened. She looked at Niall whose stance had become rigid. 'The same Tearny as…'

'There were payments to Tearny in the ledger,' Niall said. 'We at Dunross also had dealings with the man, and not to his credit. But as you know, he can't be much help to us since he is dead.' A thoughtful looked passed over his face. He shook his head sharply as if deciding not to speak his thoughts out loud.

'What are you thinking?'

'It is better not to give voice to suspicions that cannot be proven.'

'This concerns me. My land.'

'Carrick is my relative also. And my chief. There may be a perfectly innocent explanation. I will no blacken a man's name on the basis of gossip.'

She recoiled at the fierceness of his tone. He was right. He was Carrick's relative. Set to watch over her by that very man, his clan chief. He would not go against him without very good reason.

She turned back to the vicar. 'So there is no one to prevent me from visiting the house.'

'No one,' the old man said. He laced his fingers together. 'I am not sure I did the right thing, sending for you. It was an old man's fancy that you could turn things around, but I fear it cannot be. The people are gone. The house, in a sad state of disrepair...'

She gasped. 'Disrepair?'

'It was never very good in your father's time, but it is much worse now, I think.'

'There was nothing wrong with it.'

'You were young. Perhaps you did not see. It needed a new roof even then. And he had closed one wing completely.'

She remembered a long corridor where the furniture was covered in holland covers. She'd thought nothing of it then. 'The house is huge. There were only two of us living there. We had no need for all those rooms.'

'It would probably be better to look at it before you make up your mind,' Niall said gently, clearly believing Mr Hughes's account.

'It can't be that bad,' she said firmly. 'I am going to be married. We are going to live there.' She winced and looked at Niall, whose face showed nothing of his thoughts.

'You are affianced?' Mr Hughes said, his face lighting up. 'To this young gentleman? You will let me perform the marriage ceremony, will you not?'

'Actually it is another gentleman who is the bridegroom.' She hadn't barely given a thought to her betrothed since the night they left the cave on the beach. She'd been too busy trying to survive. Oh, was she going to lie to herself? The truth of the matter was that she'd been too taken up thinking about Niall Gilvry. She straightened her shoulders. 'A Mr Murray.'

Mrs Hughes frowned at her, her cheerful round face becoming serious. 'You never did tell me how you came to be travelling without your maid and a lady companion, Lady Jenna. I have trouble believing Lord Carrick so lax in his guardianship that he would have allowed it.'

'He didn't,' Niall said grimly. 'The fault is mine.'

Mr Hughes gave him a stern look. 'Explain yourself, young man.'

'No,' Jenna said. 'It was no one's fault.' And she set about pouring out the story of what had happened that had led them to travel to Braemuir in Sean's wagon. She didn't tell the whole of it, yet both the Hugheses looked thoroughly shocked.

'There is no help for it,' the doughty cleric said gravely at the end of her recitation. 'You must marry Mr Gilvry.'

'No,' Jenna said stepping back. 'It is not—'

The flash of pain at her rejection in Niall's eyes stopped her cold.

Before she could say more, his expression shuttered, became coolly remote. 'No,' he said. 'My duty as a member of Lord Carrick's clan was to guard Lady Jenna's person. I may have done a poor job of it, but there is no need for her to wed me. She is betrothed to Mr Murray, who is no doubt even now awaiting word that she is well and safe.'

Mr Hughes's gaze was sharp as it rested on his face. 'Have it your way, then, Lady Jenna, if you think this other young man will stand by you after such an adventure.'

'He has no reason not to,' Niall said harshly.

Jenna could tell that Mr Hughes did not believe him and felt her face go red.

Chapter Twelve

Upstairs in the small guest room, with Kitty the scullery maid helping her, Jenna shed the trappings of a gypsy and donned her freshly pressed gown. She'd done as Mr Hughes requested first and written Lord Carrick, telling him she was safe and sound. She'd also asked that Mr Murray join her here for their nuptials.

Since the afternoon was still young, she was determined to visit her home. Just the thought of looking on it again made her heart flutter. Not nerves. Joy. She could not wait to make ready to celebrate her wedding there in three weeks' time.

Kitty finished lacing her gown. 'Will that be all, miss? I mean, my lady.'

Somehow the plump-cheeked girl with lively brown eyes and a quick smile had managed to get Jenna's unruly hair plaited and wound around

her head in a thick coronet with the help of pins
borrowed from Mrs Hughes. 'Yes, thank you.
You have done very well.'

The girl flashed her little smile and scurried
away.

Now to face Niall. To explain why she'd been
so quick to reject any thought they might marry.
Not that he'd offered, not really. But clearly the
speed at which she'd rejected the notion had hurt
his manly feelings.

She went downstairs and found him in the parlour, so engrossed in a book he did not look up
when she entered.

'Good book?' she asked.

He did look up then and for a long moment he
just gazed at her, his face expressionless, perhaps
even a little bleak. She had indeed wounded him
with her rejection. She wished she could recall
the bluntness of her words.

He rose and put the book aside. *'Voyages
Round the World by Kippis.'*

'Ah, Captain Cook. And were you planning
on following in his footsteps?'

His expression tightened. 'Just passing the
time.'

The end of that line of conversation. 'Where
is Mr Hughes?'

'He was called out to one of his parishioners.'

She clasped her hands at her waist. 'About

what I said earlier, with regard to us not marrying—'

'You don't need to explain,' he said stiffly. 'You are betrothed.'

'If he'll still have me.' She coloured a little and looked down. 'I promised my father that I would marry well. My father inherited his father's debts. He did everything he could to make sure I was not burdened the same way. Apparently, he even sold off some of our land. But Mr Hughes is right. He wasn't able to do all he wished with the house because the estate needed so much. He was terrified he'd lose it. I promised him I would make sure the title and the estate remained with the family.'

'In other words, he charged you with the duty of marrying a well-to-do member of the aristocracy and providing an heir.'

'If you must be so blunt, then, yes. It was his dying wish.'

'Let us hope Mr Murray is up to the task.'

Heat coursed up her face at the matter-of-factness in his tone. 'I very much fear he may wonder why we did not return to the castle once we escaped our abductors.'

'Clearly, I could not take the chance of the brigands finding us on the road to Carrick.'

'You are taking responsibility for the decision, then.'

'It was mine to make.'

She looked down at the floor. He had clearly given this some thought while she was bathing and dressing. 'And how did we get here? How did we travel so great a distance with no one seeing us, yet remain respectable?'

'By oxcart. With a farmer and his wife. A Mr and Mrs McFadden. Unfortunately I was so glad to arrive, I forgot to ask them for their directions. And besides, we travelled incognito, to preserve your reputation.'

'You think Lord Carrick will believe us? And Mr Murray?'

'They will be only too pleased to believe it. A man who would risk his neck for a bird's egg is unlikely to give up the prize, provided there is a reasonable explanation.'

'Mr Hughes says we can be married the moment he arrives.'

His expression didn't alter. It remained cool. Remote. 'Then let us hope it is verra soon.'

She managed a fleeting smile of agreement, though her heart felt heavy. It was a good thing Mr Murray wasn't around to see her lack of enthusiasm. Not that he had any illusions that theirs was a love match. It was simply an arrangement that suited them both.

Was it too much of an imposition to ask Niall for one last indulgence? 'Will you walk with me up to Braemuir?'

'You didna' think I would let you walk up there alone, did you?'

At the severity of his tone, the breath left her chest in a rush. 'You think we are in danger here? At my home? Surely those men wouldn't think to look for me here?'

'I think it wise to take precautions. Whoever was behind this seemed to know a great deal about you.'

Her mouth dried. Her heart raced. But what if he was using fear to make her do as he wished, to protect her? Since she did not want to walk to Braemuir alone, she wasn't going to argue. 'Are you ready?'

He nodded and picked up a hat from the table. He looked at it with an amused smile. 'Courtesy of Mr Hughes. He seemed to think it would not look well if I was not to appear like a perfect gentleman. We are also to invite someone called Kitty to join us.'

'Kitty is serving as my maid.'

'There you have it. A perfectly respectable outing.' He ushered her out of the room.

The shade of bitterness in his voice was something best left ignored. Outside she took his arm and Kitty, who had been waiting in the hallway, fell in behind them. As he had said—a perfectly respectable outing for two disreputable people. No, really only one. He was a gentleman. She was the one who had behaved like a hoyden last night. But heaven help her, if she was to have the time all over again, she very much doubted she would do anything different. Never in her life had she felt so happy, or such extraordinary pleasure.

As they walked through the village, she saw that at least half the cottages were empty. At the tavern, she waited outside while he went in to drop off their letters for the boy to take to the post. Sadly she noted the inn's air of decay. When she moved back into Braemuir, there would be work for people. She would need to staff the house and the stables. Yes, coming back here was the very best thing she could do for those that remained.

Niall strode out of the tavern, pulling on his gloves. He smiled briefly. 'A rider will take the letters to the post office later this afternoon.'

What would Carrick think? Would he be angry with her? With Niall? Surely he would see they had no choice.

They strolled down the lane, slowly leaving the village behind. Somehow she managed to restrain her urge to run to Braemuir's gates. She kept remembering Mr Hughes's warning. Surely it could not be that bad.

They turned a bend in the lane and arrived at the arch bearing the Aleyne crest. The boar on one side of the shield and the bear on the other. When she married, the crest would change to incorporate her husband's coat of arms. *Family Before All.* As always, the familiar Gaelic words pressed down on her shoulders. Duty. Responsibility. Weighty matters lain upon her by her father.

The gates were open and she passed through with some trepidation. She peered down the gravel drive, overgrown with weeds, that cut across a tree-edged lawn that looked more like a hayfield. It looked abandoned.

She gave herself a mental shake. It would not take long to mow the grass or weed the gravel. A little care would soon restore its appearance. Yet she could not ignore the feeling in the pit of her stomach growing colder and heavier the closer they came to the house itself. It was not quite as large as she remembered, the columns over the portico not quite as towering as they had seemed when she was a child. She frowned. Many of the windows on the first floor were broken. The house looked like a lonely old crone. Not for long. She had come home. A rush of happiness filled her. Home at last.

They stood at the bottom of the steps to the front door, looking up into the two-storey portico standing grandly on its Doric pillars. Paint hung in shreds from the wooden trim above their heads and rust had eaten away at the impressive wrought iron lantern. She glanced at Niall. His face revealed nothing. Yet there was a grimness about him she did not like.

'Naturally, it requires some repairs,' she said blithely. 'It has been empty for quite a while.'

'Aye.'

So taciturn. But then this was not his home. He did not have the warm and welcoming memories she had carried with her all these years. The fact that her father would not be there to greet her was the cause of her hesitation, that was all.

She took a deep breath and strode boldly up the steps and tried the door. It swung open with an ominous creak. Oil would take care of that. She stepped into the entrance hall.

Time fell away. It was just as she remembered it. The carved staircase. The cavernous entrance hall with its tiled floor and panelled walls. The carved ceiling. The doors leading off it to the formal rooms.

Joyfully, she stepped inside and turned around slowly, beaming. 'It is just as I remembered. Oh, the outside needs sprucing up. The windows. But—' she opened her arms wide '—is it not just the most magnificent place you ever saw?'

There was no doubt that he was impressed as he gazed around him. 'It's a beautiful auld place.'

'It needs some dusting and polishing.' She ran her gloved hand over the balustrade and it came away black. 'I will hire a couple of women from the village.'

He was frowning. His gaze fixed on the staircase.

'Where shall I go first?' she murmured, hardly able to contain herself. 'I have this craving to see my old room. It has a wonderful view of the gardens and the glen.'

'Lady Jenna,' he said. 'Wait.' He stepped towards her, but she already had one foot on the bottom tread, which was covered in spider webs. She put her weight on it. The wood crumbled and her foot disappeared. She lurched forwards and the railing beneath her hand broke away and hung drunkenly.

Niall grabbed her and pulled her back.

'Wh-what happened?' she said, staring at the jagged hole in the step and the bits of crumbled wood lying on the black-and-white tile.

'Some sort of rot, I am thinking. I have read about it, but not seen it.'

'I don't understand. It looked so perfect, just as I remembered it.'

'The wood dries from inside. It might be why no tenant ever moved in.'

'Or it happened because no one cared for it these past ten years. Still, I suppose the staircase can be replaced.'

He had a look on his face that she didn't like. Sympathy. Worry.

'What is it?'

'I know only what I have read, but if it is in the staircase, it might be all through the house.'

She shook her head. 'No. It can't be. I can understand why this part would need work. The hall and the staircase are the oldest parts of the house. The rest was refurbished by my grandfather.'

'I'm no expert, but from what I have heard and read about ships that have gone the same way, all the wood must be replaced. The beams and joists and floors.'

Her stomach fell away. She felt sick. As if the roof had caved in right before her eyes. It could not be true. This house had been her lifeline. Her way back to the family she had lost. The only constant in her life.

'I'm sorry,' he was saying.

'No. I am sure the rest of the house is fine.' She would not accept that time would be so cruel to the home she loved.

He turned back to Kitty, who was lingering wide-eyed in the doorway. 'Wait outside. We will be but a few minutes.'

The little maid looked relieved and scuttled out into the sunshine, leaving the door open behind her.

Taking a deep breath, Jenna strode to the door into the front parlour. It only opened a crack, pressing against some obstruction on the other side. What she saw through that small opening was a knife to all her hopes. A large piece of the panelled ceiling had fallen and now blocked the door. Horrified, she backed away, shaking her head. 'I don't believe it. I won't.'

He caught her by the arms. 'Jenna. Love. It's just a house.'

She shrugged him off. 'It might be just a house to you, but it is everything to me.'

She went from door to door: the drawing room, the dining room, the library. In every room the story was similar. Some were in better shape than others, but all showed signs of neglect, and wherever Niall applied pressure to window frames or doorways, they disintegrated in his hands.

The pain inside her was almost unbearable as the true enormity of the damage became clear.

When they came to the back of the house it was an overwhelming relief to see that the kitchen and servants' quarters, all built of stone, were in good shape. The servants' stairs showed no sign of rot and one or two of the smaller bedrooms at the back of the house, her own included, were solid. This was the extension added early in the eighteenth century and was nowhere near as old as the rest of the house.

The public rooms at the front of the house were on the verge of falling down. Like this one. Her father's stateroom.

Niall stared up at the ceiling. 'I'm nae so sure it is only dry rot,' he said. 'The roof seems to be leaking.'

Pride came before a fall, they said. And this had been her pride and her joy. She had bragged about this house to her suitors. She flushed hot, then froze from the inside out. She would have to tell Murray.

Unable to stand any more, she fled down the stairs and out the front door. She sank down on the stone steps where she had sat when her father lay dying, looking out over the glen, dreaming of knights on white chargers who would somehow put the world back the way it belonged.

It wasn't going to happen.

Kitty approached her. 'Are you all right, my lady?'

All right? Jenna stared about her.

Had her father known? He had fussed about repairs being needed. Had even sold some of the furnishings to pay for repairs in the attic. Had Lord Carrick known? Was that why he had seemed so reluctant to find her a suitor? And would Mr Murray be willing to spend what would be a fortune to put right a decaying house? While he might be the easiest of her three suitors to manage, he wasn't a complete fool.

Nor would she want him if he was. Not really. But he would have to be told that there was no grand house in the country, no crofters. Nothing but sheep belonging to some as-yet-unknown tenant.

Niall sat down beside her. 'The stone walls are good,' he said. 'The inside can be rebuilt.'

'It would cost a fortune.'

'Aye,' he said softly, regretfully.

Ever since the day she left here, she had dreamed of coming back. Of coming home. A bright light in the darkness of loss that she had nurtured deep in her heart. The one thing she had always thought she could do to make up for not being the hoped-for son was to continue the Aleyne name here at Braemuir, just as her father had asked. She took a deep breath. 'It will be up to Mr Murray, I suppose.'

'Aye. I suppose it will.'

And what if he refused? What then?

She got up and began walking, wandering through what had been the formal gardens, the hedges overgrown and untidy, the roses struggling to push through the weeds. Niall and Kitty trailed behind her.

She had the oddest feeling that the house and the grounds were trying to tell her something. That there was a story here she was missing.

She strolled through the hedge and out into the park where once the magnificent lawn had swooped down to a planting of trees.

None of it was unfolding at all the way she had envisaged. And it was not what she had described to her suitors with such pride. She felt like an idiot. A complete and utter fraud. She turned to Niall, who was following her at a distance, his face grim. They had left Kitty behind in the gardens. Jenna could see her through a gap in the hedge sitting on a stone seat.

'Do you think the boy at the tavern has left with that letter yet? We need to get it back.'

He stared at her. 'You have to let them know where you are, Jenna. It is wrong to let them worry.'

'Yes, of course I do. But there is something I have to change. Quickly. Before it is too late.' She trotted back towards Kitty. She had to stop that letter.

'What is going on in that head of yours?' he asked as Jenna beckoned Kitty to follow and quickened her pace.

'I am going to tell Mr Murray the truth.' And give him a chance to change his mind. It was only fair. And for some ridiculous reason, it made her feel a whole lot better. She picked up her skirts and ran.

Niall paced the inn parlour. The letter was before her, and twice she'd hushed him, but the confusion inside him would not be silenced. 'You aren't going to wed Murray?'

She looked up. 'No. Yes.' She shook her head impatiently. 'Unless he is prepared to make the repairs required, which I am describing in detail, I am releasing him from his promise.'

'And if he is no prepared?'

She straightened her shoulders. 'Then I will have to seek someone who will.'

'McBane? Oswald?' Just the thought of either of them made his blood boil, because he certainly wasn't in the running.

'Not them,' she said scornfully. 'Someone I can trust. Someone who will care.'

For one blinding moment he wanted to say *marry me*. But care or not, there was nothing he could do to help her restore the house she loved.

'Mr Murray might not mind.' She bent her head over the paper.

'If he wants the title badly enough, you mean.'

She must have heard the chill in his voice, because her clear green eyes met his again. 'Of course. But he should know what is required in order to gain it. What else would you have me do?'

There was no room for discussion. He could see that on her face.

'Then I will hire a carriage and take you back to Carrick Castle. There is no sense in remaining.' He would leave her at Carrick and set out for America to look for Drew. It would take his mind off her and Murray.

'No.'

He recoiled at her vehemence. 'What are you talking about?'

'I will stay until either Mr Murray arrives to wed me, or Lord Carrick sends his carriage.'

'Why?'

'I can't go and leave the house to rot.'

'What can you do to stop it?'

The haughty wee faery was back. He could see it in the way she looked down her nose at him. 'I can make it look presentable in case Mr Murray arrives. A little less derelict.' She tapped her pen against her lower lip, gazing through him. 'The back of the house is mostly sound. I could tidy up the rooms at the front.'

Nothing but a fortune would make it look presentable. He didn't want her near the place. 'You canna go poking around in there. It will fall down around your ears.'

'This is my home, Niall. I've waited years to see it again. There are things in there that have belonged to my family for centuries. Perhaps some of it can be salvaged. I can move them into safer parts of the house.'

'Where will you live?'

'Here, if the Hugheses will have me.'

And short of bodily carrying her back to Carrick Castle, he could see he could not move her. He had no choice but to stay and help her prepare for Murray's arrival. And be there, in case Murray changed his mind.

It would all depend on how badly the man wanted that title. 'I'll help you, then.'

She shook her head. 'I really don't expect it.'

Another rejection. He ignored the pain of it. 'I am paid by your cousin to act in his stead in his absence. I can't believe he would want me to leave you here alone.'

'I won't be alone.'

'No, you won't.' He gave her a hard smile. 'I will be here.'

'As you wish.' She folded the letter and sealed it. 'Please have the landlord take this to the post as soon as possible. Now I must find Mr Hughes and tell him of my decision.'

The best he could hope for was that the vicar would refuse to house her. Somehow he didn't see that occurring.

It seemed he was going to take up a new career. Labourer.

Since coming to her decision the day before, she'd stopped calling him Niall. She was strictly formal in all of their dealings as if their friendship and…and, well, what had happened in the gypsy cart, had never occurred. He couldn't help resenting the loss of closeness. But he understood. After all, he was the one who had pointed out that by staying, he was only doing his job.

And since the Hughes had no room for him in their small house, he had made an arrangement at the inn for room and board in exchange for chores. He'd risen at first light, helped the innkeeper with his barrels and mucked out the stables and then come to the vicarage. Jenna was waiting for him in the garden. Dressed in a practical blue-cotton gown of a country lass and a white kerchief covering her bright hair, she was admiring a trellis covered in yellow roses arched over a garden seat. The scent of roses filled the air.

'I see you are ready, my lady,' he said.

She spun around with a smile. 'I was beginning to think you weren't coming.'

'We said nine, did we not?'

Somewhere in the house a clock struck the hour.

'I am anxious to get started.' She picked up the basket sitting at her feet covered by a white cloth. 'A little sustenance, though I am expected back for dinner. Dear Mrs Hughes. I had to dissuade her from sending the maid along. I assured her I'd be perfectly safe with you.'

Safe was not a word she should be using with respect to him.

They followed the same path as they had taken the day before. The birds were singing, the sky was clear of all but a few fluffy clouds. The air was clean and mild and scented with spring. He could almost imagine they were just a country couple on their way to work in the fields. Almost.

He resisted the temptation to tuck her arm

within his and kept a respectable distance. A challenge. Even so, it was impossible not to enjoy the morning.

At the curve in the drive, she stopped, staring across the overgrown lawn at the house. 'I thought it was so beautiful when I was little. I recall it as much bigger. Now it looks small and sad.' Her voice was little more than a whisper. 'I should have come back sooner.'

'Things always seem bigger and better when you are a child,' he said softly, wanting to fix things and knowing he could not.

The look she gave him said he didn't understand. And perhaps he didn't. 'Where do you want to start?'

'Perhaps we should look at the stables. Mr Murray seemed quite keen on his horses and keeps a large stable. It would be an advantage if we had decent accommodation in that quarter.'

They strolled around the back of the house and into the long, low, red-brick building a short walk from the back of the house.

'They look fairly new,' he said. 'And clean.'

'Father had them built not long after he married my mother. She loved her horses and insisted on proper stabling. I think he spent a bit more than he could afford.'

The stalls were clean and empty. 'My father's stable master was a good man. The building is in better shape than the house.'

In the last stall was a pile of rotting sacks. He pulled one apart. 'Mouldy fleece. It will have to be disposed of.'

'It smells awful.'

'Yes. It's too bad. It would have been worth some money.'

They walked around to the back of the house and into the kitchen. Jenna pulled a bunch of keys from the basket. 'The housekeeper left them with Mrs Hughes.' She unlocked the pantry and some of the cupboards. There were pots and pans and china on the shelves. Everyday china used by the servants. 'The good china was all sold, Mr Hughes said.' Her voice was a little shaky. 'Carrick never told me about the debts. Apparently they were significant.' She forced a smile. 'But at least I can make a cup of tea.' She pulled a wooden box from the basket and placed some cloth-wrapped packages inside the pantry. 'Now to see what we can do in the drawing room.'

Three hours of hauling out lumps of plaster and pieces of wood and it didn't look much better. Each time they cleared something out, something else fell. And the carpets had mildew. He doubted if they could be saved. The roof had to be leaking.

Jenna picked up another armload of bits of plaster and carried them outside. He followed with a pile of oak panelling that ought to have been too heavy for one man to carry. And was not. She'd found a few treasures, too: a couple of pictures, some figurines. Those they had locked in one of the cupboards in the kitchen.

She dropped her armload on the growing pile on the lawn and dusted off her hands. 'Will you join me for a bite to eat and a cup of tea?'

Surprised by the visceral surge of pleasure at her invitation to sit down with her, he hesitated. He wanted to say yes. Desperately. He wanted to recapture the companionship they'd shared on their journey. If that had been all he wanted, then he would have said yes at once. But he wanted so much more. And that was impossible.

He clamped his jaw on the surging sensations and shook his head. 'Mrs Hughes meant the food for you.'

'There is enough in that basket to keep an army marching for a week. And I owe you something for all your help.'

Gratitude. It was her only reason for asking. And to refuse would indeed be churlish.

Against everything he had sworn when deciding to stay to watch over her, he found his lips forming an acceptance. 'Verra well. I am honoured to take a bite with you.'

A smile lit her face. 'Wonderful. I'll go and lay out the food. I'll call you when I'm ready.'

He was looking forward to sitting down with

her. To conversation, rather than orders and pleases and thank-yous.

As she walked indoors he could not help but notice the spring in her step. Perhaps it wasn't only gratitude that had made her invite him. Perhaps she still considered him a friend. If so, perhaps he could convince her to give up this madness. Each time she walked into one of those rooms he was sure something would come down on her head. Once Murray came, or Lord Carrick sent the carriage for her, he would never see her again. He'd failed to keep her inside the castle. He'd failed to keep her safe. He just hoped the mess he had made wouldn't land at Ian's door.

He glanced down at himself. If he was going to be her guest, he had better wash up. Which meant a nice cold sluice under the pump in the courtyard.

It brought to mind the dip they had taken together and the ever-present arousal pulsed at the recollection. Not something he should ever think about again. Thank God for the blood-chilling benefits of cold water.

Chapter Thirteen

She was so glad he'd said yes. Jenna put the cloth across one end of the long kitchen table. He'd worked so hard, she would have felt awful if he'd gone hungry while she ate the delicious meat pie prepared by Mrs Hughes's cook. Not to mention the fresh crusty bread to go with the cheese and pickles. She put them out on the table and put the kettle over the fire Niall had built when they first arrived.

She had enjoyed working with him today. The easy camaraderie they had was like nothing she had ever known before. He was a friend. More than a friend. She blushed, remembering how much more. Something inside her yearned for a repeat of that closeness, the carefree bliss she'd known with him in the gypsy cart.

If only… But friendship wouldn't help Brae-

muir. She needed a man with the financial where-
withal and the desire to put the estate in order. A
faint pang twisted in the region of her heart. An
echo of the pain of loss. A pain she never wanted
to feel again.

The estate would always be here. Houses did
not die like people did. They could be restored.
Rebuilt. They were permanent. People were not.

She did not want to become attached to Niall.
But she would enjoy the small amount of time
they'd been granted.

The kettle boiled, so she made the tea and put
the teapot ready on the table and went outside
to call him.

He was standing at the pump, making himself presentable for her. She couldn't keep from
smiling at those lovely broad shoulders, the muscles shifting beneath his skin as he rubbed his
wet hair on what looked like a handkerchief. His
physical beauty inspired her with awe, but he
must have sensed her watching because he looked
in her direction.

Caught staring again. She waved. 'The tea is
ready.'

He grabbed his shirt from the pump handle
and pulled it over his head. 'On my way,' he
called out.

'That was the best pie I have ever eaten.'
'Mrs Hughes's cook has a light hand with pastry.'

'And the company made it taste even better.'

Was he flirting with her? Or simply being kind? Likely the latter. She didn't dare imagine it was anything else.

'I don't think we should do this any more,' he said.

'Eat together?'

'No. You. Clearing out the house. It's too dangerous. I can't allow it. There is nothing we can do to make it look better in a week. I'm sorry.'

It seemed that this conversation she had been leading up to had started before she was ready. 'I know.' She did know.

'At last you are listening to reason.'

'But no matter what happens, I am not leaving Braemuir. I need to be here. I cannot abandon it again.'

'What if Murray doesn't want to live here?' His voice was calm, flat, as if he did not care one way or the other, but there was something else in his eyes, something that looked like pain, but he lowered his gaze to look at his hand clasped loosely on the table before she could be sure.

'I sincerely doubt he will accept my conditions for the marriage. His family will advise against such a bad bargain.'

'Not true, Jenna,' he said sharply, looking at her again, a deep frown on his face. 'You have a great deal to offer. And not just the title.'

The thought that he wanted her to marry the

other man gave her a cold feeling in the pit of her stomach. And a pain in her chest, close to her heart. Which was nonsense. What had happened between them had been an interlude she could blame on gypsy magic. She just wished she could get it out of her mind. Stop the ache inside her for more of the same. Stop the feeling of loss, knowing he would soon depart. It was something she did not want to feel.

He wanted her no more than she wanted him.

Not true. She wanted Niall in the worst way possible. Carnally. And... She cut off the thought and poured the tea. 'Let us hope Mr Murray sees it your way.' She handed him his cup and saucer.

'And if he doesn't, then Lord and Lady Carrick will take you to Edinburgh next year for the Season,' he said.

'What if no one wants to put the house to rights? Now that I know how bad it is, I could never pretend otherwise.'

'You put too much store in this building of yours.'

'Unlike people, buildings are for ever. Or at least a long long time.' She grimaced. 'Or they are if cared for properly.'

'And how do you plan to manage that if you do not have a husband?' he asked, sounding unconvinced.

'There is the income from renting the land. I'll ask Carrick to make it over to me now I'm of age.'

The doubt must have shown on his face, because her voice became fierce. 'I'm just as capable as any man. Carrick will see it eventually.'

'You can't live here alone,' he said in a low, dangerous voice. 'It is not suitable for a woman of your station. And Carrick will not allow it, no matter how old you are. It isn't safe.'

As she opened her mouth to speak, he made a wide sweeping gesture. 'Oh, it is fine enough now. But what happens in the winter, when the snow fills the glen? When you run out of fuel for the fire and your pantry is empty?'

He meant when he was gone. Her heart dipped. 'I will manage.'

'You are not bred to this life.'

Her hands shook a little as she poured herself another cup of tea. 'I am not made of spun sugar.'

He stood up, his chair scraping across the flagstones. 'I won't allow it.'

The back of her neck bristled. Anger. And disappointment that she wasn't prepared to examine right now. She faced him, across the table, only too aware of his height and his breadth and the flare of fury in his eyes. 'It is none of your business, Niall Gilvry. None. I didn't ask you to remain here. Indeed, I wish you would go.' The longer he stayed, the harder it would be when he left.

'If I leave, it will be with you. Back to Carrick Castle.'

'By force, I suppose.'

He rose, came around the table and stood toe to toe with her, looming over her, his expression fierce. 'Yes. If you will not come willingly.'

They stood there staring at each other, sparks of anger charging the air between them. Anger and desire. Opposite sides of the same coin she realised, as her body caught light.

He caught her by the shoulders as if he would shake her, but instead hauled her hard against him. She lifted her face and he pressed his mouth to hers, hard, savage, searing, and she was no less savage in plundering his mouth with her tongue, tasting him, inhaling the clean smell of soap and a deeper masculine scent of warm man.

Pressed hard against his chest she could feel every inhale and exhale and feel the heat of those deep unsteady breaths against her cheek as he delved the depths of her mouth. Her heart pounded, her breathing became laboured. Little thrills low in her belly made her arch into him and his thigh pressed deep between hers as his large hand cupped her bottom and drew her close.

The same sensations she had felt that night in the gypsy wagon spiralled out of control. The deep need to shatter.

Finally he broke away on a groan. 'Jenna.' The anger was gone. Now there was only hunger. A note in his voice that tugged at her centre, weakened her knees and left her arms feeling too heavy to cling to his shoulders.

'Niall,' she whispered. 'Please.'

His trembling fingers cradled her jaw, as he gazed down into her face, his throat working as he swallowed. 'You don't know how you tempt me, Jenna. I want you. More than I can say. But—'

'I want you, too.'

'I can't promise to restrain myself, like before.' He closed his eyes briefly. 'Say no, Jenna. Say it and I will walk you back to the vicarage.'

The thought that he might go elsewhere to find his ease was a sharp knife between her ribs. She knew he wouldn't stay at Braemuir much longer. The way he'd spoken of what would happen in the winter left her with a feeling of panic. The sense that she might never see him again, once he left here. 'I want this,' she said, smoothing his hair back from his face. 'I want you.'

Acceptance chased by intense desire crossed his face in quick succession. He swept her up in his arms and carried her up the narrow back stairs. At the landing he hesitated.

'First door on the left,' she said.

He looked down at her, his face boyish, his beautifully sculpted lips curving in a smile. 'You read my mind.'

He stopped at the door and she turned the knob. The bedroom was the one she'd had as a child, but the bed was big enough for two and the mattress and pillows were covered with a dust-sheet. She smiled up at him as he set her down gently on her feet. He dropped to his knees before her, encouraging her to lift one foot. She placed her hands flat on his shoulders and looked down on his lowered head and felt an unfamiliar clench in her heart. A tenderness. This was not about tenderness, it was about the fulfilment of desire. She would do well to remember it.

He gently removed her shoes, then her garters. Skilfully, he rolled her stocking down over her knees and off. He sat back on his heels and ran a hand down first one shin, then the other, cupping her calf in his palm. He looked up, smiling, his eyes gleaming. 'I love your legs. So shapely.'

Her heart lurched. How strange to be so affected by admiration of her legs. She'd had compliments before, but none that meant quite so much.

His hand caressed upwards, his fingers skimming behind her knees. She shivered.

He leaped to his feet and tilted his head, looking at her gown.

'Laces at the back,' she managed to say, turning to face the bed, glad of the chance to hide her blushes. It didn't take him long to pull the laces free, from both her gown and her stays. Kisses brushed across her nape and her shoulders as he eased the gown over her shoulders, arms and hips, until she stood in nothing but her chemise.

Gently he turned her around. She looked up at him and there was no trace of anger or doubt. His face was pure seduction, heavy-lidded eyes, full lips parted, as his gaze ran down her scantily clad body. She ought to feel ashamed, but the look on his face gave her power and strength.

He teased the skin at the edge of her chemise, running one finger beneath the lace, tracing the rise of her breasts and the dip between. Her breasts tightened, felt heavy and full. She moaned. He swooped down to kiss the top of her breast, easing the fabric down with his thumb, hot mouth kisses until his tongue laved and teased at her nipple, then suckled. Thrills shot to her deepest core. She dropped her head back, clinging on to his shoulders and shuddering with the sensation rippling outwards from her centre. She cried out softly when his mouth left her and he blew a little puff of air across the sensitised peak.

He laughed quietly, a sound of delight, and moved to the other breast. The sensations started over again, only deeper, more resonant, and she could only moan and arch against him to ease her growing need for release from this wonderful torture.

He brought his mouth to her lips again, plunging deep into her mouth while his hands caressed her hips and buttocks and she felt his hard male length against her stomach. He groaned deep in her mouth and drew back with tender little kisses on her mouth, her cheek, her eyelid.

'I can't wait, lass.' He picked her up and lay her on the bed, the mattress giving beneath her weight. She lay back against the pillows, her arms above her head, her legs relaxed and open. A wanton offering.

She watched from beneath heavy eyelids as he tore off his clothes, first struggling out of his coat, then discarding his waistcoat and ripping his shirt over his head, all the while his gaze roved her body with searing heat. He had to sit to remove his boots, which he did with frantic haste. Did he think she would change her mind?

The thought made her smile a little. How could she? She had thought of nothing but this moment since he had brought her such shattering ecstasy in the wagon and had left himself unfulfilled. Despite the delicious bliss he had brought her, she had wanted more…closeness. A oneness, she had called it to herself.

He stripped off his breeches and revealed his naked glorious arousal. At dusk by the burn he had been impressive, what she could see of him, large and very male. In the warm light from the window, he was gorgeous. The muscles of his chest and arms were clearly defined. His skin gleamed golden, emphasising the triangle of dark crisp curls across his chest that continued in a narrow trail down to meet those around his rampant male member. Rampantly demanding.

She wanted that glorious body against her, skin to skin, as she had not that first time. She wriggled the chemise up over her hips and pulled it off.

Startled, he stared at her, his gaze drifting down her body and back up to her face.

Had she gone too far?

'My God,' he said. 'You are more lovely than I remember. Take your hair down.'

She took out the pins and let it fall around her shoulders to her waist.

'I love your hair. It looks like fire, yet feels like cool silk against my skin.'

She smiled and opened her arms and he fell into them with a soft groan. He lay at her side, breathing hard, his lips nuzzling at her neck below her ear, his hand warm, gently kneading one breast, one heavy thigh between her legs, his hips flexing against her flank. 'Jenna,' he said, his voice hoarse. 'You are a virgin, still. But if we continue, you will not be. Now is the time to change your mind, sweeting. But quickly.'

Sweeting. Not since she was a child had she heard such a tender endearment. It thrilled her as much as his caresses.

'Jenna,' he said, his voice sounding strangled against her throat.

She grabbed his hair and pulled his head back

so she could look into his eyes. 'I want this. I want you, Niall. I won't change my mind, I promise.'

He muttered something under his breath that sounded like thank you, then he raised up on one elbow and took her mouth in a ravishing kiss, and the slow burn inside her flared bright behind her eyes, and scorched through her veins like hot smoke and she hugged him tight against her and kissed him back.

Permission. Savage lust surged through Niall. *Control. Don't lose control.* A shred of civilisation dragged him back from the edge. He hauled in a deep breath. He would not disgrace himself. 'Jenna,' he ground out through clenched teeth. 'Be sure.'

'Please, Niall,' she whispered, dragging on his shoulders, moving beneath him, opening to him.

He came over her, sank into the soft cradle of her hips, felt her widen her thighs to accommodate his body. Not a surrender. Never that with Jenna. An impatient urging. A demand. One that he had no intention of denying as the blood roared in his ears with the sound of waves crashing on shore. A hard pounding rhythm in time with his heartbeat. Yet he held himself back, determined to make it as good as it could be, this first time.

He wooed her mouth, stroking the soft flesh behind her lips, tasting her tongue, exploring the hot sweet depths of her mouth before slowly re-treating. To his delight, she aggressively followed his lead, scraping his tongue with her teeth and then sucking.

His shaft hardened unbearably as he surrendered to the pleasure. And then she was kissing him as if she could not get enough of his taste, his mouth, and their tongues mingled and danced for a lifetime until they had no breath left and they broke apart by mutual accord.

He moved lower, trailing kisses down her throat, the rise of her small but bounteous breasts, rising up on one hand so he could shape each velvety peak in turn with his palm and closing his lips around the tightly furled buds, teasing them with his tongue and teeth until she squirmed and gasped and cried out.

Her nails dug into his shoulders and his back. More pain to go along with the ache in his shaft—it was delicious torture.

Raising his head, he captured her demanding cries in his mouth and slid his hand down her body to her hot liquid centre. *Ready, thank the heavens. So very ready.*

His shaft pulsed a demand and every part of his being wanted to pound into her, to take her and claim her. *No. No. She was... She hadn't...* He took deep steadying breaths, clung to what little reason he had and took himself in hand, guiding his throbbing flesh against her entrance, carefully parting the slick folds. *So small. So tight.* His muscles bunched and strained to be let loose, but he held back the terrible urge to plunge deep.

Instead, he flexed his hips, a tiny movement that sent searing heat to his brain as the head of his shaft encountered the hot wet flesh that slowly gave way. Holding himself above her on his hands, he gazed into her flushed face and sensually pouting lips. Never had a woman looked more beautiful or more trusting than she did at that moment. 'This is going to hurt,' he managed to say through teeth gritted to hold himself back.

She bit her lip.

She was going to change her mind. He was going to have to—

'Go,' she said. 'Go quick.'

Courage shone in her face. And a great feeling of tenderness swept through him, but there was no time to think about what it meant. She arched beneath him, destroying all thought, and he surged forwards into her heat, felt the pressure of tight silken flesh around his shaft and her gasp of pain. She tensed, rigid.

He'd hurt her. It was a stab to his heart. 'I am sorry.' He started to withdraw. 'I should never have—'

'No,' she said, still clutching at the sheets. 'It is nothing. I am all right now.'

Body shuddering with the strain of holding himself back, not touching her anywhere but at the point of their joining, he sought the truth in her face. Bravery, yes, but he had hurt her. 'I—'

'Really. It feels strange…but nice. Please, Niall.'

Nice. It needed to feel better than merely nice and the plea was more than any man could handle. Slowly he pressed deeper and watched her eyes widen and her lips part on a gasp with deep satisfaction.

'Oh, my,' she said.

He withdrew and pressed deeper yet. Her eyes, forest-dark and glazed with desire looked up at him slumberously. She wrapped her legs about him, pulling him closer as he once more slid deeper. Unable to stop himself, he picked up the rhythm, driving harder, faster and deeper, listening to her cries and moans of pleasure, longing for the moment when he knew she was there, so he could bring them both to climax.

He was too close to the edge to wait for her. He burrowed between them, seeking and finding the little nub high and deep above where they were joined, pressing and rubbing, feeling his vision darken, his breathing an unsteady rasp in his ears as he drove home to the hilt over and over. She cried out. Her inner muscles gripped him hard. She was there. He tightened and he broke through into brilliant light, soaring with her.

It lasted for hours and was over in seconds, the aftershock of her climax squeezing his pulsing shaft. Leaden-limbed, he collapsed. On her. On her tiny fragile body. He groaned and rolled to the side. To his blissful delight, she curled against him, breathing hard, her head resting on his shoulder, her hand splayed across his sweat-slicked chest.

What the hell had just happened? Never in his life had he felt so shattered during or after. He could scarcely move. He could barely keep his eyes open. Somehow he managed to cradle her close against him with one arm, his other hand enfolding the one on his chest and lost himself in warm peaceful darkness.

Jenna awoke with a start. An unfamiliar movement beside her. A deep sigh blowing against her ear. Niall. It all flooded back. The overwhelming desire. The pleasure. It seemed almost like a dream. But the evidence lay large and warm and sated beside her.

What did it mean for the future?

The sun was high in the sky, casting little sunbeams into the room through the windowpanes. Sparrows chirped in the eaves. A dove cooed softly. How long had they slept?

The room itself was filled with shadows growing shadows.

Lying there, staring at the ceiling, she listened to the even sound of his breathing. Should she wake him or not? Finally she risked lifting her head to look at him, asleep, a darker shadow curled partly around her, one arm across her chest. As if he would keep her safe while they slept.

What had she done? The pleasure of the flesh was why she had done it, the desire and attraction she felt for him, but what havoc had she wrought by giving way to her passion? To her sense that if she did not take this opportunity, she would always regret it?

A man with a strong sense of honour, he would offer her marriage, whether he wanted to marry her or not. Her heart squeezed. She would like nothing better. To be married to him, she realised, startled. To have his children. Here at Braemuir. A hand crept to her belly. Even now, his seed might have taken root. Because if she wasn't mistaken, it was more than attraction that had made her take such a risk. She was falling in love.

A cold wave of fear washed through her. No. Love did not come into this. Attraction. Friendship. Liking, even. But the idea of love was too painful to contemplate. No, indeed. That she might have chosen him, had he been one of the suitors approved by her cousin, didn't mean she loved him.

She couldn't. One way or another she would have to let him go. And losing those you loved was far too painful to be borne.

Nor did she imagine he loved her. He was simply doing his duty and, like any man would, he had slaked his lust.

So what would she say if he asked? She wanted to say yes.

She lay back and gazed at the ceiling. But what of Braemuir? Had she abandoned her solemn promise to marry well and fulfil her father's dream of returned wealth and glory to the name of Aleyne? Was her father looking down on the daughter who should have been a son with sorrow in his heart?

If she married Niall, the title would continue, there might even be a son, but her home, the house she'd sworn to rebuild, would crumble to dust. Her shame. Her failure. Her broken promise.

The ceiling blurred.

'What is it, *mo gràdh*?' Niall murmured, leaning over her, brushing her cheek with his thumb. 'Why are you crying?'

My love? A casual endearment, surely? She looked up into his handsome face with its new growth of beard and his worried eyes, and tried to smile.

He cursed under his breath. 'Regrets, I suppose.'

'No,' she said. And that was the truth. She had no regrets about what they had done. None at all.

His lips twisted with disbelief. 'Why else would you be crying?' His voice sounded harsh.

Only the truth would do. 'I was thinking about Braemuir.'

'It is only a house, Jenna. A building.'

'It is my home. My father's home and his before him. I swore I would care for it.'

His lips thinned. 'A house is not a home unless it has a heart within it.'

She stared at him blankly, annoyed by his easy dismissal. 'You know nothing.'

'I know that Dunross Keep was naught but empty stone walls on a hill until Selena and Ian moved in.'

She dabbed at her still-moist eyes. 'Your brother and his wife?'

'Aye.' He pushed himself back to sit up against the headboard, his gaze fixed somewhere off in the distance. 'Many a Gilvry lost his life to the cause of getting it back. The most recent, my older brother. For what? Bricks and mortar. We were poor, practically landless and happy. Trying to get it back ruined one life for each generation. My mother can't bring herself to speak to Ian, because she blames him for what happened to Drew.'

Never had he revealed so much about his family. 'Do you blame your brother?'

He shook his head and looked at her, his eyes bleak. 'I blame myself.'

A loud knocking sounded below. 'Lady Jenna,' a voice called. 'Are you there?'

Her mouth dried. She looked at Niall in horror. 'Mr Hughes.'

Niall shot out of bed.

'Don't let him see you,' she said, and wished she'd bitten her tongue when she saw the hurt in his eyes. 'Please, Niall. He was my father's friend. And he is a vicar.'

'Lady Jenna,' Hughes yelled, banging again.

'I'm coming,' she called back. She looked at Niall. 'Help me dress.'

Silently, brusquely, he did as she asked. He was angry, but she did not have time to smooth his ruffled feathers.

'You'll have to go out of the window on the other side. There's a tree there you can use.'

He paled. 'Not a chance.'

'Oh, no, of course not. But you will have to stay out of sight. I have known him since I was a child. I will not lose his friendship for a little inconvenience.'

His jaw hardened. 'So it is an inconvenience I am.'

'That is not what I mean and you know it.'

'You'd best tidy your hair,' he said.

She put a hand to her head and turned to look in the glass. She looked as if she'd gone through a hedge backwards, or been well-bedded. 'Hand me my cap.'

Somehow it had ended up draped on a bedside candlestick.

He tossed it to her and she made a quick knot of her hair with pins and tied the cap on tight. Curls escaped it all around her face, which was fiery red from embarrassment at being caught, and trying to hurry, and from the disappointment in Niall's eyes.

'Please, do not come down until he is gone.'

He glowered. 'I won't embarrass you, Jenna.'

'Oh, Niall,' she said, 'I'm sorry.'

'You will be more than sorry if he decides to come upstairs to find you.' The wry twist to his lips made her feel a little better. She turned and ran downstairs, breathlessly trying to smile. 'Mr Hughes. I am sorry to keep you waiting.'

His mouth pursed in disapproval as he glanced around the kitchen. 'I'm very glad you came home, Jenna. I wanted you to see for yourself what was happening here. But I really think you should leave all of this work to your future husband.'

'Mr Gilvry is being a great help.'

He did not look any happier. 'I can't say I approve of you spending all day with only that young man for company, Lady Jenna.' He harrumped, then held out a note. 'I accepted an invitation to tea for you and Mrs Hughes for tomorrow afternoon. News of your arrival has travelled quickly. Gilvry can drive you over in the gig.'

She blinked at him. 'It was kind of you to come

out of your way to tell me, but surely it could have waited until I came home for dinner?' Heaven help her if he had arrived an hour or so earlier. She would have been ruined. 'But I really don't think—'

'Drummond sub-leases your pasture for his sheep from your lessee, Mr Fraser, from the next glen.'

The leasing convolutions were hard to follow, but the resultant money should have been spent on the house. It hadn't, for some reason only Carrick knew.

'But still—'

'There is a small matter of apparel, Jenna. Mrs Hughes has it in mind to alter a gown of hers to fit you. But she needs your presence. Which is why I am sent here post-haste.'

She glanced down at her cast-off gown with a smile. 'Mrs Hughes is a gem. She thinks of everything.'

He gave her a smug smile. 'I think so, too. Now, if you will excuse me, I have a parishioner further up the glen who is expecting my visit. A sad case, you know. Not likely to last out the year. But my visit brings him comfort.'

'Then I am doubly grateful for you taking the time to relay the invitation.'

He bowed and left. She watched him climb in the gig and drive away.

Niall clattered down the stairs and joined her in the kitchen. 'News?' he asked.

'I am invited with Mrs Hughes to take tea with a neighbour tomorrow afternoon. In the meantime I must hurry back to the vicarage to be fitted for a suitable gown.'

He raised a brow. 'Then we are all done here for the day?'

'Yes, I believe we are. Would you mind driving us in the gig tomorrow?'

'You didn't think I'd be letting you go by yourself, did you?'

'There is no danger, surely?'

He gave her a teasing smile. 'Nothing but the usual footpads, lame horses and gypsies.'

She laughed. 'I hope not.'

He shook his head. 'No, there is no danger. Not here. And hopefully not at Carrick either if Dunstan has done his duty.'

'Then let us hurry and tidy up. Mrs Hughes is waiting.'

Chapter Fourteen

Stubborn to a fault. The woman was impossible, even if she was amazingly sensual and passionate. Niall shifted on the hard seat of the gig and forced himself not to think about what had occurred the previous day. What? Had he thought making love to him would make her forget all about her quest for a rich husband?

Hardly. He glared between the cob's ears at the lane winding between the heather-clad hills at the end of the glen. Why could it not be raining this afternoon? Then he would be spared the task of driving two ladies who had done nothing but share local gossip since they departed from Braemuir an hour ago.

Niall glanced over his shoulder. She looked beautiful. The borrowed forest-green gown, though modest, fitted her slim figure to perfection, and a jaunty little hat with a curling feather, while not fashionable, played to her elfin looks.

If she hadn't decided to visit her neighbour, he would have spent the afternoon convincing her to marry him as she really should. Or, since he didn't actually expect that she would agree to wed a man with so little to offer, convincing her to return to Carrick Castle where she would be safe.

From him.

A glen opened in front of them. A loch gleamed like polished steel, reflecting on one side the steep hills rising like a craggy spine and on the other a huge mansion, all round turrets and pointed roofs at varying levels fronted by an enormous columned portico set above a rustic lower level.

Behind him, Jenna gasped. 'I don't recall this house.'

'The land went to pay off your father's creditors,' Mrs Hughes said. 'Mr Drummond must have purchased it.'

'Lord Carrick sold it?' Jenna sounded disappointed.

'A ninety-nine-year lease, as I understand it. The glen was always too narrow for farming. The gypsies camped here beside the stream every summer.'

'Yes, I remember,' Jenna said. 'There was no loch then.' She stared at the house for a long time.

'The house is huge. Does Mr Drummond have a large family?'

'He is no married yet, though it is well past time,' Mrs Hughes replied. 'Every time he returns from Edinburgh or London we expect him to come back with a wee wifey, but he never does. Still, he is a man in the prime of his life. There is plenty of time.'

The closer they got, the bigger and more imposing the house became.

'It is like a palace,' Jenna said wonderingly. 'He must be exceedingly wealthy.'

'Aye, so I understand,' Mrs Hughes said. 'And generous to the poor box.'

Again Niall glanced back. He did not like the thoughtful expression on Jenna's face. He turned back and glared at the monstrosity before them. 'Who would need a palace here in the Highlands?'

Neither Mrs Hughes or Jenna proffered an answer.

He followed the lane around to the front entrance and drove up to yet another imposing façade at the front of the house. He brought the gig to a halt.

Before he could jump down to help the ladies out, a footman in red and gold livery, followed by a tall gentleman, hurried down to greet them. The footman took the horse's head. The gentleman, a hawk-faced man in his late forties or early fifties, judging by the grey at his temples and scattered among his thick brown hair, held out a hand to the ladies. 'Mrs Hughes. And you must be Lady Jenna. What a pleasure it is to meet you again.'

A puzzled look filled Jenna's face. 'Have we met, then, sir?'

Mr Drummond put a hand to his heart. 'And here was me, imagining you would remember. I visited your father on business in the months before he died. He introduced us once. Such an enchanting young lady you were then. I believe you were on your way to the stables. May I say the woman far outshines the lass?'

Niall wanted to gag.

Jenna, on the other hand, flushed scarlet and her lips curved in a pleased smile. 'I am so sorry, I do not recall. It was a long time ago.'

'So it was, my dear. Come, take my arm and I will escort you inside.' He turned his piercing dark eyes to Niall, taking him in with a swift judging look. 'Your man there can take the rig around to the stables. My stableman will set him to rights.'

Niall could see Jenna preparing to set the man straight. He touched two fingers to his hat. 'Thank you, sir.' He gave Jenna a hard look, a warning to let it be. For once, she did as requested without arguing. And for some reason that made him grit his teeth with annoyance.

'Come, ladies, come. Tea is waiting, but first

I would like to show you around my humble abode.' He held out his arms and the ladies placed their hands on his sleeves and he led them towards the steps to the front door.

With a last glare at the man's back, Niall clicked his tongue and set the cob in motion. The footman stepped back and followed his master into the house.

Had he been wrong? Should he have insisted on accompanying her inside? He wasn't dressed for afternoon tea. He ought to have known what a poor figure he cut and expected the assumption he was a servant, no matter how much it stung. At least Jenna had been prepared to speak for him. He could take some comfort in that. But not much. Not after the way she had reacted to the sight of this man's house.

In the stable yard, a snooty head groom came out to meet him. He looked down his nose at the gig. 'You can put it over there.' He pointed to a shed containing a couple of plough horses and some farming equipment. Not good enough to mix with Drummond's blood cattle, no doubt.

'When you are done, go round to the scullery door and the maid there will give you some bread and ale.' He walked away, back into the finely appointed stables across the other side of the yard.

'Snob,' Niall muttered. 'We don't care, do we, old girl. Those shires look like honest hardworking fellows. And I'll no be begging my bread at any scullery door.'

There was room for the gig in amongst the ploughs and the tillers and a stable for the cob beside the magnificently matched plough horses. Beautiful beasts, they were, all glossy and well fed.

Niall brushed his horse down and fed and watered her. Now for some refreshment.

'So, Gilvry, you come at last,' said a voice from the gloom at the back of the shed.

Recognising the voice, Niall peered into the shadows. 'Sean. What the devil are you doing here?'

The gypsy stalked into the light cast through the open door, though only at its very edge, his knife flickering in and around his fingers. A threat? 'I thought I would see how you and the lady were doing. How are you doing?'

'Well enough.' He glared at the gypsy. 'But I have some questions for you.' He narrowed his eyes. 'And by the way, how did you know we would be here today? We didn't know ourselves until yesterday.'

The gypsy flashed his quick dark smile. 'Perhaps I dreamed it.'

'More like you overheard the visit being arranged. That seems more your style.'

Sean's grin widened. 'Want to know what else I heard? It will only cost you a wee bitty silver.'

Niall shook his head. 'No thanks.'

'Then I will tell you for free. This *gadjo* intends to wed the Lady Jenna.'

'Don't be daft. The man is her tenant. She's here to take tea.'

'But this man can offer her so much more,' Sean said softly.

Niall stiffened, his heart sinking at the sound of the truth. 'I suppose you have dreamed of the wedding.'

'It is a choice. There are many choices, *gadjo*.'

The hairs on the back of Niall's neck prickled a warning. Ah hell, what did it matter if the man spoke the truth? Jenna needed a wealthy man if she was ever to set her home to rights. He didn't give a damn whom she chose.

Furious with the stupid ache in his chest, he glared at Sean. 'Why don't you choose to take yourself off?' He gave the cob a final pat.

The gypsy's teeth flashed white again, but this time his smile gave his face a predatory look. 'You chose to eat bread and salt. You and Lady Jenna. At my table.'

Now he was talking in riddles. Or… 'Are you hungry? Are you here for food?'

Sean's expression hardened. 'There will be no food for me at Drummond's door. He threw my people off land where we had camped each summer for years.'

Drummond? He frowned. Again the name

struck the same chord as it had when Lady Jenna
had said the name yesterday. He was sure he had
heard that name somewhere recently. Or had he
heard it mentioned at the inn? Likely that was it.

'Mrs Hughes's cook put up a basket to keep
starvation at bay. You are welcome to share with
me,' he said, climbing into the back of the gig.
He retrieved the basket and gestured for Sean to
join him.

Sean hesitated, glancing around as if checking
for lurking danger. Finally he climbed up and bit
into the chicken leg Niall handed him. 'There is
an important thing I will tell you,' the gypsy said
quietly. 'You will use it as you please.'

More riddles, when what he needed was food.

'And this is the portrait gallery.' Mr Drummond proudly gestured at the array of gilt-framed
pictures.

Jenna had never seen so many things as there
were in this house. The man was clearly a col-
lector. Of everything. Even here, where pictures
lined the walls, there were statues in every corner
and niche, tables cluttered with bric-a-brac and
curio cabinets stuffed with china. She stopped at
a picture of a fierce-looking woman in an Eliza-
bethan ruff. 'One of your ancestors?'

He frowned at it. 'Not mine. I bought it at an
auction. Quite terrifying, isn't she? The gilt frame
is worth a king's ransom.'

How odd that he would have pictures of other people's family and only care about the value of the frame. 'The artist must be well known,' she hazarded.

'Quite possibly,' he said. 'Shall we go to the drawing room now?'

He chivvied them onwards. Another wide corridor, a winding staircase, then a footman opened one of a set of double doors. The room was huge and stunningly beautiful, and stuffed with *objets d'art*. The windows overlooked the loch.

'What a beautiful view,' Jenna said, glad to relieve her eyes of the clutter inside the room.

He stood beside her. 'The second-best view from any house in all of Scotland, I am assured.'

She blinked, looking at him in question. 'The second-best?'

He bridled as if he thought she did not believe him. 'The architect who designed the house in the style of Horatio Walpole's Strawberry Hill said so.'

'What did he consider the very best?'

His face tightened a fraction. 'The view from Braemuir.'

Her jaw dropped in surprise, but he didn't notice, for he turned and nodded to Mrs Hughes. 'My dear lady, would you be so good as to pour the tea while I have a private word with Lady Jenna?'

'Oh, Mr Drummond, I really cannot...'

He threw his hands up. 'You mistake me, my dear Mrs Hughes. I do not mean we should go away in private, but merely that we should speak quietly together.' He held out his hand. 'Dear Lady Jenna, stroll with me about the room.'

It was a very long room and the windows at the far end provided yet another breathtaking view, this time down the length of the glen. 'I had the river dammed so it would fill,' he said with satisfaction as they paused and looked out.

No wonder she had not remembered this stretch of water. 'Mr Drummond, there is a matter of business I wished to discuss with you.'

His dark brows lifted, crinkling his high forehead. 'And what would that be, Lady Jenna?'

'You sub-lease Braemuir's pasture. I wonder if you would consider leasing it directly from me when that lease comes to an end.'

He frowned. 'My contract is with the man who leases your land from Lord Carrick and does not expire for another two years.'

'Oh, but I thought…'

It was as Niall had said. The payments from the land were going directly to Carrick, her trustee. But if that was the case, Carrick must be paying the money to her account somewhere? It was he she would have to approach about giving her the income.

She forced a smile. 'Then I will take the matter up with my cousin,' she managed to say with what she hoped was cheerful calm.

Mr Drummond coughed into his hand as if distressed by the topic. 'I am sure you know, Lady Jenna, that the small parcel of land on which this house stands will revert to Braemuir in a generation or two. In my opinion, the estate should never have been carved up in the first place.'

Her thoughts exactly. But there had been debts to pay on her father's death. She could not help but wonder what else Carrick had been keeping from her all this while.

'What is done is done,' she said heavily.

'And cannot be undone,' Mr Drummond agreed. 'Although perhaps that is not always the case.'

'I cannot afford to buy back your lease. And nor do I need such a grand house when I already have Braemuir.'

'Ah. Braemuir.' He smiled sorrowfully and shook his head. 'A tragedy for such a beautiful old house to be so neglected.'

'Yes. But I will put it to rights. In time.'

'Really.' His eyes sharpened. 'I doubt Murray would take it on.'

Startled, she stared at him. 'How can you know about Mr Murray? Or what is in his mind for that matter?'

'I am a businessman, Lady Jenna. It behooves

me to know what is happening in the world. I have my methods.'

It sounded rather sordid. And unnecessary. 'Why would you take an interest in my affairs?'

'I lease your land. A marriage might mean it may soon be unavailable to me.'

True. 'Well, I have not heard from Mr Murray as yet.'

'But you will. The world has heard of your trek across the country in a gypsy cart.'

Her stomach lurched. 'How is that possible?' She felt heat to the roots of her hair as he gave her a sorrowful look.

'My dear young lady, you cannot keep such things a secret.'

Sean must have betrayed them. 'There are reasons—'

He stopped her with a look. 'I am sure there are. And I am not so nice as to let such a small thing trouble me as others might.'

Murray would.

'It broke your father's heart to let part of his beloved Braemuir go. We hold the key to putting it back together.' He put a hand to his chest. 'Lady Jenna, I am offering marriage.'

Stunned, she stared at him, her jaw dropping, her mind scrambling to catch up.

'It is not the first time I have made this offer,' he continued. 'I approached your cousin some years ago and was rejected out of hand.'

'I'm sorry. I did not know, until very recently, that there had been any other offers.'

He bowed slightly. 'As I suspected. Your cousin plays a deep hand. And so I watched his machinations from afar. Your arrival here is more fortuitous than you could possibly imagine. The second chance I had hoped for.'

There was an odd note in his voice. It almost sounded as if he was gloating. 'Why did my cousin object to your suit?'

His eyes hardened. His jaw flickered with tension. 'My family are merchants, Lady Jenna. They gained great wealth through trade. Your cousin finds the idea distasteful.'

'Are you engaged in criminal activity?'

'You are suspicious, too, I see?'

'No. No, of course not. I am trying to understand.'

'I beg your pardon. It is foolish of me to be so sensitive when at long last I have the chance to plead my case with you. Your cousin was insulting to say the least.' His eyes narrowed a fraction. 'I must say I was shocked when I heard the gossip about his scheme to send eligible bachelors to your door.'

'You heard about that, too?'

He bowed. 'It is common knowledge in Edinburgh that you seek a wealthy man in exchange for a title.'

It sounded dreadful coming from his lips.

'Braemuir needs a great deal of work if it is to be saved. Expensive renovations.'

'And I am one of the few men who could afford such a restoration.'

'But would you?' She could not help feeling this was all too good to be true.

'I would. The finest view in all of Scotland, Lady Jenna, and a woman equally as beautiful. What man could resist?'

'That is your only reason?'

A small smile curved his lips. 'The title, too. I have a hankering to sit in the House of Lords.'

A guilty conscience made her face heat. 'I am not perhaps the unspoiled bargain you would think me.'

He flicked his fingers in dismissal. 'The past does not interest me. Only the future. I am a very wealthy man, Lady Jenna. Honour me with your hand and your title, and I will give you Braemuir. And the children to carry on the Aleyne traditions.'

Braemuir on a golden platter. Promises fulfilled. Responsibilities met. It was all she had ever wanted. What her father had requested with his dying breath.

And the man himself? He was reasonably handsome and his manners were impeccable. Indeed, gentlemanly, by anyone's standards, even if his surroundings declared him a little more acquisitive than was normal. Many men had interests in collecting things.

Then why was she hesitating? Why wasn't she jumping for joy, the way she had when Carrick announced she would have three suitors to choose from? Not one of them cared about Braemuir with this man's apparent passion. Not even Niall. No, especially not Niall. To him, the house, her beloved home, was no more than bricks and mortar and stone.

Yet Drummond's enthusiasm seemed almost too much. A little too smug.

Her heart seemed suddenly too weighty for her chest. Her breath did not come easily and she could not force the acceptance past her lips, because the image before her gaze was of Niall, of how he would react when she gave him this news.

She cared about Niall's good opinion. Admired his loyalty and steadfastness, and his courage in keeping her safe. But he did not love Braemuir. If she gave in to her feelings for him, she would fail her father's trust. Fail generations of Aleynes for her own shallow needs.

She squeezed her eyes shut to force the thoughts into some logical order, but when she opened them again to Mr Drummond's curious gaze, she still could not answer. A strange pressure on her heart held her back, kept the words from her tongue.

'This is so sudden, Mr Drummond. May I have

some time to consider? I assure you I will not keep you waiting long.'

'There is someone else making as good an offer?' His voice had chilled.

'I… No. But I must break off my current engagement before entering into another.'

'Ah, yes, Murray. A bit of a nincompoop in my opinion. And his finances remain under his parents' thumb, you know. I am well aware of his family.'

A threat lay beneath his words. Murray did not have control of his fortune. He might not have the authority to spend any of it on Braemuir. 'Will you grant me two days?'

'I have waited many years, Lady Jenna. From the first time I saw Braemuir when undertaking some business with your father, I have waited. What will two more days matter? But let me assure you, I am prepared to do all that is right. The proud name of Aleyne will not be ground into the dust, if you entrust me with its care.'

A prickle of alarm ran across her back. Did he mean it would be, if she did not? How could it? He had no power over her property. 'You are most forbearing.'

He took her hand and raised it to his lips. 'I believe a woman of your intellect cannot help but see the worth of my offer.'

'Your tea is getting cold,' Mrs Hughes called out.

'Allow me to return you to your companion,'

Mr Drummond said once more, holding out his arm. 'I will look forward to you making the right decision.'

Right for whom?

Oh, why did she have such doubts?

When Niall finished putting away the gig and stabling the horse, he was delighted to discover Lady Jenna pacing back and forth outside the stables. Waiting for him. Delighted was too weak a word. His pleasure was on a much deeper level. It felt like joy.

He smiled at her, then realised she was frowning, her expression clouded with worry. Had she also heard of her attackers' presence in the area? The odd part was that Sean seemed to think they were now in the pay of the man they had visited today. Could it really be a coincidence that they had found work here after failing in their kidnapping attempt? Sean had seemed to suggest it was not, in that mysterious way he had of speaking. Niall wasn't certain what to think. But he did not want Lady Jenna running scared.

'What is it?' he asked as she strode to meet him in the middle of the courtyard.

She pressed her hands together at her breasts. 'Mr Drummond is offering marriage.'

His stomach fell away so fast he felt as if he was falling off a cliff. No, it felt worse than falling, because his chest radiated pain. 'That old man?' The words left his lips before he could stop them. 'Why would you even consider it?'

She stiffened. 'He is the same age as my father when he married my mother.'

So that made it all right? Her father had died when she was little more than a child. He bit back his retort, keeping his voice calm, his expression neutral. 'You plan to accept him, then?'

She rolled her lips inwards, as if she was unsure, and that made him feel a little better. Not by much. 'He is willing to sink a fortune into Braemuir.'

'A generous offer, then.' He sounded as bitter as he felt. And she had caught it because hurt filled her eyes.

'He offered once before. Carrick refused him on my behalf.'

Drummond. Now he remembered exactly where he'd heard the name before. In Carrick's study. 'Your cousin didn't approve of him.'

'Because his family aren't landed gentry. They earned their wealth.'

'You deem him worthy, then?'

'As worthy as Murray, if not more. The man has a fortune to spend and is keen to spend it on Braemuir.' Her eyes met his and they were full of worry. 'I can't see getting a better offer. The strangest part is that he does not lease the land directly from Carrick, but has it by way of a sublease from an intermediary. Not only did Carrick refuse his offer of marriage, he also refused to lease him pasturage. So Drummond found another way to get what he wanted.'

'Did he now?' The man sounded ruthless. A strange prickling stirred the hairs at the back of his neck. A warning. 'Jenna I think you should be careful of this man.' Did he tell her about what Sean had said, or should he try to discover the truth first? If Sean was wrong, he might ruin Jenna's only chance to save her house.

She sat down on the small bench outside the stable door. 'He is prepared to pay for everything the house needs. I am no fool, Niall. I will make sure it is written into the marriage settlement.'

Numb, dead inside, and not fully understanding why, except the knowledge he would lose her, which was nothing new, Niall sat down beside her. 'Why does he want Braemuir when he already has such a fine house of his own?' Fine in some people's eyes, anyway.

She rested her elbows on her knees and her chin in her cupped hands. 'He desires to be part of its heritage through its future generations.'

Niall felt ill at the thought of future generations. He stood up. 'I see you have decided.'

She rose slowly. 'Niall, does it really matter if it is Drummond or Murray?'

Not one jot. He'd feel the same whichever man she chose, but somehow he'd begun to think, to hope, there might be a chance for him. He couldn't talk about this right now. If he stayed, he might do something they would both regret. He needed to think it through. Decide what he should say. He bowed. 'If you will excuse me, I ordered my dinner at the tavern.'

His stomach revolted at the thought of food, but agreed that a drink wouldna come amiss.

She put out a hand to stay him, a kind of desperation in her eyes. 'I thought we might meet later, at the house.'

Cuckold the new betrothed, did she mean? Surely not? His body hardened hopefully. His mind rebelled. The anger he'd been trying to suppress pushed its way to the surface. 'Thank you, but no.' He turned and stalked off.

Oh, he wouldn't leave her here alone, not until she was duly married off and under the protection of her husband, but he certainly wasn't going to have any more to do with her than necessary. He was too angry. Too shattered.

The pleasant chatter in the tavern had not suited his black mood. He'd been argumentative to the point of rude. Ready for a scrap, something most unlike him, but the innkeeper had kindly suggested he leave before he could entice anyone into fisticuffs. And the anger that had sustained him earlier had faded into melancholy. He had never been a mean drunk. He normally got mellow and affectionate.

Tonight he was neither. He kicked at a stone in the road.

Perhaps he'd been a fool not to take Jenna up on her offer of an evening together. One last night. If he thought he could have stuck to conversation, then he would have said yes. But in his heart he knew he would not.

Damn it all. What sort of man wants to make love to a woman he knows is betrothed to another? Conceivably, it was worse than what Drew had done to his heiress. Ian had sent him away, shipped him off to America, for that misdeed.

Yet he now wanted to make love to her. Badly. Ah, but would she turn him away after his show of temper? She would be wise if she did. And surely she would not have walked to Braemuir in the dark in the hope he would change his mind?

He squinted at the moon. 'What do you think, lassie?' Bright Phoebe smiled and seemed to wink.

'All right. What about this? If there is a light showing in the window, then I'll knock on the door.' He stopped and stared at the ground. 'And if not, you ask?' He thought about it for a moment, his mind wrestling with the thought of leaving and never seeing or touching her again. It felt wrong. In his heart he knew she would be there. Waiting. 'Och. If there is no light then I will know I was right the first time.'

Content with his decision, and hoping with all

his might for the faintest glimmer from inside the house, he strolled on, letting his mind wander, thinking about the strange meeting with the gypsy, remembering Sean's warning about their abductors and them being seen on Drummond's property, apparently with his permission. In his anger and disappointment at her decision, he'd forgotten to warn Jenna as he'd intended.

His heart pounded hard in his chest. What if they came for her and she was alone in the house? He started to run, stumbling in the ruts, tripping over stones in his haste.

There was a light in the kitchen window and as he drew close, he could see two shapes at the table. Who had she let in? Was she even now in the hands of those ruffians?

He burst through the door. And stopped short at the sight of the person slurping down a cup of tea. 'What is he doing here?'

Chapter Fifteen

The Tearny boy looked up in terror. As well he should.

'Where did he come from?' Niall asked, glaring at the boy who had led them into a trap.

'I'll let him tell you once he has finished his tea,' Jenna said.

There was an odd note in her voice and she wasn't quite looking at him. What the devil was going on? Niall leaned against the door and folded his arms across his chest, forcing himself to be patient. To resist demanding answers. There was an undercurrent in the room he didn't like, and he had the feeling he should not try to battle it. Not yet.

Finally the boy put down his cup.

'Are you done?' Niall asked.

The boy nodded, his eyes huge. He looked at

Jenna, who nodded. 'Tell Mr Gilvry what you told me. Take your time. Forget nothing.'

'The men...' again he looked at Jenna '...the ones who gave me the message to bring to the castle. I didn't want to, but they made me go with them.'

'I saw no sign of force,' Niall said.

'They said they would shoot my ma if I said one word.'

He could only imagine how scared the lad must have been after such a threat. Anger flared. 'Aye, well, when I am done with them they will be a little less cocky.'

'You don't have to look far,' the boy said.

So once more, Sean and his dreams had been right.

'You don't seem surprised,' Jenna said, raising a brow.

'Sean told me he thought they were in the area.'

'You saw Sean?'

'In your most recently betrothed's stable.'

Her spine stiffened. 'He is not my betrothed.'

'But he will be.'

'No, he will not.'

The determination in her voice caught him off guard. 'Why? What has he done?' The anger he'd been nursing all night flared brighter.

'Go ahead, William. Tell him what you told

me.' She frowned at Niall. 'Don't interrupt, please.'

Blinking, he sat down at the table and gave the lad a nod of encouragement.

'I've been locked in the attic in a big house that looks like a castle. When I saw you come there today, I escaped down the drainpipe.'

A cold chill swept down Niall's back. At the thought of the lad climbing down and the dawning realisation that Drummond must be involved in Jenna's abduction. He stared at Jenna, who gave him a meaningful look.

'They told my ma she would never see me again if she said one word to anyone about them taking you,' the boy went on. 'They said I would go home after the wedding.'

'The wedding to Murray?' he asked, confused.

'To Drummond,' Jenna said. 'It seems Drummond intends to wed me by fair means or foul. He said my arrival here was fortuitous. At the time, I did not fully understand his meaning. It seems in running from Fred and his gang, we ran right into the arms of their employer.'

All the pieces fell finally into place. 'Because of the title.'

'He was quite open about it. He wants to be a peer of the realm. And he also wants Braemuir.' She gave a short laugh. 'And there was I thinking I had found a man who would care for it as I did. You didn't go inside his house, Niall.' She hesitated. 'It is as if anything he lays his eyes on or touches, he has to own. To hoard it away. I can't think of any other way to describe it. He saw Braemuir, entered its doors while my father was alive and he wanted it.'

'And he has touched you.'

She shivered. 'For the first and last time.'

Relief flooded through him, swiftly followed by despair. No matter whom she chose, it would not be him. She had made that perfectly clear, no matter what Sean had said about their being married. And he didn't blame her. She had her duty, just as he had his. And his required that he get her to safety. And the way to do that was to return her to her real guardian.

'We leave for Carrick Castle in the morning.'

She shook her head. 'There's more. William, tell Mr Gilvry what you did for Mr Murray.'

The boy puffed his chest, as proud as punch. 'The part where I fetched him a gull's egg, or the part where he slipped and fell on the seaweed getting into the boat?'

Niall stifled the urge to laugh at the look of outrage on Jenna's face and tried to suppress the unreasonable feeling of delight coursing through him. 'So that puts an end to him? Jenna, are you sure? What will you do?'

For a long moment she looked at him and there was longing in her eyes. A heartbreakingly lost look. And he said nothing, refusing to speak the words hovering on his tongue in case he had it wrong. He wasn't going to grovel. If she wanted him, she would have to say so.

She heaved a sigh. 'Start again, I suppose. Next Season. In Edinburgh.'

The pain was worse than anything he might have expected. Shattering. 'Then we must leave first thing in the morning. I'm no waiting any longer for Carrick to act on your letter. You will be safe at the castle and from there we will set the authorities on Drummond and his band of ruffians.' He picked up his hat. 'Jenna, I will walk you home. Come on, lad, you can bed down in the stables at the inn.'

'You won't let them get me will you, sir?' William quavered.

He ruffled the lad's copper curls. 'No fear of that, young Tearny.'

He just wished they'd try, because right now he was spoiling to connect his fists with something that would fight back.

By the next morning, Jenna had resigned herself to the idea of returning to Carrick's protection. William Tearny had brought word early that Niall had walked to the livery stables in the nearby town and Jenna had walked with the boy to Braemuir to bid the place farewell. For a short time, she hoped. She picked her way gingerly through the grand hall and gazed up at the proud display of shields showing crests of her family's connections. They went all the way back to what her father had said was King James V of Scotland. She looked at the pathetic pile of debris of what had been the grand oak staircase. Niall was right. There was nothing she could do here without a great deal of money.

She still had to keep her promise to Father. And would have by now, had the men Carrick had picked for her to marry...

Liar. The men Carrick had chosen were perfect for the job. She just hadn't wanted any of them. She'd let emotion rule her decision. Next time she would do better.

At least she knew the truth now of exactly what she had to offer. The house was more a liability than a prize. But the land was good. As was the title. And the view. The best view in Scotland, according to Drummond. She repressed a shudder at the thought of that man.

She turned away.

A small figure hurtled through the baize door that led to the back of the house and attached itself to her waist.

'They are here!'

'Mr Gilvry is back already?' He must have guessed she would come here.

'No. Them. Those men.'

Jenna's mouth dried. Her heart picked up speed.

'They've come to take me back,' the boy wailed. 'They are sneaking up to the back of the house.'

A loud knock sounded at the front door. How had they known she'd be here? Had they been watching her?

The boy clenched harder.

'Go, up the backstairs. They will never find you up there. But be careful. Stay at the back of the house where the floors are safe.'

The boy raced off.

Another knock.

Jenna took a deep breath and wished she had a pistol. She manoeuvred around a heap of plaster and opened the front door.

Drummond pushed his way in.

Her mouth drying, her throat feeling tight, she stepped back. 'Why, Mr Drummond, to what do I owe the pleasure of such an unfashionably early call?'

'''Tis the early bird and all that,' he said with a cheerful smile as his eyes darted around, taking in the devastation. 'It is worse than I thought.' His gaze came back to her face. 'Where is that man of yours—Gilvry, I think his name is?'

'What business is it of yours?' She certainly wasn't going to tell him that Niall wasn't with her.

Another man strode in behind him. A man she remembered all too well. Fred. She turned on Drummond. So he truly was behind her abduction. She lifted her chin. 'I can't say I think much of the company you keep.'

Fred ignored her and spoke to Drummond. 'No luck so far, but I found the lad's coat in the stables. He's here somewhere.'

'My dear Lady Jenna, where is the Tearny boy?' Drummond asked gently. 'Better if you tell me now than see him punished if I have to spend valuable time looking for him.'

'Boy? Do you mean the gardener's boy who was here yesterday?'

At a sound behind her she turned to see Pip coming through the baize door. Not Niall as she had hoped. Her stomach dipped.

'Cor,' Pip said, stumbling over a pile of wood. 'What a mess. He's not back here.'

'Find him,' Drummond said, his voice as cold as ice. 'Look upstairs.'

Fred looked at the half-demolished staircase. 'Can't get up there.'

'The servants' stairs, you fool,' Drummond snarled, and Jenna recoiled from the ugly expression on a face she had thought reasonably handsome.

The two men went through to the back of the house.

'There is no boy here,' Jenna said. 'Please leave my house immediately.'

'Now, now, Jenna. Jake saw both of you leave

the vicarage this morning. Didn't your father teach you it was wrong to lie?'

So they had been watching her. And probably had been when she was at Carrick. Under this man's orders. 'Telling the truth is not a lesson you have learned,' she snapped.

As if he had not heard her, he pushed at a pile of rubble with the end of his riding crop. 'There isn't a man alive who would want this wreck of a place.'

'Except you.'

He gave her a small smile and bowed. 'Except me. Don't be a fool, Jenna. I will put it to rights for you.'

'I wouldn't marry you if you were the last man on earth. You had your men abduct me.'

'Aye, and if not for Gilvry, we would have been married by now and Braemuir would be in my hands.'

'Why?'

He looked surprised at her question, then he laughed. 'You don't know what it is like to be poor, do you? You've never lived fourteen to a house. Been scorned for your lowly beginnings. Well, I intend to have the last laugh when I am a peer. Let me see them turn their noses up then.'

'But you built that awful monstrosity you call a house. You don't need Braemuir, too.'

His face darkened. 'My house is better than this.' He kicked at a length of timber and it crumbled to dust. 'But it doesn't have quite the same cachet.'

The sound of heavy footsteps came from upstairs at the front of the house. Hopefully they would fall right through and break their necks.

'My father would never have approved of a man like you.'

He blanched, his smile transforming into a sneer. 'Agree to marry me and I will let the boy go. Otherwise...' He spread the fingers of his gloved hand and shrugged. 'Well, who knows what can befall a small boy far from home?'

The threat made her throat close.

Fred returned. 'We'll never find him in that rabbit warren up there,' he whined. 'Half the floors are rotted through. Nothing holds my weight.'

Jenna swallowed. *Niall, please, hurry.* Oh, but she'd told no one of her intention to come here. She folded her arms across her chest. 'There is no boy here. And you, sir, have outstayed your welcome. Go.'

Drummond's lip curled. 'Take care, Lady Jenna. You will pay for your insubordination once we are married.'

Jenna stared at him, horrified. How could she have thought him even close to being a gentleman? 'Get out! Now.'

He put his hands on his hips and glared at

Fred. 'All right. If you can't go up, we'll smoke the little rat down. Light that pile of wood.'

'No!' Jenna yelled. 'Don't you dare.'

Fred looked at his boss.

'Do it,' Drummond snarled.

Fred took a piece of timber and soon had one end alight, like a torch.

'Perhaps you would like to tell the boy to come down of his own accord, Lady Jenna. I am sure if you shout loud enough he will hear you.'

'You can't get away with it. It is murder.'

'Ah, so he is up there. Marry me, and I won't burn the place down.'

'Burn it down and you lose Braemuir,' she said, desperate to stop him.

'I will soon build another.'

'But it won't be Braemuir.'

'Of course it will.'

'No. It can't be. It would be new.'

He laughed. 'You are as mad as your father. How he hated handing over that parcel of land to me.'

'I understood it was Carrick who let it go?'

'Did you? Your father owed me money. I threatened to take everything if he didn't give me Braemuir. That is when I learned about the entail. He was so pleased with himself that day, only able to give me a ninety-nine-year lease on a tiny piece of land. But it was what he said just before I left that made me realise what I should do.'

'What did he say?' she said, her voice quavering.

'That the man who would get everything would be your husband. And it would never be me. He was wrong.' He turned to Fred. 'Light it.'

'Why harm the boy?' she asked.

'He knows too much.'

And a man cornered was a dangerous man. He would not hesitate to kill the boy to save his own life. 'All right. Let me go to the backstairs and call him down.' She headed for the green baize door.

Drummond grabbled her arm. 'Not until you agree to our wedding.'

The front door crashed back, revealing a furious-looking Niall. 'Release her.'

Drummond pulled her close to his side, his eyes narrowed. 'Ah, your lover.'

Jenna blushed.

Niall's eyes blazed. 'Let her go,'

Pip was circling around, picking his way around the piles of rubble to get to Niall.

'Niall!' Jenna called out. 'Watch out.'

A hand clapped over her mouth, but she'd warned him in time. He backed up against the wall.

'Light it,' Drummond ordered.

Jenna struggled. He took his hand from her mouth and put his arm around her throat, cutting off her air, forcing her to remain still.

Niall's fists clenched as he waited for Pip to close in.

Jenna struggled. She could not let them burn the house, not with the boy upstairs. 'I'll do whatever you want,' she gasped. 'Just don't set fire to the house.'

Niall cast her a look of disbelief and disgust.

'Are we to be married then, Lady Jenna?' Drummond purred. 'According to Scottish law, before these witnesses?'

'No, Jenna.' Niall said, glaring at her. ''Tis only a house.'

The anguish in his voice, the look of helpless fury on his face, pierced her heart. But he didn't know about the boy. 'Yes,' she said. 'We are.'

Drummond smiled in triumph. 'Let us be off, then. We have a marriage to celebrate. Come on, lads.'

'Damn you, Jenna,' Niall said and turned to leave.

'Ouch,' Fred said and dropped his torch, shaking his hand and batting at the embers glowing on his sleeve.

The dry wood from the staircase flared to life the moment the torch landed.

'No,' Jenna yelled.

Drummond uttered an oath. 'Clumsy fool. Put it out.'

Fred stamped on the flickering flames, but his efforts only served to spread them more.

'Niall,' Jenna shrieked. A lungful of smoke made her cough.

He didn't turn back.

'Niall, the boy is upstairs. Trapped.'

He spun around. 'What?'

'He ran up there when he saw Fred. They were going to smoke him out. It is why…'

Niall glared at Drummond. 'You dastard. You coward.'

'The smoke will bring him down soon enough,' Drummond said carelessly. 'Or you can fetch him down yourself.'

The flames were leaping higher, the heat of them like a blast from a furnace. Drummond pulled Jenna out of the front door and out into the fresh air. His two men followed, coughing and gasping. Smoke poured out of the front door, then flames were licking at it and at the lower windows. She could hear the cracking of glass. It seemed like only minutes and the whole ground floor was ablaze. And there was no sign of Niall. She tried to pull free and go back in the house, while Drummond tried to pull her into his carriage waiting on the drive.

Somehow she broke free. 'No. There is no marriage. You broke our bargain and set fire to the house.'

He grabbed her again. 'By accident. And you don't have a choice. By your own admission we are married.'

'Consider us divorced.' She kicked him in the shin with her sturdy boot.

He howled, let go and fell to the ground, clutching his shin.

'No court will uphold a promise made under duress,' she said, glaring down at him. 'Now get back in there and help find that boy.'

'There,' Fred shouted. 'Up on the roof.'

Jenna stared up. And saw them. The man and the boy clambering painfully slowly across the roof. So high. Her heart clenched in terror.

A farmer galloped up on a horse. 'I saw the smoke,' he said, dismounting.

'There's nothing to be done,' Drummond said. 'Let it burn. Come on, lads, let's go.' He climbed into his carriage. Fred took the reins and, with the others sitting beside him, they drove away.

'Cowards.' The farmer shook his fist at the retreating coach. 'Damnable cowards.'

But Jenna had no time to spare for them. All she could do was stare at the two figures, one large, one small, desperately slipping and sliding on the grey slate tiles, heading up to the ridge.

Oh, God, Niall and his fear of heights. If he froze…

A breath caught fast in her throat. The blood drained from her head so fast she felt dizzy.

She couldn't bear to watch, but could not take her eyes from the two on the roof. Smoke was curling up from under the eaves now. At any moment the roof would be alight. Or collapse beneath them. Oh, why had she ever cared about this house? Niall was right. It was only bricks and mortar.

'Hell,' the man by her side said. 'He's got courage, whoever he is.'

Courageous. And honest. And loyal.

There wasn't a man she'd ever met to match him.

It was like a veil being stripped from her eyes. He was all those things, but he was so much more. He was dear to her heart. She loved him.

No. No. She didn't want to love anyone. Would not.

But there was no stopping it. Her heart had known for ages. But she had been too afraid to listen. And now she was going to lose him. To the house. And she didn't think she could bear it.

She clenched her hands. *Just let him live. I'll never ask for anything else as long as I live, if you just let him be safe.*

'He seems to be making for the chimney,' the farmer said. 'Probably plans to jump for it. He'll break his neck.' He looked around him. 'We need something to break their fall.'

Her mind scrambled to keep up, while her gaze remained fixed to his precious form so high above her. 'There are sacks of old fleece at the back of the stables.'

'Right. You, there,' he yelled at a couple of labourers from the village who had arrived breathless and now stood staring, helplessly. 'Help me.'

'Do we fetch water?' one of them asked.

'Too late for that. Come on, men.' He strode off, the men in his wake.

Sick to her stomach, once more Jenna raised her gaze upwards. So high. So far above the ground. And yet there he was, helping the boy inch by inch along the narrow ridge. He slipped. She felt her heart dip in a nauseous rush, her breath catching in her throat.

She sank to her knees, her hands clasped at her breast, not wanting to look, scared to look away in case it made a difference.

Somehow, he caught himself, kneeling, clinging on to the tile. The boy skipped along the ridge to the chimney and stood looking back, clearly encouraging Niall to follow.

He did so on all fours, slowly, painfully, while Jenna bit her knuckles so hard she drew blood. Finally he reached the chimney, put one arm around it and sat. Jenna watched as he pulled a rope from his pocket and tied it around the narrow part of the chimney. This must have been his plan all along.

Her body was shaking with fear. For him. For herself. She could only imagine how he must be feeling up there with the flames only feet away. And yet he was still trying to save that little boy, because that was what she had asked him to do.

The tears filled her eyes and ran down her face and she watched him struggle to tie that rope.

Once he had it fastened, he looped a knot in the free end and lowered it down the side of the end wall. It dangled a good few feet above the ground when stretched to its full extent. The farmer and his helpers ran back and forth at desperate speed, piling sacks out from the wall.

More people from the village were arriving. 'Shall we try to put it out?' the tavern owner asked Jenna.

She shook her head, numbly.

''Tis a sad day,' a woman said. 'What on earth started the fire?'

Not what, but who. But she did not care a fig for that now, as Niall once more got to his feet on that narrow ridge, knowing how hard it must be for him to stand there, knowing how hard he must be shaking, because she was shaking, too.

He helped the boy with the rope and the lad shimmied down to the knotted end. He was grinning from ear to ear as if it was some kind of game. At the bottom, he let go and landed with a whoop in the sacks.

Niall, on the other hand, was gripping the chimney as if he would never let go.

He had to. Every part of her being willed him to climb down that rope as the boy had done. The flames were at the upstairs windows now. The roof might give way at any moment. He must climb down that rope.

Without thinking she got up, drawing closer, standing beside the sacks of wool, looking straight up the length of rope to where Niall stood.

'Your turn,' the farmer said, waving at him.

'Niall,' she called out. 'You can do it.'

Their gazes met and he straightened, grabbed the rope and started down, hand over hand. She covered her mouth with her hands in case she should cry out and somehow disturb his determination. When he reached the knot, he hung there, not looking down, but staring straight at the stone wall for what felt like hours but could only be moments.

A loud crash.

Voices cried out in horror.

The chimney shook and bits of tile rained down from the roof. The roof had fallen in.

'Niall,' she shrieked. 'Now. Let go now. Please.'

He released the rope with a yell and landed heavily amid the sacking. Her knees gave way. She collapsed on the ground, sobbing.

He ran at her. 'Quick,' he said, pale as a ghost, grabbing her arm. 'Get away from here. The chimney could come down at any moment.'

Everyone was running away from the building, and then they turned to watch as the roof fell inwards. Niall dropped onto the grass and put his head in his hands between his knees.

She sank down beside him. She looked at his dear brave face and the tears flowed anew. She couldn't speak, she was so happy he was safe.

'I'm sorry, Jenna,' he said. 'So sorry. There was no way to save the house.'

There was blood on his face. 'You are hurt.'

He touched a finger to his forehead. 'I banged it on the window, climbing out onto the roof.'

'I can't believe you did that.'

He gave a shaky laugh. 'Nor can I.'

Sitting on the grass together, they watched the chimney topple, bricks and rubble and dust flying upwards to join the smoke from the fire.

'That is it, then,' she said, and was surprised that she felt almost relieved. She hid her face in her skirts.

Niall patted her back. 'I'm so sorry.'

'So it has come to pass.'

Jenna looked up to see Sean standing beside them, his hat in his hand, the flames from the fire glowing in his eyes. It was eerie to say the least.

'Don't tell me you saw this in your dreams,' Niall said. 'If so, you should have warned us.'

'Choices, laddie,' Sean said softly. 'It is all about choices. My time here is done. Drummond will pay for his crimes, no doubt.'

Niall stared at him. 'Is that what this is all

about? Your retribution for him building on that land.'

The gypsy's eyes flickered. ''Tis a smart man you are, Niall Gilvry. I just hope you make the right choice.'

At that moment, Mrs Hughes hurried up. 'Oh, my poor dear, I am so sorry. I came the moment I saw the smoke. Your poor father must be turning in his grave.'

Getting up, Jenna looked around for the gypsy, wanting to ask him what he meant, but he seemed to have melted away. He was very good at disappearing.

Niall rose beside her. 'It can be rebuilt.'

He sounded so weary, so dispirited, she wanted to say something to comfort him, but what could she say? What she wanted to say required privacy, and right now they had an audience.

They stood silently with the others, watching the house as it continued to burn.

The farmer who had first come to their aid, walked over and shook Niall's hand. 'Ewen Lithgow,' he said.

'Niall Gilvry.'

'A fine rescue, sir. If I can ever be of service, I would be proud to be of assistance.' He bowed. 'And to you, ma'am.'

'Thank you for your help, sir.' Jenna dipped a curtsy.

Lithgow looked back at the house. 'Nothing

more to be done, I'm afraid. It could burn for days.' He went for his horse, tipped his hat and rode off.

'He is right,' Jenna said to Niall. 'All that could be done, has been done.'

'Come back to the vicarage, child,' Mrs Hughes said. 'We'll have a nice cup of tea and think about what to do next. I never did like you coming out here alone.'

She hadn't been alone. She had been with Niall. She just hadn't fully appreciated his presence.

'Listen, Jenna,' Mrs Hughes hissed in her ear. 'A letter has arrived from Lord Carrick. His carriage will arrive first thing tomorrow to take you back home.'

Carrick Castle wasn't her home.

She looked back at the smouldering house. Nor was Braemuir. Her home had been where she had lived with her family, not the walls that had surrounded them. And her family had been gone for many long years. She just hadn't acknowledged it.

Numb, she let Mrs Hughes hook her arm around her elbow and chivvy her along the drive and down the lane.

Niall fell in behind with William, who was happily chattering about balancing on ridgepoles and climbing down ropes. Every time she tried to turn around to say something, Mrs Hughes pulled her along even faster, deliberately widening the gap.

The lady leaned closer. 'Your cousin says if you do not return at once he will swear out a warrant for Mr Gilvry's arrest for abduction.'

Horrified, Jenna stared at her. 'Mr Gilvry did not abduct me. Drummond did.'

Mrs Hughes's face showed disbelief. 'Well, as I understand it, the two of you ran off together. Carrick is just trying to put a good face on it, for your sake. My dear, you would be well to keep your distance from that young man from now on, if you wish to keep your reputation.'

'I have to speak to Niall.'

'I think not. Your cousin has given you to Mr Hughes's care until you leave tomorrow. You will do as I bid. I will not have Lord Carrick turning my husband out of his living.'

She really did not want that, either.

Mrs Hughes ushered her through the garden gate and turned back to prevent Niall from entering. 'You will stay at the tavern, Mr Gilvry,' she said loudly. 'There is a letter here for you from Lord Carrick.' She pulled a note from her pocket and handed it over. 'I understand he has terminated your employment.'

Jenna caught a glimpse of his face before he turned away. Grim resignation was the only way to describe his expression.

'Inside, Lady Jenna,' Mrs Hughes said. She

lowered her voice. 'Please. We have served your family well all these years. Do not by your recklessness ruin our lives as well as your own.'

The admonition was well deserved. She had been thoughtless and reckless. Trying to recapture something she'd lost a long time ago. Not her home. But the love she'd felt there. In so doing, she'd lost something far more important. Niall.

Back in that field she had promised that she would ask for nothing for herself if only Niall was spared. Another promise she had to keep. Didn't she?

Chapter Sixteen

Niall sat in the corner of the taproom, nursing his whisky. The letter from Carrick had been to the point. He was appalled and would be taking the matter of Niall's behaviour up with Ian. He was not expected back at Carrick. And if he came anywhere near Lady Jenna, he would be charged with abduction.

So much for doing his family proud.

But none of that really mattered. It only mattered that Lady Jenna was safe.

He was going to miss her.

Self-disgust filled him. He'd taken her innocence, let his base urges override reason. He just hoped she would not pay the price for his inability to behave like a gentleman, that in time she would find a suitable husband and that one day her precious home would be rebuilt. She was a determined wee lass and he had no doubt she would find a way to do it.

He loved that about her. Her determination. Her courage. Such a brave lass.

He loved her? Aye, he did. He loved the way she'd fought to achieve her father's plans for her and her land. She had far more courage in her little finger than he had in the whole of his body. Look at the way he'd frozen on that roof. Turned into a mindless lump of cowardly jelly. Only the sound of her voice had enabled him to let go of that rope, or right now he'd be ashes.

But he did love her. And that was why he must disappear from her life.

Yesterday, in Drummond's barn, Sean had said it was as plain as the nose on his face they were meant to be together. Gypsies. What did they know of the real world? It was Sean's fault they had spent so much time alone together. He should have taken them straight back to Carrick Castle.

And by now Jenna would be safely married to Murray.

They were not, as Sean had insisted that afternoon, married. Sharing bread and salt at a gypsy fire did not constitute a wedding. It might be all right for gypsies, but it was not all right for a lady. Any more than Drummond's forced declaration had been right. Which reminded him: he needed to speak to the magistrate in the town. William had agreed to give evidence, so he could have them charged with the lad's abduction without Jenna's name having to be mentioned. Not that they were likely to lay their hands on Drummond any time soon. According to the tavern owner, Drummond had been seen heading, not for his own house, but south. No doubt planning to leave the country. A villain he might be, but not a fool. He'd known it was time to cut his losses.

And Jenna would be gone in the morning.

He would likely never see her again.

Just as well.

His heart contracted to the size of a pea. A painful sensation. One he had better get used to. And yet, how could he let her go without at least saying a proper goodbye? They had gone through too much together to just walk away without a word.

He wanted to tell her how much he admired her. Her courage. Her determination to keep her promise, even though it left him out in the cold. He pushed his chair back from the table and strode out of the tavern door.

And stopped short at the vision before him. It was as if his mind had somehow conjured her up, standing there in the cloak she'd worn the night they left the Castle.

'Jenna?' he said, questioning his sanity. Feeling his heart leap with hope at the sight of her.

'Niall. Thank goodness.'

'Good God, woman, what are you doing hanging around outside a tavern door?'

'I came to find you,' she said, with a shy half-smile. 'Once I got here, I realised what a foolish notion it was to think I could just walk in and ask for you.'

'Foolish, aye.' And utterly fearless as usual, but not to the point of stupidity. 'Come. I will walk you back to the house.'

Most of the houses along the lane still had lamps burning beside their doors so the path was easy to see as they fell into step, not touching.

She wrapped her arms about herself as if she was cold and he had the terrible urge to pull her close, to warm her with his heat, in more ways than just holding her. He widened the distance between them.

'Where were you going?' she asked.

'Where?'

'You were leaving the inn.'

A clever girl, his Jenna, except of course that she was not his. And would never be. 'I wanted to bid you farewell. We did not have a chance earlier.'

'Where will you go?'

'I haven't decided, but most likely home.' To face the music. To let Ian know he had managed to make a mess of things, first. But he would not stay there. He did not belong at Dunross.

They reached the vicarage. She stopped at the

gate. 'How were you planning to see me? Everyone is asleep and my chamber is on the second floor.' She tilted her head in that pixy gesture she had. 'Don't tell me you were going to climb through the window?'

He grinned. 'I thought I might chuck a few pebbles at the glass.'

'In hopes I might wake? It would take more than that. No, laddie, you would have had to have climbed.' There was laughter in her voice.

'Aye, well, when a man has a strong enough reason, he'll do anything, even risk his life.'

'Like climbing onto a roof to save a boy?'

He swallowed, his mouth drying at the recollection. 'Aye. If he must.'

He took her hand, loving the smallness of it in his palm, knowing it would be the last time, and led her through the gate and around to the back of the house. He seated her beneath the arch of roses and sat down at her side, half facing her. The lamp over the kitchen doorway cast shadows and bars of light over her face.

'Jenna,' he said softly. 'Why did you come to the inn tonight?'

She hesitated, as if trying to choose her words carefully. 'I wanted to thank you for all your help. For saving William's life.'

His hopeful, fast-beating heart sank. 'It was little enough I did. I couldna' save the house.'

'It can be rebuilt.'

'Young Murray will do it for you nae doubt.'

'You really think I should wed Mr Murray even though he also cheated?' Was that disappointment he heard in her voice? Or was he simply hearing what he wanted to hear?

'I want your happiness. Your comfort. Your security.'

'And you think Murray can give me all these things?'

He didn't answer. What he wanted to say and what he ought to say were at odds, so it was better to say nothing.'

'What if I said I wanted you?' she whispered so softly he was sure he must have misheard.

He lifted his head to look into her eyes and saw the glaze of tears. That he had caused them tore at his heart. 'Never in a million years could I rebuild your Braemuir,' he said brusquely. 'You would have to choose me over the house. I know you can't do that.'

'This is what you were coming to tell me?'

'I thought to tell you…how much I admired your courage and your determination to keep your promise to your father.' He took her hand in his, gazed down at her small fingers, so dainty in his large fist. 'Jenna, I wish you great joy in your life.'

'Niall, couldn't we—?'

'Hush. Jenna, it is a pathetic man that I am. A coward to the bone. You saw. You know.'

Her eyes widened, and he felt his heart clench and he could not bear the idea that she would turn away from him, or that he would see the disgust in her eyes, so he gazed down at the dark between his feet. 'A man terrified of high places. You saw me hanging there too scared to come down.'

'A coward would not have gone up there in the first place,' she declared roundly, vehemently. 'A coward would not have tried to save that boy. Niall, it was the bravest thing I have ever seen. You are a good man, Niall, with a true loyal heart.'

He shook his head slowly, heartened by her words even as he despaired. 'Don't mistake what I did for bravery. If not for you, I might never have made the attempt.'

'Then together we are stronger than we are apart.'

'Oh, Jenna, can you not see?' He looked at her pale face, at the hands pressed tight against her bosom, and his arms longed to hold her. 'A good man, a man of worth, protects the woman he loves. Gives her what she needs.' He squeezed his eyes shut. 'I can't do that. I would see you with a better man than me. A braver one at least.'

'And so you will leave. I can't ask you to change your mind,' she said softly.

He nodded. 'I know.'

'I cannot ask, because I swore I would ask for nothing as long as you came safely down from that roof. But, Niall, it is very cruel of you to be breaking my heart.'

'Jenna,' he whispered, his voice hoarse, almost broken. '*Leannan*. I do not want to hurt you, not for all the world. I love you too well.' He could not keep the pain from his voice.

'I love you, too, Niall. When I saw you on that roof, I knew my heart would be torn from me if I lost you.' She reached over and took his hand in hers, bringing it to rest in her lap. 'I have lost so many of the people in my life that I love, I could not bear it if I lost you, too. I had been denying my love for days and it came to me that if you died up there on that roof, and I had never told you how I felt, it would be far worse than anything that went before.'

Her voice broke and he curled his hand around hers. 'Jenna—'

'I wanted to raise my children in that house, Niall. Give them the same joy as I had as a child. But it wasn't the house. It was Mother and Father. Their love. You were right, Niall. A house is nothing but bricks and mortar. And it was nothing compared to your safety. And if you being safe means we must part, then so be it, but it hurts, my love.'

Tiny tendrils of hope reached into the corners of his soul, forcing light into the darkness he hadn't even realised was there. 'I would walk through fire for you, if that was your desire.' He would find the courage from somewhere.

She half-laughed. 'You did. How do you think I would have felt if you had not survived, knowing I was the one who asked you to save the boy?'

'I have nothing to offer you,' he warned. 'No wealth. No position.'

'We have something better. Something far more valuable. We have love.'

He gripped her hand hard. 'Did you hear nothing of what I said?'

'You said you loved me. That is all that matters.'

He turned and took her face in his palms, felt the cool of her skin against the cradle of his fingers and saw the love and hope shining in her eyes and could deny her nothing of himself. 'I will love you always and for ever, if you will have me, darling girl.'

Reaching up, she twined her arms around his neck and kissed his lips so sweetly he thought he might expire on the spot, but instead he wooed her mouth with his until they were breathless.

When they finally broke apart, he gazed into her eyes and drank in the love shining there until it filled all of the empty places inside his heart. '*Leannan*, I can't quite believe this is really happening, but there is no going back now. Whatever Carrick says. Or Ian.'

He held her close and she leaned her cheek

against his shoulder, while they waited for their breathing to settle and their pulses to return to normal.

'Niall, what did Sean mean about us being married?'

'Sean is a troublemaker.'

'Tell me.'

His imperious little faery. 'It is some nonsense about a gypsy wedding ceremony where the bride and groom eat bread and salt together and afterwards they...' His blood thickened. 'Well, you know what happened afterwards.'

'If we are married, there is no reason for you to go back to the inn, is there?'

His shaft hardened hopefully. 'You, my lady, are a wicked temptation.' He lifted his head and looked around. 'Are you saying you consider yourself no better than a gypsy?'

'Definitely not. Though I would like a proper marriage, too.'

Desperately, his gaze scanned the garden.

'What are you looking for?'

'A ladder. So I can take you up to your room.'

'You would climb a ladder for me?' she asked softly, trying not to laugh at his pained expression.

'I would do anything for you, *leannan*.'

She smiled her secret faery smile. 'And I for you. But we can use the stairs. You see, I have a key to the back door.'

He chuckled. 'It is a clever woman you are, Lady Jenna.'

She put her arms around his waist as he rose to his feet. 'I know. I found you, did I not?'

'We will be married properly. Right away,' he warned. 'Tomorrow.'

'Yes, dear heart, we will.'

Epilogue

'So, is it Lord Aleyne we are to call you?' Logan asked with an elbow to Niall's ribs as they stood together in Dunross's great hall after the dinner his brother had laid on. All the clan were gathered to celebrate his marriage, even though the ceremony had taken place at Braemuir the previous week.

Niall glanced across at his lovely fiery-haired wife talking to his mother, who had deigned to cross the threshold of Dunross Keep for the first time since Ian's marriage. Poor Ma, she looked so shrunken and frail, but like the rest of them, she had fallen under Jenna's faery spell.

Wearing a gown of pale blue with roses and leaves bordering the hem, she looked very much the harbinger of summer. As she moved, the light from the chandelier caught the silver pin at her breast, the faery pin that had been the only jewellery he'd had to give her on her wedding day. Not that she'd complained. Indeed, she'd been as enchanted as if it had been a string of diamonds.

Sean, who had met them outside the church on their wedding day, had said it would bring them good luck. Not that he believed any of the things Sean said.

'You will call me as you always have,' Niall said, answering Logan's enquiry after another jab in the ribs.

'At least she's a proper Scottish lass,' his brother said with a glower at Selina.

Scottish or faery, Niall didn't care. Jenna was his and he would do everything in his power to make her happy. 'How is the smuggling business?'

'Oh, aye, never been better. The guagers dinna get any smarter.'

'Don't rely on that, Logan. One of these days luck will be on their side.'

Logan snorted and Niall wanted to give him a shake, but had no chance to say more as a grinning Ian joined them.

'She's lovely, your Lady Jenna,' he said. 'You have done the family proud.'

For once. He shook his brother's hand. 'Thank you. And thank you for this fine reception.'

'What are your plans now?'

'To Edinburgh to study law. McDougall put me

in touch with a lawyer friend of his who will take me on. I hope I can help this family, too, in time.'

'Edinburgh, is it?' Logan said. 'You will no doubt be mixing with the nobs and too proud for us.'

'You'll bring me a half dozen bottles of whisky every time you bring a cartload for that scurvy friend of yours in the Wynds, or I'll know the reason why,' Niall said, punching him on the upper arm.

'Oh, aye.' Logan slapped him on the back and wandered off.

'Thank you for looking into the matter of Tearny,' Ian said in a lowered voice.

'I'm sorry I was unable to unearth more than I did.'

'I will take the matter up with Carrick. The more I think on it, the more I think there must be something behind those payments to the man.'

'If there is, you will need to take care. Carrick is a powerful man. And I'm afraid he's none too pleased with me.'

'I know it. Ah, here is your lovely bride coming to join us.'

Jenna smiled at both of them. 'What a lovely old keep this is,' she said.

Lady Selina, who had come up behind her, laughed. 'Lovely and draughty.' She was heavy with child and glowing. 'The school is going to miss you, Niall.'

'I'll look for a new schoolteacher for you when I reach Edinburgh,' he promised.

She smiled her thanks. 'I think you can't wait to disappear inside all those dusty law books.'

Jenna smiled at him, her eyes dancing. 'Oh, no doubt he'll be enjoying himself. But I'll make sure he doesn't forget his other duties.'

He took her hand and raised it to his lips. 'With you around, my love, it could never happen.'

Ian put an arm around his wife's shoulders. 'If you are half as happy as I am, you will be the most fortunate man alive.'

'I expect I will be far happier.' He drew Jenna close to his side.

Lady Selina snorted. 'Brothers.'

Jenna chuckled.

The piper was tuning up his pipes and the clansmen were clearing the tables from the middle of the floor. 'Come,' Niall said to Jenna. 'It is time to dance at our wedding feast.'

And dance they did until they fell into bed, exhausted. But not so exhausted that they couldn't take advantage of a soft bed and thick walls of stone.

* * * * *

A sneaky peek at next month...

HISTORICAL

IGNITE YOUR IMAGINATION, STEP INTO THE PAST...

My wish list for next month's titles...

In stores from 2nd August 2013:

- ❏ Not Just a Governess – Carole Mortimer
- ❏ A Lady Dares – Bronwyn Scott
- ❏ Bought for Revenge – Sarah Mallory
- ❏ To Sin with a Viking – Michelle Willingham
- ❏ The Black Sheep's Return – Elizabeth Beacon
- ❏ Smoke River Bride – Lynna Banning

Available at WHSmith, Tesco, Asda, Eason, Amazon and Apple

Just can't wait?

Special Offers

Every month we put together collections and longer reads written by your favourite authors.

Here are some of next month's highlights— and don't miss our fabulous discount online!

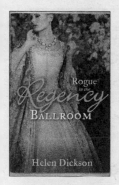

On sale 2nd August   On sale 2nd August   On sale 19th July

Save 20%
on all Special Releases

Find out more at
www.millsandboon.co.uk/specialreleases